THE PARTY'S OVER

The masks started to come off. Everyone was talking and laughing again.

Peter stood and stretched. "Great party."

"Well," Benny chuckled, "I don't think that guy enjoyed it." He indicated the table behind them.

They all looked. There was a man slumped in a chair.

"Some people can sleep through anything," Benny said.

Walter stood up and grabbed his cane. "He may not be sleeping." He moved toward the man. Peter and Benny went with him.

The man was dressed as the Phantom of the Opera. His long black cape covered his shoulders and extended almost to the floor. Walter looked at Peter. "You'd better alert Jessie. He's dead."

"Jesus," Benny said. "I'll get her."

As he turned to leave, Walter added, "You'd better have her call the police. This may not be a death from natural causes . . ."

MORE MYSTERIES FROM THE
BERKLEY PUBLISHING GROUP . . .

FORREST EVERS MYSTERIES: A former race-car driver solves the high-speed crimes of world-class racing . . . "A Dick Francis on wheels!"

—Jackie Stewart

by Bob Judd
BURN   SPIN
CURVE

THE REVEREND LUCAS HOLT MYSTERIES: They call him "The Rev," a name he earned as pastor of a Texas prison. Now he solves crimes with a group of reformed ex-cons . . .

by Charles Meyer
THE SAINTS OF GOD MURDERS   BLESSED ARE THE MERCILESS

FRED VICKERY MYSTERIES: Senior sleuth Fred Vickery has been around long enough to know where the bodies are buried in the small town of Cutler, Colorado . . .

by Sherry Lewis
NO PLACE FOR SECRETS   NO PLACE LIKE HOME
NO PLACE FOR DEATH   NO PLACE FOR TEARS
NO PLACE FOR SIN   NO PLACE FOR MEMORIES

INSPECTOR BANKS MYSTERIES: Award-winning British detective fiction at its finest . . . "Robinson's novels are habit-forming!"
—*West Coast Review of Books*

by Peter Robinson
THE HANGING VALLEY   PAST REASON HATED
WEDNESDAY'S CHILD   FINAL ACCOUNT
GALLOWS VIEW   INNOCENT GRAVES

JACK McMORROW MYSTERIES: The highly acclaimed series set in a Maine mill town and starring a newspaperman with a knack for crime solving . . . "Gerry Boyle is the genuine article."

—Robert B. Parker

by Gerry Boyle
DEADLINE   BLOODLINE
LIFELINE   POTSHOT

SCOTLAND YARD MYSTERIES: Featuring Detective Superintendent Duncan Kincaid and his partner, Sergeant Gemma James . . . "Charming!"   —*New York Times Book Review*

by Deborah Crombie
A SHARE IN DEATH   ALL SHALL BE WELL
LEAVE THE GRAVE GREEN   MOURN NOT YOUR DEAD

GHOUL OF MY DREAMS

RICHARD F. WEST

BERKLEY PRIME CRIME, NEW YORK

This is a work of fiction. Names, characters, places, and incidents are either the product of the author's imagination or are used fictitiously, and any resemblance to actual persons, living or dead, business establishments, events or locales is entirely coincidental.

GHOUL OF MY DREAMS

A Berkley Prime Crime Book / published by arrangement with the author

PRINTING HISTORY
Berkley Prime Crime edition / November 1999

The Penguin Putnam Inc. World Wide Web site address is http://www.penguinputnam.com

ISBN: 0-425-16983-9

Berkley Prime Crime Books are published by The Berkley Publishing Group, a division of Penguin Putnam Inc., 375 Hudson Street, New York, New York 10014.
The name BERKLEY PRIME CRIME and the BERKLEY PRIME CRIME design are trademarks belonging to Penguin Putnam Inc.

PRINTED IN THE UNITED STATES OF AMERICA

10 9 8 7 6 5 4 3 2 1

For my children—Valerie, Cynthia, Diana, and Richard.
For their love, for their help, for their friendship.

Sadly, Henny Youngman is no longer with us. He once said that he didn't have new material, just new audiences. He has left us and future audiences many hours of laughter. I am grateful for that and for the humor he contributed to this work. He will be missed.

AUTHOR'S NOTE

This is a work of fiction. The characters, the places, the events are all contrived. However, the speech that Warren Styck makes at the Halloween party, where he talks about his daughters Valerie and Cynthia and his wife, is all true. It happened to me. And I want to thank my wife and our children for showing me that life is more mysterious and intriguing than I would have otherwise believed.

—Richard F. West

GHOUL
OF MY
DREAMS

CHAPTER

1

The hand moved with agonizing slowness across the page. It held the pen tightly, the fingertips white with the effort, and advanced with the deliberation of a child learning to write. The hand was misshapen—the knuckles knobby, the skin mottled; beneath the deep tan the wormy blue veins were visible around the fingers and across the back of the hand. It was a hand that had seen years of hard physical labor, and had suffered for it. Slowly the letters and the words formed beneath the tip of the pen. Ever so slowly the hand guided the pen, the fingers tightening harder and harder, as they tried to control the writing, the impressions of the letters digging deeper into the paper. But the letters, the words that were formed did not betray the effort it took to make them. They were smooth and firm, with gentle curves and straight, bold strokes. A penmanship of the old school.

Suddenly the hand stopped, trembled, cramped, and dropped the pen to the paper. The fingers flexed and stretched woodenly, trying to relieve the cramp. The flexing continued for a few moments before the hand

RICHARD F. WEST

picked up the pen, and again attacked the paper and the
labor of writing. A few more letters were formed on the
paper; then the trembling returned without warning, and
the pen created an uncontrollable scrawl across the page
before the hand could release it.

The hand dropped the pen, and in trembling anger
slapped the palm down, splayed the fingers out over the
paper, then pulled into a fist, dragging the paper together
in a crumpled mass, and threw it into the waste basket.

"Suicide? I find that difficult to believe," Peter Benington said. He was sixty, a David Niven look-alike complete with white hair and mustache, as well as the flavor
of an English accent. He was dressed in khaki shirt and
trousers, with belt and shoes a shade of soft cream.

Peter was seated with others at a table in the coffee
alcove off the lobby of Coral Sands Assisted Living Retirement Residence in Sarasota, Florida. The lobby, a
broad, three-story affair with a glass roof and glass elevator, was fit for an upscale hotel. It was done in muted
pinks and reds, and plants, sofas, and easy chairs were
scattered about.

A cup of coffee with cream sat on the table in front
of Peter. Against the wall were a coffeemaker and four
carafes of coffee on warming burners, the whole unit
surrounded by empty cups, sugar, stirrers and the like.
The urns that had been there for years had been removed
a week before to make a place for this new system.
Beside the urns was a platter with an array of pastries.

"I don't know, Slick," Benny Ashe said, a short,
tough, seventy-three-year-old from Brooklyn who was
wearing his favorite baseball cap, dark blue with "NY"
in faded white lettering. His red plaid shirt and light blue
pants had been worn so often there was no life in them.
He, too, nursed a cup of coffee—black. "You take a
look around you. There're a lot of people suffering
through their golden years." He grunted. "Golden years,

that's a laugh. The only gold in them years goes into the hands of the doctors.''

"Well, that is true," Doctor Walter Innes said, ignoring the slight to his profession. "However, the statistics are there for you to read." A thin, knobby man, he was dressed in an assortment of colors and patterns whose only purpose in being combined was to disturb each other and the viewer. He leaned forward in his chair, resting his hands on the handle of a wood cane.

"But the statistics don't tell the whole story." Walter sipped at his cup of coffee. "The Centers for Disease Control, in the last figures I saw before I stopped practicing, put suicide as the ninth leading cause of death among people over fifty-five. That, I might add, is reported cases. The elderly have more tools at their disposal to disguise what really happened. That's why I believe the actual figure probably approaches the leading cause of death in the elderly."

"Tools?" Betty Jablonski asked. "What tools?" Betty was a dumpy, nervous little woman with black hair that matched her black button eyes. The light blue dress she wore had the look of silk and sported a conservative pattern of pale yellow flowers. The dress was struggling to contain her body.

"Why do they want to cover up their suicide?" Eleanor Carter asked. A tall, attractive woman with light blue eyes and soft brown hair that hung to just above her shoulders. She was wearing soft tan slacks and a white cotton blouse with a large gold chain and pendant, the chain tucked under the collar of the blouse. She had the regal bearing and grace of Lauren Bacall, a resemblance that had caught Peter's eye and imagination. They had been seriously "going together" for the past three months.

"The elderly are not out to demonstrate how badly the world has treated them, forcing them to take their own lives," Walter said. "They are not looking for sympathy after death, so they don't leave notes, don't create a commotion around their deaths. Nor do they want to embarrass their friends and family. With them it's strictly personal."

"What kind of tools?" Betty persisted.

"Heart disease is the killer holding first place. But how many people stop taking their heart medication? Pneumonia and bronchitis are up near the top. How many with those diseases simply stopped eating? Or overdose on their medication? We chalk those things up to accidental occurrences. It's easier. And speaking of accidents, they are high on the list. How many simply drive their cars into a tree, or deliberately fall down a flight of stairs?"

The hands stopped the wheels of the wheelchair one inch from the edge of the stairs. The stairs descended to a landing, which turned the stairs around to continue descending to the next floor down. There was another landing by the door leading to the floor below—the second floor—and in the same fashion the stairs continued down to the first floor. A window was set in the wall of the landing, and through it bright sunlight was coming in to light up the area and give the metal edges of the steps the gleam of sharp knives.

"You are speaking of death, no?" The accent was French. The man who stepped awkwardly to the table had set his cup of coffee down and, with a hand stiffened to the point of not functioning well, was clumsily maneuvering a chair so he could sit with them. He was a tall man, but his back was bent and crooked, and it was clear by the difficulty he had in moving around that there were other physical things wrong with him. "I could not help but to overhear as I poured out the coffee."

"Sit down, Henry." Benny smiled. "Everybody, this is Henry Gaston. Just moved in yesterday." Benny made it his business to know everyone in Coral Sands. Seventeen years ago Benny had crossed a gangster in New

York by the name of Bobby Dee. Bobby went to jail, and Benny went into hiding, took an assumed name, and ensconced himself here in Coral Sands with Bobby Dee's money. Since then Benny had been looking over his shoulder for Bobby Dee's muscle squad to find him, so he checked on everyone who moved in or sniffed around. Better safe than dead. "Henry," Benny said, pointing to each of them, "that's Peter, Betty, Eleanor, and"—he grinned—"Walter Innes, M.D.—retired."

The man with the French accent bowed to those at the table. "Henri Gastonne, from Paree by way of Philadelphia."

"Welcome to Coral Sands, Henri," Walter said, pronouncing the name correctly. "We hope retirement is all you expect it to be, and"—he hesitated and grinned—"we hope it takes you a long time to realize it isn't."

Henri smiled. "I, too, hope it is a long time. It would be too disappointing to have so short a time of joy after waiting so long a time on the list to be allowed here." He sat down. "It is much pleasure to meet . . ." He broke off as he looked at his coffee cup, his eyes growing wide. "My God! What is this?" There, floating in the brown liquid, was a palmetto bug—a large cockroach by any name.

Benny laughed, and the others sighed patiently. Henri looked puzzled at Benny. "We got this guy in the place," Benny struggled to say through his laughter, "who likes to play practical jokes."

"Benny," Eleanor said, "let's not be sexist. There are no grounds to say it's a man." Benny was still chuckling, holding back the belly laugh that wanted so badly to come out.

"We call him the Mad Joker," Peter explained. "He plays practical jokes." He pointed to the palmetto bug in Henri's coffee. "Like placing a plastic bug in the coffee carafe."

Henri moved his face closer to the cup and peered at the bug. Then he raised his eyebrows, pulled back, and shook his head, "Ah, but it is not plastic."

"What!" Benny exclaimed, eyes wide, the laughter gone instantly.

"Ugh!" Betty said, "that's disgusting!" She made a bitter face and flapped her hands about.

Gagging and screwing up their faces, everyone around the table looked at their own cups filled with coffee that had come from the same carafe.

"Oh, my," Walter sighed, looking suspiciously at his cup of coffee. "Do you all realize that two-thirds of the world eats insects?"

"Why doesn't that make me feel better?" Eleanor asked, grimacing as she slid her cup away from her, touching it as if it held a fragile bomb.

"How could this happen?" Betty said, annoyed, moving her lips as if trying to find the taste of an insect, anticipating its bitterness. "We pay for an exterminator!"

"Have you ever examined a lobster?" Walter persisted. "It appears to fit the description of an insect— an insect of the sea."

"Yeah, well, Frank the bug man must be slipping," Benny said, trying to figure out what to do with his cup of coffee. "I just saw him around this morning. I'll have to give him a piece of my mind over this." He looked at Henri. "Sorry about this. Don't get the wrong impression of the place. It's really top-notch."

"You need not to apologize," Henri said. He shrugged and with a nod of his head looked at everyone at the table, "I, too, like the little joke." He smiled. "The bug *is* plastic."

The clown came out of the last door at the end of the corridor. The clown had outrageously red hair, a big red nose, a billowing red-checked outfit, and large flappy shoes. Tiny bells in the wig jingled when the clown's head moved. The clown closed the door to the apartment and started down the hall, jingling with each step.

• • •

The hands on the wheels of the chair pulled back and forth nervously, the wheels moving repeatedly to the very edge of the top step, then back an inch. Back and forth, as if the person in the chair couldn't make up his mind, or needed to build the courage to act. Suddenly the hands yanked the wheels and the chair back from the steps. Then the hands tightened their grip on the wheels, the muscles of the hands tensed, and the hands threw the wheels on a reckless forward spin toward the stairs.

The clown was approaching the door to the stairway when the awful screams came. The clown froze, the painted happy face hiding shock and concern. "What the hell?" the clown said. The screams coming from the stairwell were terrifying. And there were terrible crashing and tumbling and banging sounds. It seemed a long time that the clown stood there, staring at the door to the stairway, waiting for—what? The crashing and banging grew louder and closer, the screams grew louder and closer, and the clown's eyes grew wider.

The door to the stairwell burst open, the clown's eyes grew wider still, and the clown jumped back out of the way as a man in a wheelchair, his long gray hair streaming back, screaming at the top of his lungs— "YAAAAH!"—came slamming through the door. He threw himself back in the chair, the wheels hitting the wall as the back of the chair hit the floor. Then the back raised up, but it stopped rising as the footrests gouged into the wall. The chair settled to the floor with a thump as the man's head bounced off the carpeted floor.

"I DID IT!" The man—his eyes alive, his face flushed—threw his hands in the air, and shouted up at the clown. "I DID IT, ALICE!"

"What you did, you damn fool, was nearly give me a heart attack!" Alice, the clown, shouted down at the man, murder in her eyes behind the painted smiling face.

"I ought to stomp you into the rug right now! You coulda killed me!"

"Coulda, woulda, shoulda, but didn't." The man laughed excitedly. "You're alive and well, and the only witness to a super stunt! Something you can tell everyone about! I DID IT! Two floors down in a wheelchair!"

"Warren," Alice said, her eyes still aflame, "you may have been a stuntman years ago, before you ended up in that chair, but you're also a very large jackass." With angry determination she stepped past him and continued down the corridor toward the lobby.

"Alice! Alice! Don't just walk off!" Then, in a more subdued tone, "Could you help me up?"

"It ain't gonna work, Warren," she said, not looking back. "No pity to subdue my anger. You're a jackass, and I know you can get up by yourself."

Warren Styck laughed. "You're something else, Alice me lass," he shouted after her. "Will you marry me?"

"At least now I won't have to give Frank, the bug man, a piece of my mind," Benny said.

"I don't think you can afford to give away what little is left," Walter said with a smirk.

"One for you, Doc." Benny grinned.

"The exterminator is here again?" Peter asked.

Benny shrugged. "Frank comes once a month and spends a week spraying the joint inside and out. Everybody in Florida has a bug man."

Walter said, "Two things have made Florida habitable—pesticides and air conditioning. Without them we'd all be living someplace else, and Florida would be a sweltering jungle knee-deep in insects."

"And alligators," Benny added.

"And alligators," Doc Innes agreed.

"He does the spraying of the apartments also?" Henri asked. "I do not intend to be available to escort him around."

"Don't worry," Benny assured him. "Grace at the

front desk goes around with him to the apartments. Not that Frank'd take anything. She does it more because us old folks sometimes forget where we put things. This way she can assure us Frank didn't take those things.''

Two men stepped up to the coffee carafes and began pouring themselves coffee. In the category of ''old,'' these men were up there. Both in their eighties, both lean, wrinkled, and a little bent. One was short; the other, tall and gangly. The tall man had long, thin, gray hair. The short man had a worn sailor's hat on his head and was wearing a T-shirt that read JESUS IS COMING. EVERYBODY LOOK BUSY.

''Please,'' Henri said to Walter. ''I did not wish to interrupt your discussion of death.''

''Suicide in the elderly was the topic,'' Walter said.

''You hear that? They're talking about suicide,'' the man with the sailor's hat said. The two men had taken their cups of coffee and were slowly moving past the table, toward the glass doors that led to the swimming pool area.

''You ever think about suicide?'' Gray Hair asked.

''Wished it on every one of my enemies,'' Sailor Hat said.

''No. I mean did you ever think of committing suicide?''

''Nah. If my enemies didn't think I was worth killing, why would I think it?''

Henri looked at the two men, then frowned questioningly at Benny.

''I'll introduce you to those two later, when I take you around. They hang out in the gazebo outside by the lake. We call them Tweedledee and Tweedledum.''

The questioning frown on Henri's face got deeper.

''I'll explain later.''

At that moment Alice in her clown outfit stomped past the alcove on her way across the lobby to the front door, a woman on a mission.

The questioning frown returned to Henri's face. Peter

smiled to himself, remembering his own reaction the first day at Coral Sands. He had been treated to the same surprises: a visit from the Mad Joker, the appearance of Tweedledee and Tweedledum, and now the clown. At the time Peter had thought he had moved into a lunatic asylum, and the day had just begun. What next? What had been next was no laughing matter. One of the women had died. He hoped that was not in store for today.

"Hi, Alice," Benny said. "How's everything?"

Alice stopped short and turned to the group at the table. Furious, she spat the words out: "Benny, if that wheelchair-bound jackass doesn't stay out of my way, you'll have a real funeral at the Halloween party to-morrow."

"Easy, Alice," Benny said, but Alice was already walking away.

Henri turned to Benny.

Benny shrugged. "Alice is a retired clown who still does kids' parties, and hospitals and such. She's really good people. Guess Warren got her ticked off some-how."

"This Warren individual," Henri said, "he is in a wheelchair?"

"Yeah. Warren Styck is his name. He's new here, like yourself. Been with us about a month or so. Used to be a stuntman in the movies. Got his name on a lot of films. Then he was in an auto accident. His wife was driving. She didn't make it. He ended up attached to a wheel-chair. Did work in special effects after that. Finally, so he tells it, he decided he had enough with movie people and retired."

"That is sad," Henri said. "He loses his wife, and to be with the wheelchair, too."

"He didn't talk much about his wife. And he doesn't complain about the wheelchair. Stunt stuff is all chal-lenges to the stuntman, Warren says. He treats the chair like another challenge. He's arranging the Halloween party tomorrow night. We're anxious to see what he's going to do. By the way, you'll need a costume.''

''Ah, a costume party. That will be very interesting.''

''Yes, a masked ball!'' Betty said. ''It sounds so exciting. We're trying to figure out what costumes to wear.''

''What are you going to wear, Doc?'' Eleanor asked Walter.

''You know, Doc,'' Benny said with a grin, ''you could go in a sheet—as a corpse.''

''Yes,'' Betty giggled, her hand to her mouth. ''Go as one of your patients.''

''I'm going to go naked,'' Walter said dryly, ''as a tongue depressor.''

''With all them wrinkles,'' Benny chuckled, ''it'll have to be a well-used tongue depressor.''

The man in a white peaked cap that looked even whiter because of his deeply tanned face, was about to grab the handle of the front door when Alice, coming out, shoved it open with such ferocity he jumped out of her way.

''Whoa, Alice!'' Alex Conners said.

'' 'Morning, Alex.'' It was a grumble thrown out as she went past him. She sliced through the construction crew, the men looking at her warily as they moved out of her way. She headed for the taxi parked near the entrance to the parking lot.

Alex Conners stepped inside the building, and gave Grace a bewildered look. ''What's with Alice?''

''Beats me. She whizzed past me the same way.'' Grace nodded in the direction of the coffee alcove at the other end of the lobby. ''And she shouted something to Benny when she passed him.'' Grace, in her fifties, was a tough-looking woman with a solid, stocky body, dyed brown hair, cold blue eyes, and a warm disposition. She'd been working at Coral Sands for close to eighteen years, almost two longer than Benny had been there, and for all that time she had manned the front counter.

"A clown acting like that could give a kid clowna-phobia."

"Clownaphobia?"

Alex grinned, his teeth almost as white as his hat. He stepped up to the counter. "What else would you call it—a fear of clowns?" He was a short, solidly built man in his forties, with dark hair and eyes. He wore jeans, work boots, and a short-sleeved blue work shirt.

Grace grinned. "Clownaphobia is good." She came out from behind the counter. "I assume it's coffee time for the crew."

He smiled playfully. "Not really. I just can't resist coming in to see you."

"If you're going to make any moves on me, you'd better hurry up. I'm not getting any younger." She walked toward the kitchen.

Alex followed her. "You'll always be young to me, dear one."

"Pull-ease!" She rolled her eyes. "I just ate break-fast."

Alex chuckled.

In the kitchen Manuel—short, in his early twenties, with black hair and gentle features—was putting plastic cups, pastries, a pot of coffee, napkins, utensils, sugar, and milk in a corrugated box. An apron was wrapped around his lean body. "Is ready," he said, a Spanish accent lightly smoothing the tones.

Manuel had been putting together this box of food and coffee every day for the two weeks the construction had been under way on the fountain out front and a large canopy over the entrance. It promised to go on for a long time, because those were just the first steps in the project to add a new wing to Coral Sands, doubling the capacity of the Home.

Alex picked up the box. He smiled. "Thanks, Manuel." He left the kitchen.

Manuel turned to Grace. "Maybe is good idea to put in a walk-up window?" He pointed to the far wall.

Grace smiled. "And a statue of a chef where they could line up and holler in his ear to place their breakfast orders?"

"Si. Yes." He shrugged, the hint of a grin on his face. "We could charge. Make a little money."

"If the owner, Jacobson, knew we were giving these guys breakfast, I'm sure he'd come up with that idea himself."

CHAPTER

2

Audrey Knitter was in good shape. Though by the calendar she was sixty-three, by her looks she could pass for a very healthy woman in her forties. She exercised regularly to keep her body in tone and keep her weight under control, and it worked. A good hair dye, with a touch of plastic surgery here and there to keep the aging from her face, completed the illusion.

She had been living at Coral Sands for a little over four years. Her husband, George, had died after a long and painful fight with cancer. Soon after she buried him, she left their home in Virginia and settled in Coral Sands. There was not one day she regretted the move, not one day she missed the frigid winters, not one day she hungered for the long days of dreary gray skies. Florida, with its persistent sunny days and pleasant temperatures, was where she was meant to be, and she loved every minute of it. Until yesterday.

That was when she got the phone call from Harry—long-forgotten, long-thought-dead Harry. The bastard was alive and back in her life. No amount of sunshine and warm breezes could temper the foul mood that created. Her late husband used to say, "If you're feeling good, don't worry. You'll get over it." Well, she had been feeling good for a long time, and now this. Now Harry Benson, back from the dead. George also used to say that people were no damn good. Harry was one of those near the top of the "no damn good" list.

She had married the bastard when she was too young to know any better, and spent twelve years with the abusive, conniving, manipulating son of a bitch—twelve years! Boy, was she a slow learner! But she had to give credit to Harry. He did one good thing for her—he walked out the door one day and never came back, leaving her with their two children. Nice guy Harry Benson. For a long time after that she prayed to meet him just once, so she could cut his heart out and stuff it in his mouth. It was tough for her after he left, but it was also great. She learned just how competent and self-reliant she really was. Harry had her believing she couldn't do a damn thing without him, couldn't make decisions, couldn't handle the money, couldn't raise the kids.

When she had received the telephone call yesterday, she thought it was some kind of joke. Harry had to be dead. Except she couldn't think of who would play such a joke. There was no one from that part of her life that she knew anymore, no one who would know about Harry. Except, of course, Harry.

She had never told George about Harry, and he never asked. One thing nice about men, they don't look to the past. At least not George. His view was that the past was nothing that could be changed or justified. It just was. And the present and the future were the only things under our control. That hippie philosophy that today is the first day of the rest of your life—that was George. Thank God for him. He was a nice, kind man who asked nothing of her she couldn't willingly give. He had restored her faith in the goodness of some people. Not all people. Not many people. Not Harry. Harry and good did not go together except when it was something good for Harry.

One thing that amazed her was how the hate she had buried all those years came over her when she heard Harry's voice on the telephone. It was like a dam had burst, a dam she didn't know was there, and all the slime it held back just engulfed her. She hadn't slept a wink since yesterday. All she could think about was killing the bastard—thoughts that had been buried and, she assumed, forgotten for over thirty years.

It was two in the afternoon, and she was on her way to the Denny's restaurant in downtown Sarasota. That's where he wanted to meet her. Someplace public, where there would be a lot of people around. Well, a lot of people or not, she had a gun in her handbag. This morning, when she finally got out of her sleepless bed, she had resolved to shoot him right there in the restaurant, that's how irrational, how angry she was.

But after three cups of coffee and a handful of cigarettes, she began to think more clearly. Shooting him would be worse for her than for him. He'd be dead, and she'd be in jail for the rest of her life. Not a good trade. Revenge should not inflict punishment on her. She had been punished enough by good old Harry when she was living with him. He was the one who deserved punishment, not her.

She brought the gun with her, anyway. Just in case— of what she wasn't sure. But she felt secure with the gun in her bag.

When she had parked the car and was heading into the restaurant, she suddenly wondered if she'd recognize him. After all, it had been—let's see, she was thirty-two when he headed for the hills—thirty-one years since she'd seen him. All she had was the mental picture of him as he was then—tall, slender, dark hair, thin dark mustache, light blue eyes, and always in a snappy suit.

When she got inside the restaurant, the man who signaled her with a grin and a small wave of the hand did not look at all like Harry Benson. She immediately became suspicious that this was some sort of hoax or scam or whatever, because that pudgy, balding man with the heavy jowls and wearing a polyester blue suit was not Harry Benson. No way. Then she noticed the slick grin, and the eyes, and then she could see Harry buried beneath that flesh as a sculptor sees a finished statue in a slab of marble. A knot of hot anger tightened in her throat. She walked over to him, with each step the knot growing tighter and hotter.

"Hello, Aud." Harry Benson smiled, not a warm smile, more a knowing, superior smile. He pointed to the seat opposite him at the table. "You want some coffee?"

She sat down and nodded, not trusting herself to speak just yet, the knot too tight to talk through, the heat of the anger spreading.

Harry signaled the waiter for another coffee.

"How have you been, Aud?" When she didn't answer him, just kept staring, he said, "It's been a lot of years. Heard you did rather well after I left. I was happy for you. That George Knitter guy seemed to treat you all right. And the kids turned out great. Thanks for that."

She still kept looking at him and trying to breathe, the anger now tightening her chest. Her hand rested on the handbag in her lap, feeling the shape of the gun in the bag.

"Guess it was a real surprise hearing from me yesterday?" He put on his charming smile, but it had no effect. She just kept glaring at him. "I know I have a lot to explain. But we'll have plenty of time for that. We've got a lot of time to get to know one another again, talk over old war stories and all that. It'll be good again." Her posture, her glare had not changed, and it unnerved him. "Aren't you glad to see me, Aud? We spent a lot of years together. Did a lot of fun things."

The waiter placed a cup of coffee on the table in front

of Audrey. She didn't move. Her hand kept feeling the gun in her purse, her eyes spewing hate at Harry.

"Aren't you going to say anything? Don't you have any questions?" Harry said.

Audrey swallowed, trying to open a passage through the knot in her throat. What came out was more a hiss than speech. "Why?"

Harry seemed relieved. The first step had been made. "Why did I leave? Well, I . . . ."

"No, you bastard!" she spat the words at him between clenched teeth, her hand fiercely tight on the bag in her lap. "Why did you call me? Why did you come back? Why aren't you dead and out of my life? What the hell do you want with me?"

Harry leaned back, unaffected by her outburst. He spoke evenly and softly. "Calm down, Audrey. They'll be plenty of time to go into all that."

"There's no time. You got me here today, and that's it. This is the first and the last you'll see of me. You try and see me again, and I'll have the cops on you in a flash."

"Now, I don't think you'll do that." Harry's voice was soft and oily. "Not to old Harry. You've got too much to lose." With calm eyes he looked straight into her glare. "Like all that money you inherited."

She looked at him, stunned, confused, but still angry. Just the effect he was looking for.

He leaned forward, his face close to hers, his voice conspiratorial. "Yeah, I know how much money you got from dear old George's estate after he died. The grieving wife was well provided for. Except how would it look if his children found out you were not legally his wife? 'Cause you were still married to me."

The anger faded in a flash, replaced by fear and desperate hate.

"Don't you think they'd be a little annoyed, and maybe"—his grin grew oilier—"make you give it all back?"

The anger exploded like a fireball and she lashed out at him, but he deftly caught the hand she threw at his face. He made an admonishing tsking sound, and shook his head. "Now that's not the Aud I used to know. She never would resort to violence. She was a sweet, gentle thing. George taught you some bad things."

He released her hand, and she reluctantly pulled it back. He sat back in the seat. "Now, here's the plan. Pay attention. I hear you've got a big party tomorrow night at that Coral Sands where you live. I think that would be a good time for you to introduce me to all your friends. I'm you're new boyfriend. Then after a short while we'll be publicly married, and we'll live happily ever after—you, me, and George's money. Won't that be peachy?"

He leaned forward, his face and his voice becoming hard. "Just remember, Aud, I've got nothing to lose in this. You don't cooperate, you lose everything. Nothing would be changed for me." The hardness left his voice and his face. "I sure would hate to see you punish yourself like that. And for what? Remember that half a loaf is better than no loaf."

The anger in Audrey was like a white-hot flash that seared everything. Get involved with Harry—NO DAMN WAY! The words screamed in her mind. Her hand crept back to the handbag in her lap and slipped inside to grope for the gun.

"I know being with me is not the happiest thought of the day. You can thank old George for that. If he had given you the money outright, instead of a yearly allowance, you could pay me off and that would be the end of it.

"Now, I know this is all a shock to you. But you're a smart girl, and I feel confident you'll come around to what has to be done here. I mean, you'll see that you've got no choice."

The thought was like a revelation. Yes, she was a smart girl; smarter than that slime ball Harry Benson, that's for sure. And, yes, there was no choice; she knew what had to be done. Her mind grabbed the anger, struggled with it, forced it into a corner, and held it there, away from her rational thinking. She released her grip on the gun. Now was not the time. But the time would come.

"When does this little party of yours start tomorrow night?"

"Eight," she said. She spoke as if in a trance, her mind tumbling with hate and the desperation of her situation. "It's a masked costume party for Halloween."

"Sounds like fun." He took a folded piece of paper from his pocket and placed it on the table in front of her. "I expect you to pick me up in your nice, shiny white Cadillac at seven forty-five. My address is on that piece of paper." He grinned and shrugged. "I don't want any problems getting in the door. You understand?"

She didn't respond.

"Any ideas on what costume I should rent?" he asked.

"The Devil."

He laughed.

CHAPTER

3

"So," Peter said, "how did Henri enjoy the tour?" Peter was wondering if Tweedledee and Tweedledum had raked Henri over a bit, and if Henri had met Henny Youngman. Then he chuckled to himself. *Wait until he finds out about Eugene.*

Peter, Eleanor, and Benny were seated in lounge chairs by the swimming pool, enjoying the view of the lake and the palm trees. The searing heat of summer was gone, and the chill of winter hadn't arrived. Spring and fall were the best times of the year in Florida. Fortunately for Floridians, the Northerners didn't get their vacations until summer, which left the best times of the year to be enjoyed, for the most part, by the Floridians.

"Actually, really good," Benny said. The afternoon had been sunny and pleasant until a few moments ago, when angry chunks of dark clouds began sweeping in from the Gulf. The afternoon rain was moments away.

"Tweedledee and Tweedledum didn't give him a hard time?" Eleanor asked.

"That was the real surprise. He got along famously with them."

"Now that's a new one," Peter said. He remembered when he'd first met them. Benny had introduced Peter to Tweedledee and Tweedledum as a new guy. They had said he didn't look new to them, with all those wrinkles and thinning hair.

"Yeah. He got to talking war stories, and those two jumped right in. Henri was in the French resistance during the war. Just a kid. He ended up in a German concentration camp, where they busted him up pretty bad. His hand doesn't work too good, and some other things weren't put back together just right. Anyway, I left him with them. Haven't seen him since."

"I see they moved some large equipment to the other side of the property."

"Yeah," Benny said. "They're supposed to start digging another lake over there."

Eleanor frowned. "I'm not looking forward to all the construction noises we'll have to live with over the next few months."

Frank Wilson, the bug man, came around the corner. He was wearing a heavy vest beneath the metal tank of insecticide strapped to his back—the vest to protect the tank from chafing. He held the sprayer nozzle in his left hand. From his appearance—thin, bent, and graying— Peter guessed that Frank was nearing seventy. *And still a working man,* Peter thought. Frank had once told Peter that he worked because he needed something to do. A man with nothing to do was a dead man. "I'm going to do a little spraying here. You people may want to go someplace else while I do it. Don't want you ending up on your backs with crosses in your eyes and your feet and arms up in the air."

"Hi, Frank," Benny said, as he got up from the lounge chair. "We won't stand in the way of a working man. But have you looked up?" Benny pointed to the sky.

Frank looked up. "Damn! Hadn't noticed the rain coming. Wasn't supposed to rain. Means I'll have to do some of the spraying over again tomorrow." He hooked the sprayer nozzle to the loop attached to his belt. "Guess you people can stay where you are."

With that, a few drops of rain smacked against the deck around the pool, and thunder grumbled overhead.

Peter smiled. "Guess not."

Inside, Peter left Eleanor to go upstairs and take a shower before dinner. Benny said he was going to pick up Caroline, and they were going out to eat. Eleanor smiled at that. Benny and Caroline made such an incongruous couple—she the soft-spoken, genteel Southern belle, he the tough, outspoken guy from Brooklyn.

Eleanor saw the postman at the front desk. *No*, she corrected herself mentally, *postwoman. Or was it postperson?* She headed for the front desk to see if there was any mail for her.

"How's it going, Liz?" Grace smiled as she checked the clock. It was almost four.

The postwoman was in her thirties with long blond hair in a ponytail. She smiled and shrugged. "Same old, same old." She hefted onto the counter a cardboard tray that held the mail for Coral Sands.

"Right on time," Grace said and pulled the tray toward her. It was filled to capacity. "Looks like the usual load of junk mail."

"If it wasn't for junk mail, I wouldn't have a job," Liz said. She picked up the cardboard tray of outgoing mail that Grace had put on the end of the counter. There was considerably less mail in that tray.

Junk mail was a good thing, Grace thought. *If it wasn't for junk mail, some of these old people would get no mail. And the mail was what many of them lived for. Some waited around all day for the mail to come. Nothing else in their lives.* She shook her head. *Sad.*

Audrey Knitter came through the front door. "Hi, Audrey," Grace said. Audrey didn't acknowledge Grace. She kept walking, her face hard, her thoughts, her focus somewhere else.

Eleanor stepped up to the desk. "Need help sorting the mail?"

"Hi, Eleanor." Grace smiled. "I can use all the help you're willing to give." She picked up the tray of mail and walked into the little room off the lobby where the mailboxes were located. Eleanor followed her inside, and together they went through the mail, putting it in the appropriate boxes. Besides the advertisements, Eleanor came across a letter addressed to her. She turned it over in her hand. No return address. Curious. She put it aside with the rest of her mail, and helped Grace finish the sorting. As they came out of the room, Grace spotted Ted Walden getting off the elevator and heading in their direction.

"There goes poor Mr. Walden," she said. "He's always so down."

Eleanor nodded.

"He hasn't been the same since his wife died last spring," Grace said. "She had Alzheimer's for so many years. You'd think he'd be relieved that she's not suffering any longer."

"He took care of her for so long," Eleanor said, making a token comment. She didn't really want to engage in that conversation.

"Probably was the only purpose in his life," Grace said. "I sure hope he snaps out of it soon. His depression is starting to worry me." She slipped to her post behind the counter of the front desk.

Surprised, Eleanor looked at Grace. She wasn't aware Grace had such concern for the residents.

As if reading Eleanor's mind, Grace said, "I worry about my friends."

"Are you going to the Halloween party tomorrow night?" Eleanor tried to change the subject.

At that moment Alice, in her clown outfit, came stomping wearily through the front door.

"Bad day, Alice?" Grace said.

"Was over at Hospice. Tough trying to make dying

people laugh." Alice stepped heavily to the cushioned love seat across from the front desk.

"I don't think I'd sit . . ." Grace didn't get to finish, as Alice dropped her exhausted body down on the love seat. The other half of the seat cushion swelled up instantly, and burst open with a pop, sending a tall spray of feathers into the air.

"What the hell!" Alice said, looking at the cloud of white feathers over her head. The feathers slowly snowed down over her and the area around the love seat.

Eleanor was smiling. Grace grinned sheepishly. "Sorry. I saw the seat cushion was different. I was going to check it out a little later. I guess the Mad Joker has just paid us a visit."

"God!" Alice groaned, throwing her head against the back of the love seat, trying to blow away some of the feathers that were sticking to the makeup on her face. "Is this day ever going to end?"

Still chuckling, Eleanor turned to the letter she had received. She pried open the flap of the envelope, extracted the letter, and unfolded it. There were just a few words written in what Eleanor thought was beautiful penmanship: "Dearest, I desire your full attention." No signature, no date, nothing. *Peter*, she thought with a smile. *How sweet*.

"This is a crazy place."

Eleanor and Grace looked at the emaciated man standing by the counter, his body bent, his hands trembling. *The first signs of Parkinson's*, Grace thought. *Poor man*.

Grace smiled. "No crazier than the rest of the world."

"Shouldn't be." The man was not amused. "A man deserves some peace and sanity in his last days."

"You still have plenty of time left for being bored. What can I do for you?"

"Has the mail come yet?"

"Yes, Edmund," Eleanor said with a polite smile. "We just finished sorting it." Edmund Stanton had arrived last month. Benny had done his usual welcoming of new people, had introduced him to the group, and had taken him around. He didn't speak much, and laughed not at all. Eleanor's impression was that Edmund Stanton was a depressed, bitter man. Since then Edmund had kept to himself, avoiding everyone.

"Thanks." He walked carefully, as if his legs were heavy and difficult to control, back to the mailboxes.

"See you later, Grace." Eleanor gave her a small wave and left.

The evening went well. Eleanor and Peter had decided to eat out. They went to The Beach House in Manatee County, sat on the deck overlooking the Gulf of Mexico, enjoyed the food and the live music from a combo, had a few drinks afterward, and strolled hand-in-hand on the beach. And they talked the conversation of lovers getting to know one another.

They had been lovers for three months. During that time Eleanor had revealed nothing of her past except that her husband, Matthew Carter, who had been twenty years her senior, had died, and that she had no children. The only family she had was an arrogant brother-in-law, Mark, who was bent on taking away the money Matthew had left her. After Matthew's death she moved to Coral Sands. Peter didn't press her for more about her past. Eleanor said that the past didn't matter. What did matter was the here and now.

In some respects Peter had to agree. He had not revealed to Eleanor that he had done a bit of thievery in his time. As an insurance agent he had contracted out the jewel thefts of some of his clients. Then he paid the thief, getting a cut for himself, for the return of the jewelry, with no questions asked. The insurance companies gladly paid twenty cents on the dollar rather than give the full amount to the insured, and the insured got their jewelry back. Everyone was happy. Sometimes he didn't contract out the thefts, but did them himself. The only person in Coral Sands who knew this was Benny. Shortly after Peter had moved in, the police were putting heat on both Benny and him. It was then they had exchanged confidences as souls joined together in trouble.

It was after ten when Peter and Eleanor returned to Coral Sands, said goodnight, and went to their separate apartments.

Peter closed the door of his apartment, stripped off his clothes, and slipped into shorts. Then he turned on some soft music and poured two glasses of Amaretto—hoping. Most evenings Eleanor would come to his apartment and spend the night. But he never knew when that was going to happen. There had been evenings when he finished both snifters of Amaretto and went to bed alone, and lonely. Tonight they had had such a wonderful evening. That made him feel confident she would come to him.

He still was amazed at what he felt for this woman. All those years, all those women in his life, but never one like this. Never one that touched his heart so. He was sixty years old, yet he felt like a schoolboy with his first love. Only this wasn't the dreamy infatuation of youth, this was a love—yes, love, he admitted to himself—that was rooted in maturity. He couldn't explain the difference—it was just different, more solid, more substance without the fear of life and living. He wasn't sure if this love he felt for Eleanor would last, but he knew he was going to absorb every joyful minute of it while it did.

When he heard the soft knock on the door, his heart surged, reminding him that he had to take his beta-blocker to keep the old ticker in rhythm. He stepped over to the door and opened it. Eleanor was standing there barefoot, wearing red silk pajamas. *God, she was beautiful*, he thought.

Eleanor smiled seductively. "You now have my full attention."

He returned the smile. "A man could ask for no more."

Since she had quoted the note, Eleanor had expected

Peter to say something about sending it to her, but he didn't, which made her more curious. He hadn't mentioned the note at all through the whole evening, even though she had dropped gentle hints. Now he had not responded to the direct quote. Puzzling. She wondered what he was up to.

They spent some time snuggling on the sofa and sipping their drinks while listening to the music. Then they went to bed. They lay there in the dark, comfortable with each other's presence, with the soft yellow night light giving a hint of substance to the room.

Eleanor couldn't get the note out of her mind. And she couldn't understand why he hadn't mentioned it. Finally she could stand it no longer.

"When are you going to tell me about the note?" she whispered.

There was a moment of silence; she thought Peter had fallen asleep. Then he said, "What are you talking about?"

That was not the answer she expected. "The note you sent me about wanting my full attention."

He rolled over to her and propped himself on one elbow. "I am sorry, but I have no idea what you are talking about."

"You didn't send me a note?"

He shook his head. "No. What sort of note was this?"

Now she was puzzled. "I received a note, in a beautiful handwriting, that said 'Dearest, I want'—no—'desire your full attention.' And you didn't send it?"

Peter shook his head again. He didn't like this at all. Something new had entered the scene, something Peter had never felt before—jealousy. He did not like the feeling. Who was trying to take this woman from him?

"Could it be the Mad Joker?" she said, thinking aloud. "No. It's not his style." She smirked and looked at Peter. "There I go, calling him a him. Even I'm becoming sexist." She expected a reaction from Peter, but there was none. She looked at the ceiling, her thoughts searching for some idea of who the sender might be. ''I wonder who did send it?'' she said absently. *And what did he want?* she thought.

Peter lay on his back and, frowning, stared at the ceiling. ''I wonder, too.''

CHAPTER
4

The flowers came around noon the next day. They were a striking arrangement of orange and black carnations in a black vase. Grace thought they were for the Halloween party until she saw that the envelope was addressed to Eleanor Carter. She shrugged. *Someone's strange idea of a Halloween bouquet,* she thought. She accepted the delivery and put the vase of flowers off to the side of the counter. Grace knew Eleanor had gone to the hairdresser's. She would catch Eleanor when she returned.

Just about everyone was bustling around today, preparing for the party in the evening. Warren Styck was shouting orders and directions to the workmen who were hustling all sorts of equipment through the front door and into the dining room. And there was hammering and banging, and all kinds of noises. *Enough to make you move to the peace and quiet of a retirement home*, Grace thought, grinning.

"Eugene said there would be some excitement tonight," Betty said. She was very concerned. She, Walter, Henri, and Charlie were sitting in the coffee alcove.

A table had been set up there with a spread of sand-wiches because the dining room was being decorated for the party in the evening.

"Who is this Eugene?" Henri asked. "I do not think I have met him." With all the strange people he had met so far, he was almost afraid to ask.

"Been talking with Eugene again?" Charlie asked Betty, holding back a skeptical grin. He was a tall, heavyset, retired salesman who a few months before had had a heart attack, followed by open-heart surgery.

Walter turned to Henri. "Eugene is Betty's husband—deceased."

Uh oh. Henri's eyebrows went up, and he looked at Betty.

"Oh, you two!" Betty fluttered her hands in despair. She turned to Henri. "They don't believe me."

Henri did not know what to say. He frowned and leaned back a little, moving away from Betty. *This is a strange place*, he thought.

"You mean we don't believe that you speak with your dead husband every night?" Walter said. "Of course we believe you. What we have a difficult time believing is that *he* speaks with *you*."

"Well, you'll see. Eugene said that the party was go-ing to be an exciting experience, but it was going to end on a dead note. Those were his exact words—'end on a dead note.' "

"Seems appropriate for a Halloween party." Charlie grinned, exchanging conspiratorial glances with Walter and Henri.

"I'm happy to hear the party's going to be an exciting experience," Walter said. "They sure are making a lot of noise preparing for it. Warren Styck is going to wear out the rubber on his wheels, the way he's been rolling around directing everything."

"You all have your costumes?" Charlie asked.

"Yes," Walter said, "but I'm not telling what mine is. I don't want you recognizing me."

Charlie laughed. "I have trouble recognizing all us old people without costumes. I mean, all wrinkles look alike. Sometimes I think we all look alike."

"Ah, yes, old age. The trouble with old age is there isn't much future in it," Mr. Petersen said. He was a thin, fragile-looking man, bald with a sparse fringe of gray hair around the sides of his head. He wore small, round eyeglasses set in wire frames.

"Henny Youngman, I presume," Walter said.

Mr. Petersen made a small bow. "Growing old has one advantage—you'll never have to do it again."

Now what! Henri gave Walter and Charlie a puzzled look.

"Now that I'm old enough to know my way around, I don't feel like going."

Charlie chuckled. Betty giggled. "Oh, Henny," she said.

"The way to live to be a hundred, is to reach ninety-nine, and then live very, very carefully. And I leave you with this parting thought. An old man is a man who is ten years older than you are." Mr. Petersen waggled his fingers in a wave, and walked away.

Henri was stunned. He looked at Walter. "Who . . . what? I do not know the question to ask!"

"That's Mr. Petersen," Betty said. "He's perfectly harmless."

This, Henri thought, rolling his eyes, *comes from a woman who speaks with her dead husband.*

"He's a retired chemical engineer, I think," Charlie said. "There are times when he thinks he's Henny Youngman, or Sherlock Holmes, or Fred Astaire, or a whole lot of other people."

"Perhaps," Henri said, pointing to his forehead, "he was too close to his chemicals."

Frank came in and poured himself a cup of coffee. He was still wearing the vest, but not the tank of insecticide.

"How's it going, Frank?" Walter asked.

"Good. Just finished spraying the ground around the pool area. So tonight, when you go outside for the party, you won't have bugs out there"—he smiled—"except the residents."

Henri could relate to that.

"Look, Ms. Cummings," Alex Conners said, "my men are doing their best, but it's hard to get work done with those equipment trucks in the way." He was standing by the front counter, talking with Jessie. Grace was at her post, listening but keeping a low profile. Grace could see that Jessie was not a happy camper. In her role as manager of Coral Sands Jessie had been riding herd on Warren Styck and his workmen as well as Alex Conners and the construction crew outside. At forty, an attractive woman with black hair touched up by chemical magic, Jessie was fighting the war of fat, and barely holding her own.

Jessie sighed with exasperation. "We can't move them until they're finished setting up in the dining room for tonight's party. I told you earlier in the week there might be a problem."

"Yes, you did. And from the looks of the stuff going into this place, it's going to be a great Halloween party. But I can't guarantee we won't damage one of those trucks. I've got heavy equipment widening the hole for the fountain. It's already a tight maneuver with the cars in the parking lot. Now we've got trucks crammed in as well."

"All right." Jessie walked around to the front of the counter. "I'll let you work this out with Warren. He's handling all this. Maybe he can do something about it."

Grace watched them walk to the dining room. *Good luck with Warren*, she thought, smiling.

Peter came in the front door, carrying his costume on a hanger under a black plastic bag. He nodded to Grace, then saw the flowers out of the corner of his eye. "Very nice decoration," he said, nodding in the direction of the vase.

Grace smiled, "Not mine. They're for Eleanor." She regretted saying it as the words left her mouth; he would have recognized them if he had sent them.

Peter frowned, stepped over to the vase and looked at the envelope addressed to Eleanor. Then he turned and walked away, his mood black.

"Uh-oh," Grace said under her breath.

Jessie came back to the desk. "Grace, the next time I let Warren Styck do something like this, you have me taken out back and shot."

"Giving you a hard time, Jessie?"

"If I were a man, I'd have strangled him." Jessie held up a fist so tight the knuckles were white. "Hell, if I was his mother, I'd have drowned him in the bathtub when he was a baby. Would have saved a lot of people, including me, a lot of aggravation through the years."

"Letting him get to you, eh?" Grace spoke calmly.

Jessie sighed and shrugged in surrender. "Yes. You're right. Since day one. I shouldn't let him do that to me. I guess it's just that the place was so peacefully quiet before he came. He's always doing something to disturb all that. Yesterday he gouged out that chunk of wall in the hall."

"He did arrange to fix that, didn't he?"

"Yeah. But that doesn't take back the aggravation it caused. And now this racket he's raising decorating the hall is really grating on me."

"Remember the motto of milk of magnesia . . ."

Jessie nodded with a grin. "And this, too, shall pass. You're right again. In a couple of days this will be only a bad memory." She made a face. "Then I'll just have Alex Conners and his problems to deal with."

"And maybe we'll all enjoy the peaceful quiet a little more."

"For as long as it lasts." Jessie shook her head. "The

construction promises to get really noisy soon.''

Alice came through the front door, carrying a costume covered in a black plastic bag.

"Had your clown costume cleaned for the party?" Grace asked.

Alice smiled. "Not funny, Grace. You'll have a tough time picking me out of the crowd."

"No we won't," Jessie said. "Not if you speak."

"Oh, boy." Alice looked to the sky for help. "A *pair* of comedians, now. See you guys tonight at the party," she said over her shoulder as she walked away.

"We'll be there," Grace and Jessie answered in unison.

"I'll be in my office having a well-deserved cup of coffee, if you need me." Jessie went through the door behind the front counter.

Eleanor came in. Her hair was done to perfection. The color was so natural, and the hair coifed so elegantly. *I must ask her who her hairdresser is*, Grace thought with envy. "Hi, Eleanor," she said.

Eleanor smiled.

"Those are for you." Grace pointed to the black vase.

"Me?" Eleanor frowned. She stepped to the vase and carefully picked off the envelope. She removed the card. "I hope I am getting your attention, Dear One," it read. The card was unsigned. This time the penmanship was a little shaky in places, but still quite flowing. She looked at Grace. "Do you have any idea who sent these?"

Grace shook her head. "No. Some florist brought them a little while ago. I was busy and didn't note the name of the florist. Why? Is there a problem?"

"No," Eleanor said. *Except I haven't the faintest idea who is doing this, and it's getting me annoyed*. She started to walk away.

"Aren't you going to take them with you?" Grace pointed to the flowers.

Eleanor hesitated. "No. You can keep them there."
She turned and headed across the lobby.

Grace frowned. She wasn't sure she should tell
Eleanor that Peter had seen them. *Better stay out of it*,
she thought. She shrugged and went back to work.

CHAPTER
5

Harry Benson opened the door to Cat Woman and was immediately taken back by how she looked. She looked great. The outfit covered her whole body, even to gloves on her hands, but it clung to her like her skin. *Still a terrific figure*, he thought. Then he got annoyed. "You're early, Aud." She hadn't changed. Still didn't listen to him. Still couldn't get it through her lame brain that when he said a quarter to eight, he meant just that. "Why?"

"Sorry, Harry. I know you don't like surprises, but I have to talk to you before we go to the party." Cat Woman stepped past Harry into the apartment. She wasn't surprised by what she saw. The place was one tiny step up from shabby.

Wants to talk to me, he thought. *Not unexpected. I just hope she doesn't start that crying stuff she used to pull. It didn't work then, and it won't work now.* He closed the door and stepped into the living room. Harry was dressed in his costume except for the mask and wig.

Audrey saw the mask and wig on the sofa. She turned

and looked him over. "Phantom of the Opera?"

Harry nodded. "So what's this all about?"

"I've been thinking, Harry."

"Now, don't hurt yourself, Aud."

She put her hands up defensively. "Truce. That's what I wanted to talk about—a truce."

Harry nodded. "I'm listening." *And waiting for the crying and pleading.*

"You were right. I have no choice in this arrangement. It's taken a lot of thinking to finally accept that. You used to tell me I should learn to accept things, rather than fight them. Well, that's one of the things that has changed in me. I've learned that some things you just have to accept, and make the best of them."

Surprise, surprise, Harry thought.

"But that's no reason we should be . . ." She couldn't think of the right word.

"Miserable?"

"Well, yes. 'Miserable' is a good word. We're talking about spending the rest of our lives together. That could be a very long time. And, I mean, we *were* in love once. Though the relationship didn't work out, we did have some good times together. It wasn't a total waste of time."

"Yes, we did have some good times." He didn't expect this at all.

"And a lot of water has flowed under the bridge since then. We are different people now."

"Well, I'll say one thing, Aud," he interrupted, appraising her with his eyes. "Time sure has treated you right. You look terrific."

"Thanks, Harry. But what I mean is that we are not the same people who were married so many years ago. Time has changed us, and we should try to get along, try to get to know each other again. It might really be fun."

"I'll drink to that." He smiled. This might be a small miracle, and he'd take it. This Audrey just might be his kind of woman after all. "It's what I hoped would happen, once you got to know me again. I thought, that Aud was a wonderful woman, and maybe there was a chance we could have the magic back that we once had."

She shrugged and smiled. "We can sure give it a good try." Then she looked at him as if she had just had an inspiration. "Maybe that drink isn't a bad idea. We could drink to a new beginning, a new Harry and Audrey."

"I've got a little wine in the kitchen. That all right?"

"Perfect. Where do you keep your glasses?"

He shrugged sheepishly. "In the kitchen. I don't have enough glassware to fill a lot of cabinets."

"Well, we're going to change that. Let me get the wine." She moved toward the kitchen.

Best to treat her gently for a while, he thought. He put out a hand and stopped her. "No, Aud. Let me. I don't want you waiting on me. You did that plenty when we were married. Now it's my turn. You just wait right here."

He went into the kitchen, found the wine and a couple of glasses, opened the wine, and went back into the living room. *God, this place is a dump. In a little while I'll be out of here and living more comfortably. Goodbye, poverty. Hello, George's money.* He handed her one glass and held the other. Carefully he poured the wine in her glass, then his, and put the bottle down on the cocktail table.

"To a new beginning," he said with a smile, and clinked his glass against hers.

"A new beginning." She smiled, and sipped her wine.

Harry took a small gulp. "Aud, I think this is great. You and me again. Like old times." He looked her over. She did look absolutely great. He couldn't wait to see how she performed in the old sack.

He was about to drink again when she put her gloved

hand over his glass. "Not old times, Harry. New times. A new beginning, remember?"

"Right." He grinned. "A new beginning. That sounds terrific."

Smiling, she took the glass from his hand, and set both glasses on the table next to the bottle of wine. Then she turned to him, and put her arms around his neck. "New beginnings can start with some old things," she said seductively, and brought her lips to his. The kiss was gentle, then hungry. She pulled away, leaving Harry a little breathless.

"God, Aud, you take my breath away. I can't believe this is happening." Boy, he didn't expect any of this. Things were looking up for good old Harry Benson. He sure was feeling good about what was to come. It was possible that things could be better than he ever imagined.

She smiled. "Like I said, it could be fun."

"I'll drink to that."

Audrey turned back to the table, picked up the two glasses, and handed one to Harry. She raised her glass and smiled. "To fun."

"To fun," he said, and swallowed the remaining wine in his glass.

She took another sip of her wine, then took his glass and put both glasses on the table. She picked up his wig and mask from the sofa and held them out to him. "Time to party, Mr. Phantom."

"You betcha, Miss Cat Woman."

"But first, let me clean up a little here." She picked up the glasses and the bottle.

"It's okay, Aud. Leave it."

"Well, let me just put them in the kitchen." She walked into the small kitchen before he had a chance to object. There was not much time. She had to move quickly. She hurriedly rinsed her wine glass. There was no dish towel that she could see.

"C'mon, Aud. Leave the damn dishes."

Damn, she couldn't find the cabinet with the glasses. Her heart was racing like a front runner in the Daytona 500. She stashed the glass in the cabinet with the cups and plates, then wiped her gloved hands on her costume.

"Let's go, Aud." His voice was more firm and annoyed.

Her hands were shaking as she slipped the note from under the top of her outfit, opened it, laid it next to Harry's wine glass, and smoothed it out. "Okay!" She quickly looked around, then stepped out of the kitchen. Harry was coming toward her. "You know us women— cleaning up is a force of habit." She gave him a sheepish grin. She took his arm and guided him toward the door. "To the party, Mr. Phantom. Or is it Mr. Opera?"

He laughed.

CHAPTER

6

"My God, Eleanor, will you look at this?" Cyrano de Bergerac said. Peter's costume was complete with a half mask and prominent nose, goatee and mustache, sword, and a plumed hat with the wig sewn in.

"They certainly outdid themselves this year," Morticia said. Eleanor's costume was flattering. The long black dress hugged her body, and the long, black draping sleeves accentuated the effect. The black wig, harsh makeup, and mask took away any hope of someone recognizing her.

Peter handed the two orange passes to Minnie Mouse, who took them and dropped them in a box on the chair next to her. "Isn't it terrific!" Grace said. "Warren did a super job."

The dining room had been transformed. Crepe paper in orange and black decorated the ceiling and met in three centers where three of the ceiling fans were mounted. Cobwebs with resident spiders dripped from the crepe paper. The globes of the lights on the ceiling fans had been replaced with grinning jack-o'-lanterns or skulls. Bats dangled from the ceiling and fluttered in the air moved gently by the ceiling fans.

In one corner of the room, at ceiling level, was a large spider web. An equally large spider, its legs wriggling, clung to the web. Black drapes hung in various places, and spiders, large and small, wriggled on the walls. The walls also sported broomsticks, monstrously ugly masks, and bleeding parts of human anatomy.

One wall was lined with long tables draped in black cloths and covered with food and drink. The wall on the opposite end of the room was covered in a large black curtain. Small black tables and chairs were scattered about. Each table had a black candle in its center.

"Over here," Snow White said. "Stand by the wall. I want to take your picture." Jessie Cummings was stopping everyone as they entered and taking their picture. She intended to post the photographs in the lobby later in the week, and to send a few copies to the *Sarasota Herald Tribune*, along with a story on the party.

After they had their picture taken, leaving them with the blue dot of the flash in their vision, Peter and Eleanor headed for the food table. The place was already filled with people. The disk jockey was playing "Monster Mash," and there were some couples on the dance floor.

"See anyone you recognize?" Peter asked.

Eleanor looked around. "Well, not really." She giggled. "I saw Charlie in the hall when I came in this afternoon. He said he'll have a hard time picking out people he knows because all the wrinkles look alike."

Peter laughed softly. "This mask is annoying," he said. "I hope I can eat around this nose. The darn thing is longer than my sword."

Eleanor grinned devilishly. "Not the sword I know."

Peter chuckled. "You *are* bad."

When they reached the table, Captain Hook was arranging some food on his plate.

"Who do you think that is?" Peter asked.

"Looks like Captain Hook from Peter Pan."

Peter grinned. "You think he lost his hand while making peanut butter?"

Eleanor smiled and slapped him playfully on the arm. "You're sounding like Tweedledee and Tweedledum."

By each dish of food was a little tombstone with the name of the food on it. Peter and Eleanor chuckled at some of the names: "Maggot Salad" by the macaroni salad; "Toes Salad" by the potato salad; "Tuna Leech." By the small sandwiches were names like "Bat Only," "Liver Worst," "Hand & Knees." There were "Crypt Cakes," cupcakes with white icing in the shape of skulls. The punch was blood red, and it was in a witch's caldron. Floating in the punch was a severed hand, complete with blood and torn flesh.

"Speaking of Tweedledee and Tweedledum, where are they?" Peter asked.

Captain Hook turned to Peter. "That's them over there, dressed as Dopey and Grumpy, two of the Seven Dwarfs." He chuckled. "Never saw such big dwarfs."

"Wonder if he's got his T-shirt on under the costume?"

"Walter?" Eleanor said to Captain Hook. "I wouldn't have recognized you." Then she noticed the cane hooked onto the table.

"Understandable. I hardly ever dress like this."

"Aud, I'm feeling a little dopey," Harry said. "Must be the wine on an empty stomach."

"Why don't you sit down?" She helped him settle into a chair at a table near one of the sliding glass doors. "I'll open the door a little. The fresh air might help." She slid the door back. The cool night air drifted into the room. "You sure you didn't have anything to drink before I got to your apartment? I mean, I'd swear you were a little tipsy."

"Yeah," he said, grinning a little foolishly. "I did have a little of that wine. But, hell, not enough to make me feel like this. I'd swear I had a whole bottle of the stuff, the way I'm feeling.''

"I'll get you some punch, and something to eat. Food may help absorb some of the alcohol.''

Cat Woman left The Phantom of the Opera sitting at the table, and went over to the food table. She threw a few little sandwiches on a black plastic plate, and scooped out a large glass of punch. She brought the plate and glass back to the table and sat down next to Harry. "Here, drink this. The liquid should help move that alcohol along. Here are four aspirins to take with it.'' When he looked at her questioningly, she added, "Helps the body's tissue get rid of the alcohol faster.''

"I didn't know that.'' He took the four pills and looked at them. Not that he didn't trust Audrey, but he felt he couldn't be too careful. The pills were marked "aspirin.'' He shrugged, threw all four in his mouth, and drained the glass of punch. "Thanks,'' he said, then looked appraisingly at the empty glass. "Good punch.'' He grinned. "Could use a little spike, though.''

"Not the way you're handling it. Now, eat. Get some food in you. You don't want to miss the party by being sick or dopey.'' She stood. "I'll get you more punch.''

Grumpy turned to Dopey. "You see anybody you know?''

Dopey looked around the room. "Well, there's Queen Elizabeth. She was supposed to be a virgin.''

"Looking like that, it's no surprise.''

"And that one over there with the pink sweater is a bobby soxer.''

"Looks like Bobby didn't just sock her, he beat her up badly.''

"That guy over there is dressed like the Grim Reaper.''

Grumpy put his hand over his heart and sighed with relief. "That's a costume! Thank God. I thought my time was up.'' Then he pointed across the room.

"Who's the woman having a bad hair day?"

"Medusa. I thought I saw you going out with her the other day."

"Well, she does look like a blind date I had once."

"To go out with you, she'd have to be blind, and have a lot of dust in her attic, too." Dopey looked around. "There's the Frankenstein Monster."

"Look at the ugly stitches in that guy's face and neck. Looks like he and I go to the same surgeon." Then Grumpy pointed to another person. "What's with that guy over there? He's supposed to be in costume. He looks like just another Coral Sands resident."

"That's the Crypt Keeper."

"They did a fabulous job on the decorations," Cyrano de Bergerac said, looking around admiringly.

"You been out by the swimming pool, yet?" Captain Hook had finished loading up a plate with food, and was ladling out a glass of punch.

"No."

"It's a nice touch, but doesn't encourage any swimming. You should go take a look."

Morticia looked at Cyrano. "Let's go. Then we can come back in and get something to eat."

They walked through the sliding glass doors, out to the swimming pool deck. The area was illuminated by lights strung all around. The lights were orange jack-o'-lanterns and pale white skulls. Ghoulish dummies, illuminated from below by yellow light, had been placed behind the long bar. The lights in the pool had been changed to red, making the pool look like a large tub of blood. Plastic rats and spiders floated in the water.

Tables had been set up on the pool deck, and some people had settled outside with food and drink. The music was piped outside through small speakers.

Peter chuckled. "I see what Walter meant by not encouraging swimming."

"So what do you think?"

Peter and Eleanor turned to see who was speaking. There was a decaying, cancerous old man seated in a wheelchair. An I.V. bag of blood was hanging from a metal pole attached to the chair, and the tube of the I.V. disappeared in the tattered fabric of his clothing.

"Certainly fits the theme." Peter grinned.

"Warren," Eleanor said, "you've done a fabulous job."

"Thanks. I was thinking about having a body floating in the pool, but Jessie felt it was a bit much."

Peter smiled. "I rather like the idea."

"You would." Eleanor grinned.

"Well, Jessie thought someone might call the police, thinking the body was real. You know how some of these old folks are."

"Yes. I see her point."

"I had to change the finale, too. I was going to do a dive off the third floor balcony into the pool. Jessie didn't think it was a good idea." He smiled, showing rotted and missing teeth. "She felt if I missed, it would really dampen the party."

"Too bad. It sounds like an exciting finale," Peter said. But he had to agree with Jessie.

"Don't worry. I worked out a good finish to the party. We put together a nice show for later on."

"I'm looking forward to it."

"Me, too," Eleanor said. "And thanks for all the work you put into the party."

"I wouldn't call it work, dear lady. If you're doing something you love, you never work a day in your life." He backed the wheelchair away. "Gotta go. Preparations to make. Talk to you later."

"Aud, I tell you I'm drunk." Harry giggled. He was slumped in his chair. "I feel good." His head was wavering, and his speech was slipping into a slur.

"Just keep drinking the punch. It should pass soon. You sure you had only a little wine?"

"Scout's honor." He held up a wavering hand in the Boy Scout salute.

She grinned. "Harry, one thing I can say—you were never a Boy Scout."

"Trouble is, I'm getting dizzy and sleepy." He giggled some more, thinking how it would look with him passed out on the floor. "Wouldn't make a good introduction, you pointing to me on the floor as your new boyfriend."

"I promise you, Harry, you pass out, I'm not even going to let on that I know you. You're going to be some wandering Phantom that dropped in uninvited."

He chuckled at that. "By the way, when am I going to meet some of your friends?"

Still smiling, she gave him an incredulous look. "You gotta be kidding, Harry. When you sober up a little, then I'll introduce you around. Don't want to give everyone a bad first impression, do you?"

Eleanor and Peter had gotten some food and punch, and joined Captain Hook at a table. Sitting with Captain Hook was a dumpy little witch complete with hairy warts, pointed hat, and long, scraggly hair.

"Betty," Captain Hook said, indicating the witch, "told us this afternoon that Eugene said the evening was going to end with some excitement." Walter had removed his hook from his hand so he could eat with both hands.

"What he said," Betty said, "was that the evening was going to end on a dead note."

"Dead note?" Eleanor asked. "What does that mean?"

Peter thought of Warren attempting to dive into the swimming pool from the third floor balcony and missing. That could be construed as a dead note.

Betty made a gesture of futility. "You know Eugene. He never says things outright. Always has to tease me with these riddles."

"You think it's serious?"

"Who knows? Eugene likes to joke around." Betty was clearly annoyed with Eugene.

"So, who else is here?" Peter tried to change the subject. Eugene disturbed him.

"Well, let's see," Walter said, looking around. "That overweight Devil is Charlie. And the overweight Minnie Mouse with him is Grace."

"Yes," Peter said. "We met Grace. She took our passes at the door."

"Medusa over there is Alice."

"Alice!" Eleanor said. "My God! I would never have guessed. I thought she'd come in her clown outfit."

"Mandrake the Magician is, naturally, Mr. Petersen. And the Grim Reaper is Henri."

"You guys want to move around a little so we can sit here?"

They looked up to see a big white woolly sheep and a bent shepherdess complete with crook. They were holding plates of food.

"Benny!" Eleanor laughed. "Is that you in all that wool?"

"Yeah, yeah," he said, not too pleased. "The things we do for love. C'mon, make room." They started shuffling the chairs around.

"Caroline, your outfit is terrific," Eleanor said. Benny had met Caroline outside a supermarket last spring. She had missed her bus home, and was sitting among her groceries. Benny offered her a lift. Romance blossomed, and the rest, as they say, was history. Though Eleanor still couldn't understand what this fragile Southern lady could have in common with tough Benny from Brooklyn.

"Little Bo Peep, I presume," Peter said.

"And you found one of your sheep," Walter added.

"Okay, everybody. Turn this way and smile." Snow White was back with her camera. They all dutifully turned and smiled, and Snow White left them with the blue ghost of the flash in their eyes.

•   •   •

The evening wore on, and no one noticed the Phantom of the Opera sitting alone, passed out in a chair near the glass doors.

It was ten-thirty when the music stopped and the cancerous old man in the wheelchair moved in front of the black curtain.

"Everyone!" he shouted. "I'd like your attention, please!" His voice came over speakers placed about the room. "Those of you outside, I would appreciate it if you would come in and take a seat someplace."

The conversations died in hesitant dribbles. People came in from the swimming pool area and took seats around the tables. Everyone turned to face Warren.

When they were all settled in, Warren continued. "Thank you. We have a little event with which to close the evening. If there are any among you who have weak hearts, this may be the time to leave. Our event might get the old ticker a little nervous."

Nobody accepted Warren's invitation to leave.

"Good. Then we are all settled in. Hopefully everyone is back from the bathroom." The Grim Reaper, Little Red Riding Hood, and the Devil came into the room at that moment, and everyone chuckled. They took seats near the back. No one saw Snow White, Medusa, and Minnie Mouse slip out of the rear door of the dining room.

"Before we begin our little venture into the dark side, I feel obligated to address the skeptics among you. There are many people who do not believe things they can not touch and see, things they can not get their arms around. Unfortunately, I am one of those people. I'm from Missouri; you have to show me. I'm not going to take your word for it. Therefore, what I am about to tell you is the God's honest truth, because it happened directly to me.

"Our first child, Valerie, was a precocious little thing who was in a very great hurry to grow up. She walked at nine months, and was talking in clipped phrases before she was a year old. One night this innocent soul woke up crying hysterically. I went in to see what I could do for her.

"It took me a few moments to understand what she was trying to say through the fear and tears. Her exact words were 'Tree fall.' And she kept repeating those words. 'Tree fall. Tree fall.' Once I understood what she was saying, I took her to the window in her room, and together we looked out on the street, and the big old trees that marched down the sidewalk. She peered intently at those trees for a few moments, then she calmed down and went quietly back to sleep.

"The next morning I left to go to the bakery, and there, lying across the street, was one of the huge trees we had looked at the night before."

Some chuckling and whispered comments in the crowd.

"Again, I stress that this is a true story. But there is more.

"Our second child was born fourteen months after Valerie. This child, Cynthia, we put in the same room with Valerie, in a portable crib. Again, Valerie woke up crying hysterically. And now she had my undivided attention. 'Crib broke, baby cry!' she was screaming.

"I carefully checked the portable crib, and found the screw that held the bedspring in place had worked its way almost all the way out. I screwed it back in. And over the next months I repeatedly checked that screw, and when I found it had worked itself out, I screwed it back in.

"Now what this demonstrated to me was that the future can be seen. And it can also be changed. The crib never broke, the baby didn't cry. At least not from the crib falling apart."

Some chuckles from the audience.

"There is one more incident. This occurred to my wife—a more pragmatic woman I have never met.

"Five years after her father died, she told me he had visited her in the car that day while she was driving to the store. He spoke to her for a short time, asked her if everything was all right, then left, saying there was so much he had to see."

A little nervous stirring in the audience.

"From then on, I looked with less skepticism on those stories of ghostly visitation told by others. The pleasant stories and the gruesome ones.

"There is much we do not know about the living world around us. But there is much we suspect. We have heard many stories, some passed down for centuries. I learned that some of those stories are true. Spirits do walk the Earth. Some people can see across the boundaries that separate the living from the dead, the future from the present.

"Tonight I have asked you to accompany me, and we will all cross those boundaries together.

"This is All Hallows' Eve, when the dead walk. The unhappy dead. The tortured, restless dead. Let me take you all outside under the night sky, where we have a better opportunity to see those disquieted souls."

A screen that had been hidden by the decorations rolled quietly down over the windows. When the screen had fully descended, covering all the windows and sliding doors, the lights suddenly went out, swallowing the world around them in blackness that was impenetrable. There was some unsettled muttering in the audience.

Peter heard the thin squeaking of the curtain being opened, but it was too dark to see anything. A soft breeze flowed around him, the air cool and moist. On it was the sour smell of dank earth. The breeze rattled a few dead leaves that still clung to trees somewhere. *Nice effect*, Peter thought.

"The darkness frighten you? It is the natural ground for fear to take root and thrive. For the darkness holds things we can not imagine, creatures we dare not meet.

They make noises we can not identify, and they move close to us, where we can feel but can not see them.

"Samuel Coleridge said it best:

> Like one that on a lonesome road
>   doth walk in fear and dread,
> And having once turned round, walks on,
>   And turns no more his head;
> Because he knows a frightful fiend
>   doth close behind him tread.

He paused. "But the night is not always so dark as this."

On the screen a full moon appeared, shreds of torn clouds slowly moving across it. There were stars visible here and there through the gaps in the clouds. Peter looked up, and saw stars and clouds on the ceiling of the dining room as well. It was as if the ceiling—the entire room—had vanished, and they were outside in a frightening, dead world.

In the subdued moonlight Peter could see the shapes of those at the other tables. And in the scene on all sides beyond them, he could also see a scattering of twisted black skeletons of dead trees that poked at the sky.

"There are creatures that belong to the night. Nature doesn't rest when the sun disappears."

And the bats came, fluttering in the sky where the ceiling had been, passing before the moon, uttering peeping sounds as they darted about. Some of them were luminescent in the moonlight. A stab of fear hit Peter. It was not something he could help, or control. But it made him feel silly.

Off in the distance came the mournful howling of a wolf.

There was a distant flash of lighting, followed by a low rumble of thunder.

Peter smiled to himself. These effects were terrific! He then noticed that the shadows against the sky were not just shadows of dead trees. There were structures there as well. Oddly spaced. Some leaning awkwardly. Whether the moon had grown brighter, or his eyes had become more adjusted to the dark, the shapes became clearer—headstones, mausoleums. They were in a graveyard. An old and abandoned graveyard, the grounds unkempt, the headstones off-kilter.

A cool mist began to rise around them.

"Appropriately for this night when the dead will rise, we are in a cemetery, a place of the dead. A border where the physical world meets the world of lost souls. And where, on such a night as this, those souls cross that border to mingle with the living."

The chilling creak of a rusted gate drew Peter's attention to a large mausoleum on the left. In the moonlight he could see the metal gate slowly struggle to open, dust falling from it. The creaking sent chills up his spine. And then there were other creakings as other mausoleums around them began to open. Bodies—disfigured, horribly decayed—pushed open the gates. They slowly stepped out and walked stiffly and purposefully toward them.

Somewhere behind him Peter heard a person sigh as if the air had been let out of him. He understood Warren's warning about people with weak hearts. His was doing a stumbling tap dance even though he had taken his beta-blocker before the party started.

"There is a peculiar sound that is heard on this night when the dead walk. It is written in the annals of ancient civilizations and in the experiences of those of more recent times. It is referred to as the note of the dead."

Betty poked Walter. "See," she whispered. "Eugene was right."

Eleanor squeezed Peter's hand at the announcement of the note of the dead. "The amazing Eugene," Peter whispered.

"It is the sound of tortured souls, yearning for relief of their suffering, yet hopelessly despairing of any respite."

A low rumbling moan began, and Peter felt the trembling pressure of that sound on his heart and in the vibrations in the table and in the chair he was sitting on. It was as if the sound had substance, filling the space around him, pressing in, vibrating his very bones down to the roots of his teeth. He squirmed against the sound, but couldn't escape it.

"Should we fear the dead? Should we cringe from their sight? Are they here to hurt us? I think not. For they were once us, and they are us. We should embrace them, welcome them on their short visit with us."

The figures had taken on a soft luminescence, and continued their labored walk toward them. And then, to Peter's surprise, they walked among them! The grotesque bodies, glowing like apparitions, were now wandering around the tables and among the audience, as if in search of someone.

"Do not show fear. Extend the warmth that only humans can extend to one another. Their nature is our nature. Reach out to them. Take the hands of love offered to you. Remember, they are humans."

The half-dozen specters stopped at tables and extended their hands to the people sitting there. One of them stopped by Peter. An ugly creature in tattered clothes, with decaying face and hands, covered with dirt and dust from the grave. It extended a hand to Peter. Not a healthy human hand, but something gnarled and crippled and dirty. Peter made no move to take the hand. Touching it was not something he wanted to do.

"Go, on," Eleanor whispered. "Take its hand!"

Peter did not want to look cowardly in front of Eleanor. Especially with that mystery admirer lurking in the background. So he slowly reached out for the disgusting hand extended to him.

Suddenly the dining room filled with light. Peter winced at the sudden, painful brightness, his eyes forced to squint. The night, the graveyard, the bats, the full moon were gone. The creature standing before him was not one of the walking dead, but someone in a hideous costume. Peter and Eleanor laughed, a laugh of nervousness and relief. The laughter grew around them. The creature removed its mask, and there was Jessie Cummings's grinning face. "Gotcha!" she said.

"What a great show!" Peter laughed and started applauding. The applause picked up until everyone had joined in.

"Thank you, thank you," Warren said. The black curtain behind him was open, revealing a complicated array of equipment. "I'm happy you enjoyed the show. Please extend your applause to include all those who assisted me."

The applause grew louder, and there were whistles and shouts of praise. The apparitions, all unmasked, took their bows. Peter recognized Alice and Grace among them. They must have slipped out unnoticed and changed costumes for the show.

"And now, everyone, it's time to unmask! The party is over."

The masks started to come off. Everyone was talking and laughing again. Peter was glad to get rid of his mask—he'd been sweating under the darn thing. Some people had gathered up front around Warren, giving him his due praise. Others were talking to Alice and Grace and the other apparitions.

Jessie Cummings had stepped to the front and taken the microphone from Warren. "Please, everyone, as you leave, take some of the food remaining on the tables. Otherwise, we'll have to throw out what's left. There are some containers on the tables for you to use."

Peter stood and stretched. "Great party."

"Well," Benny chuckled, "I don't think that guy enjoyed it." He indicated the table behind them.

They all looked. There was a man slumped in a chair.

"Some people can sleep through anything," Benny said.

Walter stood up and grabbed his cane. "He may not

be sleeping." He moved toward the man. Peter and Benny went with him.

"You think he might have had a heart attack?" Peter said. "The show was rather frightening."

Walter did not answer. He stepped next to the man, and gently felt his neck for a pulse. The man was dressed as the Phantom of the Opera. His long black cape covered his shoulders and extended almost to the floor. Walter looked at Peter. "You'd better alert Jessie. He's dead."

"Jesus," Benny said. "I'll get her."

As he turned to leave, Walter added, "You'd better have her call the police." He pointed to the pool of blood beneath the man's chair. "This may not be a death from natural causes."

"Damn!" Peter thought of Eugene. Was this what he had meant?

CHAPTER

7

"I saw them at the table together earlier in the evening," Charlie said. It was nearing one in the morning. He was still in his Devil outfit, and he was tired. It had been a long night for him. Since his heart surgery, he had been getting to bed at ten every night, and was out walking by eight the next day. "She was bringing him drinks."

"Did you know her?" Ralph Ardley asked, looking up from his notebook. A detective with the Sarasota Police Department, he was a big man with a sweat-stained white shirt, a bulging waist, and a thick head of gray hair. He, too, was tired. It had been a long day for him as well. They were seated in the dining room. Ardley had already interviewed most of the guests.

"No."

"Was she a resident?"

"Couldn't tell. We were all in costumes and masks."

"Yeah, but you could still recognize people, even in costume."

"Some of them, yeah. But others, no. You see, her

costume had a tight hood that covered her head. In fact, the only thing showing on her whole body was her eyes, mouth, and chin. I couldn't even tell you what color her hair was."

"Well, was there anything familiar about her? Her walk? Her height? Like that."

"No. She did have a nice figure, though." He grinned. "That's why I noticed her. Not many people in this place with dynamite bodies."

"She had a dynamite body?"

"She was wearing some kind of cat outfit, black, that really hugged her body. Looked dynamite from where I was looking." Charlie smiled. "Of course, at my age I'm less discriminating about those things. They say that women get prettier as you get older. Worked for me."

Ardley looked around at those remaining to be interviewed, then flipped through the pages of his notebook. "I don't recall interviewing anyone in a cat outfit."

Charlie shrugged. "She could have left early. After she stabbed . . ." He nodded in the direction of where the dead man had been found. The police had removed the body a short while before, after pictures were taken and the body examined. Now technicians were at the table, dusting it for fingerprints.

"When was the last time you saw her?"

"Let me think." He looked off in the distance, trying to run through the events in his mind. "It was on the bathroom break before the show started. I got up to go to the bathroom, and she was leaving the dining room. I assumed she was also going to the bathroom."

"Sounds like you were really keeping an eye on her."

"Well," Charlie said, "I remember that time because I thought I might bump into her. You know, strike up a conversation."

"When you returned, she wasn't around?"

"I didn't see her."

"Did anyone else leave or come back at that time?"

"Well, now . . ." He shifted in the chair, trying to get

comfortable. It had been a long night of sitting, and the chair was no longer his friend. "I don't remember anyone else leaving. But I came back in at the same time a couple of other people did. There was the Grim Reaper and Little Red Riding Hood. We sat in the back so as not to disturb the show."

"Do you know who the Grim Reaper and Little Red Riding Hood were?"

He nodded. "The Grim Reaper is that new guy, Henry something or other. Don't remember his last name. And Audrey Knitter was Little Red Riding Hood. She's got a pretty nice figure, too. But the outfit didn't show it off."

"You recognized them?"

He shook his head and smiled. "Only after they took their masks off. We were together in the back of the dining room at the unmasking."

"What about the murdered man? You have any idea who he is?"

Charlie shook his head. "Never saw him before."

"Did anyone leave during the show?"

"Henry, the Grim Reaper, left for a few minutes."

"Any idea why?"

"Bathroom break, I think. Came back with the smell of the bathroom soap on him."

"I thought you said Henry had just gone to the bathroom before he came in with you and"—he looked at his notes—"Audrey Knitter."

Charlie shrugged. "May have. Not sure. I just remember him coming in with me." He shifted his weight. "You have to remember, at our age sometimes there are a lot of trips to the bathroom."

Ardley nodded and wrote in his notebook.

"He isn't one of the residents," Jessie Cummings said. She had changed from the costume while she waited for the police. She knew the press wouldn't be far behind the police, and she wanted to give some credibility to an interview with reporters. Who would take her seriously if she was dressed in the tattered clothes of the walking dead? "I've never seen him before tonight. Didn't he have any ID on him?"

"No," Ardley said. "His pockets were empty. How did he get into the party, if he wasn't a resident?"

"Many of the residents are single, widowed. So we let each resident bring a guest."

"How did they do that? Did they have to tell you who they were bringing?"

"No. We just gave everyone two passes. We kept it simple."

Ardley took a card from his shirt pocket and held it up for Jessie to see. It was a simple orange card with "Admit One—Halloween Party" printed on it in black. "Like this one?"

"If you knew, why did you ask me?"

"Sorry. Force of habit." Then he indicated the swimming pool area outside. "Anyone could simply walk into the party from outside. They wouldn't have to go through the lobby to the dining room and present this card."

Jessie sighed in annoyance. "This is not a college fraternity party we're talking about here. In fact, we don't even serve alcohol at these parties. We don't get gate crashers. We have a limit of one guest per individual resident, because many of these people would invite their entire Elks' lodge or bridge club unless we exercised some restriction."

Ardley put the orange card back in his pocket. "Did you recognize the woman that came in with the victim?"

Jessie shook her head. "No, but there were a lot of costumes that made the people unrecognizable. Part of the purpose of wearing costumes and masks."

"I was told by some of the people that you were taking pictures all evening."

"Yes! That's right! I took a picture of everyone who came tonight. I caught them at the door and took their picture before they could get into the party. I've got a picture of everyone as they arrived. I also went around and took pictures at some of the tables.''

"May I have that film? I'll have it developed for you free of charge.'' Ardley made an attempt at a grin, but it was unsuccessful.

"I left the camera in my office. I'll get it for you.''

"All right.''

Jessie got up and left the dining room. Ardley looked around. The technicians were gone, and there was only one man in uniform left to help him. The policeman was standing over the last two people left to interview. Ardley yawned wide and long. *Finish with those two, and I can go home and get some sleep*, he thought. Jessie returned with the camera and a roll of film.

"There's a roll in the camera, and this one I finished shooting.'' She handed the camera and the roll of film to Ardley. Ardley took them, and signaled the policeman to come over. "Will I get the pictures back? I mean, you aren't going to keep them as evidence or anything?''

"You'll get the prints back from each picture. We'll keep the developed film in case we need to blow up some of the pictures and look at them more closely.'' The cop came over, and Ardley handed him the camera and film. "See that this film and the roll in the camera get developed. I want three eight-by-tens of each frame.'' The cop nodded, and put the film and camera in a plastic evidence bag he took from his pocket.

"There is one thing you can do for me, Ms. Cummings.''

"I thought we agreed you could call me Jessie.''

He grinned weakly. "I'm sorry, Jessie. It's been a long day. But there is still one thing you can do for me.''

"What's that?''

"I'd like a complete list of the residents.''

"Why?''

"Well, somebody came to the party with the victim. *I've* questioned all the people that were here at the end of the party. I'll need to question those who weren't here. It's likely that the woman in the cat costume . . ."

"Cat Woman costume," Jessie said. "It's from Batman. You know, Batman and Robin? She's one of the villains, I believe."

Ardley wrote that in his notebook. "It's likely that the Cat Woman slipped out after the deed was done. It's also likely that someone who didn't attend gave their passes away. I'd like to find out who they gave them to. So, I'd like to talk to all the residents I didn't interview tonight."

Jessie nodded. "I'll have Grace provide you with a list tomorrow."

"Thanks."

"Did you lose a bet or something?" Ardley asked. He was trying to keep a straight face. He was sitting at a table with Benny and Peter. He'd decided to interview the two of them together.

"You don't like my costume?" Benny was clearly annoyed. He'd been taking abuse for the sheep costume all night long, and he'd had enough. He had told Caroline that he felt silly in the costume, but she said he looked darling. And they were a theme together—Bo Peep and her sheep. He had said to her, "Why don't we go as Jack and Jill, or Bonnie and Clyde, if you want a theme?" But he gave in, reluctantly, because he liked Caroline and didn't want to offend her. And she did look kinda cute in the Bo Peep outfit. Given the opportunity, he wouldn't do it again.

"On the contrary"—Ardley couldn't hold back the grin any longer—"I love it."

Peter tried desperately to keep a straight face. Benny was his friend, and he felt he should not join in the ridicule of his costume, but it was difficult.

"This is why you kept me here, so you can make fun of my costume?"

Ardley swallowed the grin. "Did either of you know this guy who was killed?"

"I have never seen him before," Peter said.

"Me neither," Benny said. "And I can tell you he ain't a resident. I know everyone who lives here."

Ardley nodded. He was very much aware of Benny's role. Jessie had referred to Benny as the mayor of Coral Sands. "What about the woman who was with him? The one in the Cat Woman outfit."

Peter shook his head.

Benny said, "Didn't recognize her. She could have been a resident."

"Your table was just in front of where the man was found dead. Did you see anything or hear anything? Snatches of conversation?"

"When I came to the table to sit with these guys"—indicating Peter—"I passed his table. The guy looked passed out. Like he was drunk or something."

"You didn't notice any blood anywhere?"

Benny shook his head. "The guy wasn't dead. He was breathing, and moving his head like he was trying not to sleep. Like a drunk."

"The only thing I can tell you, Detective," Peter said, "is that during the show, I did hear someone behind me let out a long sigh. It was dark, and the show was potentially frightening. I thought it was a reaction to that fear. In fact, after the show, when we saw the man slumped in the chair, I thought he might have had a heart attack."

The knock on the door was light but urgent—a gentle knocking, but rapid and impatient.

"Alice," Betty whispered through the door, the whisper no louder than the knocking. "Alice! Alice! It's me, Betty. I must talk to you. Alice!" She repeated this for a long time, but nothing happened. What should she do? She couldn't go away. This was too important. She had to speak with Alice. Just had to. "Oh, dear," she said in a worried whisper. She looked around, as if the answer would be somewhere nearby. "Oh dear, oh dear," she said again.

Then Betty did something she would never have done if this wasn't an emergency, a real emergency. She opened the door, and leaned into the darkened apartment. "Alice! Are you there?" There was still no answer.

Betty was fretting now, clearly dealing with a conflict between decorum and the urgency of the situation. But the urgency could not be denied, and she stepped inside the apartment. She leaned forward as she carefully took one step after another. "Alice! It's Betty! Alice!" Finally—in for a penny, in for a pound—she straightened, and switched on the lights. The sudden light was bright enough to make her squint. Alice's Medusa costume lay sprawled on the sofa along with the tattered clothes and mask of the dead.

With the determination of a woman on a mission, she walked into the bedroom. She turned on the lamp on the dresser. Alice's still body was on the bed, bundled under a light cover. Betty stepped cautiously toward her. "Alice!" she whispered. "Alice! It's Betty. Alice?" She reached out a tentative hand as she approached the bed. Then she laid the hand lightly on the body's shoulder and shook it. "Alice!"

"Jesus!" Alice jumped awake, throwing off the cover and blinking her eyes, trying to get them to work. Wide-eyed with fright, Betty stumbled backward, colliding with the dresser, a pain shooting up her back that made her wince.

Alice stared for a moment, trying to get a handle on reality and shake off the fog of her dreaming. "God damn! Betty! What the hell are you doing here? What's going on?"

"Oh, I'm so sorry, Alice," Betty said, clearly upset, wringing her hands excitedly. "Please believe me. I had to talk to you. This is very important. Very, very important.'' She stressed the words, as if saying them that way would make Alice understand that she wouldn't have intruded otherwise.

Alice rubbed her face, trying to clear her mind. "It's okay, it's okay. Jesus, Betty, you scared the wits out of me.''

"I'm so sorry. I really am.''

"It's all right, it's all right. Just stop saying you're sorry. Please.'' Then Alice took a deep breath to calm herself. She looked around the room, and felt embarrassed. The bedroom was a mess.

"Could we at least go into the living room?'' Alice said.

"Oh, yes. Yes, of course,'' Betty said, and hurried from the room.

Alice got out of bed and untangled her nightgown. The damn thing was useless, always ending up around her neck by morning. She grabbed a light robe that was lying across the back of the chair near the bed, slipped it on, and went to the living room. Betty was standing near the door to the corridor, and she was still fretting.

"Okay, Betty,'' Alice said. "How about you calm down, and tell me what's going on?''

"Well, after that terrible thing that happened at the party . . .''

"You mean the dead guy.''

"Yes, yes. After that, I went to my apartment and contacted Eugene.''

Oops, Alice thought. She had seen what Eugene could do. She could not take anything he said lightly.

"And, you know, we talked about what had happened, and everything. I mean, Eugene said something terrible was going to happen at the end of the party, and it did.''

"Yeah. Yeah.'' She hadn't heard anything about Eugene making a prediction, but she believed it.

"Well, then Eugene said something about you.''

"Me?''

"Yes, and it worried me so much I couldn't sleep without telling you."

Great, Alice thought. *So now you're gonna tell me and I won't sleep.*

"I didn't know if you were going out tomorrow morning. I was afraid you'd be gone before I could catch you and tell you."

"Well, I do have a gig tomorrow morning." Alice looked at the clock. "I mean, later *this* morning, at a house on the bay. Another rich kid's birthday."

"See. I was right to come to see you now."

"I guess you were. Now, will you *please* tell me what Eugene said?"

"Yes, yes. Of course. He said . . . Now let me think exactly how he said it." Then she gave Alice an annoyed look. "You know, Eugene is so cryptic sometimes. He talks like those pieces of paper in the fortune cookies. I don't understand why he doesn't just give me a direct answer."

On with it, already! Alice thought.

Then Betty closed her eyes, trying to look into her memory. "He said, 'Alice should watch out for traffic tomorrow.' That's what he said. Those were his exact words—'Alice should watch out for traffic tomorrow.' "

"Without spelling errors?" Alice asked.

Betty gave Alice a puzzled look.

"Sorry, Betty. Just a stupid joke. Your using the Ouija board and all."

"Well, I'll go now," Betty said. She sighed with relief. "I feel better that I told you."

"I'm glad you came," Alice said, but wasn't sure that was true. "I'll make sure the taxi driver is careful when he drives me to the gig. And I'll definitely watch out for the traffic."

"Good." Betty opened the door. "Good night, Alice."

"Good morning, Betty."

"Oh, yes." She smiled. "Good morning."

She closed the door after Betty had left, and Alice wondered if she'd get any sleep at all now. Watch out for traffic. *Damn you, Eugene. Couldn't you be more specific?*

CHAPTER
8

"I know," Peter said, and stood up. He reached for the ashtray to put out his cigarette, the first one of the day. "You must spray, and we must move." Frank the bug man had just come into the swimming pool area. The tank of insecticide was mounted on his back over the workman's vest, the sprayer nozzle in his left hand.

"No, no," Frank said carelessly waving his right hand. "Stay where you are."

It was after ten in the morning, and Peter, Eleanor, Doc Innes, Betty, and Charlie had come outside just a few minutes before to enjoy the pleasant weather. They were seated at one of the tables with cups of coffee in front of them. The table's umbrella was up, taking the sharp edge off the sunlight.

"I'm not going to spray here. Sprayed this area yesterday." Then, more seriously, "I wanted to find out what happened last night. I saw Alice over an hour ago. As she was getting in a taxi, she told me somebody died at the party last night."

"I hope she's careful," Betty said to Eleanor, who

was wearing a pink silk blouse and shorts the same soft brown as her hair.

"Killed is more accurate," Walter said. He had grabbed his cane to get up. Now he leaned his cane back against the chair. "We were just talking about it. The topic of the day. Maybe even the week."

"I went to Alice's apartment last night to tell her what Eugene said."

When he heard Eugene's name mentioned, Peter tried to listen to both conversations.

"Killed?" Frank was incredulous. "At the Halloween party?" He shook his head. "I find that hard to believe."

"Eugene said something about Alice?" Eleanor said. "Was it bad?"

"Stabbed in the back," Charlie said. "Right under our noses, and nobody saw it."

"Well, he told me to tell her to watch out for the traffic today."

"Stabbed! What kind of party was this?"

"It had me so worried I couldn't sleep until I told her."

"Not a party to get that excited about," Walter said. "We had punch with a severed hand floating in it, and maggot salad. Not something to kill for."

"Who was it? I mean, after three years of working here, I know a lot of the people who live here."

"But I felt better after I told her. I don't think anything will happen, now that she has been warned."

Eleanor nodded. "I'm sure Eugene would not have said anything if there was nothing Alice could do about what was going to happen."

"No one from the Home," Peter said. "In fact, no one anybody knows. The man had no identification on him."

"Yes," Betty said. "That's what I thought, too."

"And Alice will pay attention to Eugene. She'll be looking around her."

"A mystery guest. Maybe a mystery lover?" Peter looked at Eleanor when he said it. She saw him turn to her, and she gave him a look that said, Don't be dumb. Dumb or not, he felt the green-eyed monster taking over. Now that he had found a woman he truly cared for, someone was trying to muscle in. He didn't like that one little bit, but he didn't know what to do about it. Or if there was anything he *could* do about it.

"That's a relief." Frank sighed. "I mean, it's bad that someone died, if you know what I mean. But . . ."

Walter interrupted, finishing the thought. "It is not as bad as if it were someone you knew." He shook his head sadly. "That is the way it always is. Read a newspaper headline about a hundred thousand people dying in a monsoon in India, and you turn to the sports page and sip your coffee. But if you knew one of them, what a difference that would make to your day."

True words, Peter thought. *That guy last night was a nobody to me. His death was tragic. No, not even that. It was just a death. The death of a child would have been tragic.* He looked at the people around the table. *But if it had been one of my friends here, that would have been a different story.*

"The cops are looking for a mystery woman who was with the guy," Charlie said. "They think she did him in." He made a stabbing motion with his hand.

"Sounds like something from that TV show, *Murder She Wrote*."

"Life imitating art," Walter said. He was wearing a faded blue fisherman's hat that had lost its shape and looked as if he had kept it rolled up in his pocket. His short-sleeved shirt was a red and white plaid, and his shorts were hunter green. Blue reflector sunglasses hung off his nose.

Peter looked at Walter and raised an eyebrow in surprise. "Art?"

Walter shrugged and grinned. "Well, entertainment, then."

"Well," Frank said, "I'm sure glad it was nobody I know. At my age you're always losing friends. You check the obituaries every day to see who has gone. Thanks for the information. I'll get back to my spraying, now. Got lots to do."

"Heads up, down there!"

Everybody turned toward the building. Henri had just come through the sliding glass doors from the coffee alcove, and was walking stiffly across the deck toward them. He looked up when he heard the cry. A sack the size of a duffel bag came sailing off the third floor balcony. Henri, shocked, threw up his arms protectively and stumbled quickly to one side. The sack missed him and landed with a loud smack on the concrete deck four feet from the edge of the swimming pool, a yard to the left of where Henri was standing.

"What the hell?" Peter said. Eleanor let out a small cry; Betty cringed and screeched. Charlie stiffened and grunted. Walter did not react. He was blasé about everything.

"What do you suppose that is all about?" Walter said.

"What kind of place is this!" Henri shouted.

Up on the third floor a head peered over the railing. It was Warren Styck, his long gray hair moving in the breeze. "Everybody okay down there?"

Henri threw up his hands in disgust. "I am here two days! There is a bug in my coffee! I meet all kinds of crazy people! Then some one gets killed!" He glared down at the duffel bag. "And now *I* am almost killed by whatever that is!" He waved his arms at them as if it was all too much to bear, turned, and headed back inside.

Charlie chuckled. "What does he expect for only two days?"

Peter was sympathetic. Henri's image of retirement, like Peter's when he had first arrived, was not based in reality. It was a dream of paradise. The reality was Looney Tunes. It was tough to adjust quickly to that let-down.

"Is he all right?" Warren called down.

"Just a bit temperamental!" Walter shouted up to Warren.

"What are you doing?" Eleanor asked.

Warren leaned over the railing and pointed at the bag on the deck. "I'm working on a stunt. I'm going to vault out of the wheelchair, off this balcony . . ."

Grinning, Charlie interrupted. "From the looks of that bag, it's a stunt you're going to do only once!"

"Well," Warren grinned back. "I anticipate landing in the swimming pool."

"Quiet this morning, Alice. What's the matter?" Bert was the taxi driver she got most of the time. She'd let him know her schedule, and he'd be sure to be free to pick her up. Bert was a nice guy—all heart, and he liked to talk. Friendly and even—surprise, surprise—courteous. He always needed a haircut, and he was on the fat side. Alice thought the closest he ever got to soap and water was watching the Zest ads on TV. And he smoked cigars. You could tell Bert was near when he was a block away. She always rode with her window open.

"Just thinking, Bert."

"Don't hurt yourself, now." He grinned at her in his rearview mirror.

Alice gave him a forced grin. "Who's the clown in this car?"

As they drove through the city streets they always drew stares, the taxi with the clown in the back. Bert enjoyed that.

"How was the Halloween party last night?"

"All right." She didn't want to talk. Eugene was on her mind. Damn Eugene! "Look out for traffic." What the hell was that supposed to mean? Cross at the corner, only when the light was green? What? And when? This morning, or later this afternoon when she took back her costume? Or this evening? Though she didn't have any plans for the evening. Was it going to be a runaway car, some old guy with his foot on the gas instead of the brake? Some truck jumping the light and running her down? Or some jerk on a bicycle thinking traffic laws weren't for him?"

"Nothing special, huh?"

"What?" She hadn't been listening.

"The party last night. Nothing special?"

"Nah. You'll read about it in the papers."

"They're gonna put it in the paper?"

"Yeah, the comic section. Speaking of papers, that reminds me, we gotta stop someplace to buy a news-paper."

"What's the matter? My conversation skills slip-ping?"

"Never been much better than your driving."

"What's wrong with my driving?" He feigned being hurt. "I'm a good driver. I do it for a living."

"That should tell you why you're no millionaire. I need it for a prop. To make a eucalyptus tree. There are little kids at the party, and they get a kick out of that sort of thing. So find a place where I can pick one up."

"Eucalyptus tree?"

"Yeah. You roll up the pages, then tear halfway down the length of the cylinder." She saw Bert watching her intently in the rearview mirror and not watching the traf-fic. Eugene popped immediately into her mind. She waved her hand and shook her head. "Never mind, Bert. Someday I'll show you."

Bert nodded.

"And I need to borrow a dollar. I've got no money on me in this outfit."

"You want to borrow money from me?" He gave her a look of disbelief. "Does that sign on the top of my cab say 'bank'?"

"Give me a break, Bert. I'll pay you when you take me home."

He let out a weary sigh of surrender. "All right. I could never resist a woman."

"Even with bells in her red hair, and size 24 shoes?"

Bert shifted his weight, and reached into his pocket. The cab wandered around in the lane as he struggled to get the money out of his pants pocket. When the cab started to swerve, Alice looked anxiously around. *Is this it! Should I look for the traffic now?* Bert righted the swerve, and pulled a wrinkled dollar out his pocket. Alice was still looking nervously around. He held up the limp bill.

"I'm trusting you, now."

Alice leaned forward, and snatched it from his hand. "Sucker."

Bert shook his head. "Never trust a woman. Especially one in size 24 shoes." He signaled and made a right turn at the corner. Then he looked around and moved into the center lane. He put his blinker on and made a left onto Main Street. "There's Sarasota News down on the corner. That okay?"

"Great."

He eased the car down the street and pulled to the curb. "You want me to go in and get it for you?"

"Nah. We'll give them a treat. Something to talk about all day. 'You see, this clown came in for a paper. Honest to God, a real clown.' You know how it goes." She opened the door and stepped onto the sidewalk. Already some people were looking at her. She had closed the door and taken one step toward the store when she heard a crash and Bert shouted, "Damn!" She whirled around and saw that a car had jumped the curb, knocked aside a metal trash can, and was flying along the sidewalk between the palm trees and the buildings, straight at her. She reacted instantly and dived for the doorway. No fancy drop and roll, just a straight dive. Even as she left the ground, she knew she wasn't going to make it. Damn Eugene!

CHAPTER
9

"I saw a truck from the local TV station outside this morning. Must have been a great party." It was ten-thirty. Alex Conners had come in for coffee and he was standing at the front desk talking with Grace.

"Murder always gets their interest."

"Murder!" Alex Conners said, his eyes wide. "My God! Who?"

"Nobody knows the guy who was killed." Grace didn't elaborate.

"Jesus, Grace, don't leave me hanging like this. What happened?"

"Can't wait for the six o'clock news?" she teased.

Alex Conners made a face. "Do I have to go to Benny for the story?"

She told him all she knew.

Ardley came through the front door. He had a large brown envelope tucked under his arm. He didn't look any better than he had last night. Obviously he needed a good night's sleep. Grace smiled at him. "Good morning, Detective. I've been expecting you."

He nodded, then looked questioningly at Alex.

"This is Alex Conners," Grace said. "He's the project manager for the construction going on outside."

Ardley extended his hand. "Ralph Ardley."

Alex took his hand and shook it. "Pleased to meet you."

Ardley turned to Grace. "Ms. Cummings said there would be a list of the residents for me."

"Got it right here." She handed him two sheets of paper. "Thank God for computers. Took only a few minutes to get the information you need."

"Thanks. Is Ms. Cummings available?"

"I'll check, if you'll wait a moment."

Grace went into Jessie's office. She knew Jessie was there, and that she could hear everything that went on at the desk. Going into the office gave Jessie time to decide whether or not she wanted to see the visitor. Jessie met Grace just inside the doorway. "It's okay, Grace. Thanks."

She followed Grace to the front desk. "Good morning." Jessie smiled at Ardley. "You want to come into my office?"

Ardley stepped around the counter and followed her into the office. He took the chair facing the desk, and Jessie sat down behind the desk. From the brown envelope he slipped a thick stack of eight-by-ten photographs, leaned over, and placed them before her on the desk.

"As I promised"—he gave her a weary smile—"free developing."

Jessie leaned over the pictures. The top photograph showed the Phantom of the Opera and Cat Woman just after they entered the Halloween party. "That's her," Jessie said, "but her face is turned away." She was disappointed. She hoped the other photographs hadn't turned out so badly.

"Anything at all familiar about her? Something in the way she's standing, or holding herself?"

"No."

"There are two other pictures beneath that one."

She moved the top photograph aside. There were the two of them sitting at a table. The Cat Woman's hand was a blur in front of the lower part of her face, as if she were raising her hand when Jessie took the picture. No help there.

She removed that picture. The one beneath was of Charlie in his Devil costume. The Cat Woman was visible in the background, at the food table. She was in profile, and a little blurred. *Outside the camera's field of focus,* Jessie thought. She peered at the picture, but there was no recognition.

Ardley reached into the envelope and pulled out a magnifying glass. He placed it on the desk next to the pictures. Jessie looked at him. "Sherlock Holmes, I presume?" Ardley produced the weary smile again. Jessie took the magnifying glass and held it over the picture. The Cat Woman loomed large in the glass, but no clearer. Jessie examined the picture for a few moments, then put the magnifying glass down.

"I have no idea who she is."

"Well," Ardley sighed, "I'll arrange with Grace to set up interviews with the other residents."

"Have you found out who the man was?"

"No. But it won't be long." He stood. "I've got a couple of men out with those pictures, visiting costume shops to see who rented those outfits. Usually those sorts of places either accept a credit card or get some ID so people can't run off with the costumes. We'll probably locate them both that way." He picked up the magnifying glass and put it back in the envelope.

"What's with all that construction outside?"

"Jacobson thinks he's going to be knee-deep in wealthy baby boomers in a few years, so he's getting ready. He's putting in a fountain and an upscale canopy out front, and he bought the property next door. He's having a new wing built, complete with its own lake, which should double the size of Coral Sands. Of course, he isn't going to hire any help for me, I'm sure."

Ardley gave her a grin. "From what I've seen, I'm confident you can handle it." He turned toward the door. "Thanks for your time."

"You should try and get some sleep."

He shrugged and grinned. "You sound like my wife." As he left the office, he said, over his shoulder, "I'll be seeing you soon."

She nodded, but she wasn't pleased. She had seen too much of Detective Ardley already.

Grace appeared in the doorway. "Jacobson, our esteemed employer, is on the phone. And he is not making happy sounds."

"Yeah." Jessie shrugged wearily. "I called him earlier and left a message on his machine. Thought I'd get to speak to him before he saw it in the newspapers." She looked at the clock. "Obviously he's read the newspapers."

"Probably wants to thank you for all the wonderful publicity you're getting for his Coral Sands." Grace made a face and rolled her eyes.

"I guess I'll talk to him." Jessie said it as one surrendering. It was not something she really wanted to do. Jacobson was a shouter when he was angry. And in the ten years she'd worked for him, she had found that just about everything made him angry.

"A girl's gotta do what a girl's gotta do," Grace said, giving Jessie a small wave as she headed out of the office.

The package, addressed to Eleanor Carter, arrived a little before two. A young teenager dropped it on the desk in front of Grace. She grabbed the kid's arm. "Where did you get this?"

The kid shrugged her hand off his arm, gave her an angry look, and started backing toward the door. "Some old guy asked me to bring it here. He gave me five

bucks. Can't turn down that kind of money. Why?
Something wrong?'' By that time he was at the door.
He turned, opened it, and ran off.

Grace made a face, and looked at the package. About
two inches high, half a foot by a foot, was her guess.
There was nothing on the brown wrapper except Eleanor
Carter's name and the address of Coral Sands. The handwriting looked the same as on the note with the flowers
yesterday. She remembered Eleanor's reaction to the
flowers. She remembered Peter's reaction, too. *This was
not going to be good,* she thought.

Peter and Eleanor came back close to two-thirty. They
had left around eleven, returned their costumes, and
stopped for a leisurely lunch. Grace was at the desk
when they came in the front door. They both greeted
Grace with a smile as they passed the desk. Grace returned the smile and said, ''Eleanor?''

They stopped, and Eleanor came over to the desk.
''Yes, Grace. What is it?''

Grace turned her head toward the package on the
counter. ''That came for you.''

Eleanor looked over at the package, then gave Grace
a questioning look.

''Some kid brought it.'' Grace shrugged. ''I asked
him about it. He said some old guy gave him five dollars
to deliver it.''

Eleanor reached over and drew the package to her.
Frowning, she examined the outside with the care of one
defusing a bomb, her hands gently sliding around its
surface and examining the seams of the brown wrapper.
Peter came over to her. ''A problem?'' he asked.

Eleanor did not respond, her full attention focused on
the package. She carefully pried open the folds at one
end of the package, then tore the wrapper full length and
pulled it off. A two-pound box of Russell Stover chocolates. There was a small white envelope taped to the
top. She pulled the envelope off the box, tore open the
flap, pulled out the note, and unfolded it. ''I know these

are your favorites. Sweets for the Sweet. Friends will leave. But you and I will have each other to the end." The handwriting was getting shakier in places, but it was the same as the other two notes.

"Your secret admirer?" Peter asked.

"My secret asshole." Eleanor spat out the words. It took Peter back. He had never seen her that angry, and had never heard her use such language. But he also felt good to hear her talk like that. It meant he had nothing to fear from this man vying for Eleanor's affections. The green-eyed monster of jealousy was put to rest for the time being.

Eleanor hastily crumpled the note and stuffed it in her bag. To Peter she said, "Let's get a cup of coffee." Then to Grace, "Enjoy the candy."

"You don't want it?"

"No. Share it with whoever you want or keep it for yourself." She turned to Peter. "Let's go."

Grace watched them walk away. Then she looked at the box of candy. Chocolate was not on her list of dietetic foods, but it was certainly on the list of her favorite foods, right at the top. She shrugged. *What the hell?* she thought. *You only live once.* She raised the top of the box, and the aroma of chocolate invaded her mind. *Enjoy it, girl. It'll take you a week to remove the weight it'll put on.* She carefully chose the first piece. As she gently put it in her mouth, she hoped it was a vanilla cream. The first bite told her she was right. *Wonderful!*

Peter and Eleanor had poured themselves coffee. "Let's go outside," Eleanor said. "It's too stuffy in here. I need some space."

"Sure." It was obvious Eleanor was upset, and Peter was willing to do anything to help her.

They walked out the sliding doors to the swimming pool area. It was a little warm in the sun, but there was a pleasant breeze. As they looked toward the lake, they were surprised to see the gazebo was empty. The favor-

ite spot of Tweedledee and Tweedledum was unoccu-
pied! How could that be? They exchanged glances, and
each knew what the other was thinking. It would be a
quiet place to talk. They walked across the deck of the
swimming pool, then across the grass to the gazebo.
They sat in the chairs facing the lake. Such a pleasant
spot—looking out over the lake with the surface a soft
ripple, on the opposite side the fronds of the palm trees
gently waving like the swaying arms of dancers, the sky
a blue that went on forever, the white birds floating by
overhead.

"You can't ask for more than this," Peter said with
a sigh.

Eleanor didn't respond. She was looking out over the
scene, but she was someplace else. Peter couldn't guess
where. They sat there quietly for a while. Peter kept
looking at her, but her eyes did not stray from the scene
in front of her. Finally, he could stand the silence no
longer.

"Do you have any idea who it is?"

Eleanor did not respond. At first he thought she hadn't
heard him. Then she said, "No." She looked at him a
moment, then turned back to the view. "I was just thinking how nice things had been before I got that note. It
reminded me of something someone once said a long
time ago. So long, I don't remember who said it, but the
words have stayed with me. 'Life is all ups and downs.
Whenever you're up, remember there's a down coming.' "

"Pessimistic."

"Maybe. But true, nonetheless." She turned to Peter.
"I've been on an up since I met you."

"Me, too." Peter, meeting her eyes, smiled warmly.

"For a while there I thought that maybe there would
be no more downs." She looked away. "Then this note
came."

"You feel that it's a bad thing—a secret admirer?"

She shrugged. "Maybe it's a woman thing. A feeling

of vulnerability. There's always the fear of becoming the focus of some stranger, of being stalked, attacked, raped. Once, when I was very young, I was on a train, and a man suddenly took an interest in me. I changed my seat. He changed his, too, closer to mine. I moved to another part of the train. He followed. And I became frightened. I was afraid to get off the train for fear he would follow me, and do . . . something. This secret admirer thing feels as ominous.''

"Then maybe we should go to the police about this.''

"If I had confidence that they could do something about it, I think I would.''

"Would you feel better if I were to keep a constant vigil?''

She smiled. "You're pretty constant now.''

It was then they heard two men talking, and they looked around. Tweedledee and Tweedledum were coming toward the gazebo.

"Looks like our privacy is over,'' Peter said. "Want to go inside?''

She shook her head. "It's nice here. Let's stay a while. There are enough chairs for them.''

When the men got close, Peter could read Sailor Hat's T-shirt. NEVER PUT OFF UNTIL TOMORROW WHAT YOU CAN DO TODAY . . . UNLESS IT CAN WAIT.

The two men slowly stepped into the gazebo, nodded to Peter and Eleanor, and sat down.

"Like I was saying, they took pictures of the inside of her head,'' Gray Hair said.

Sailor Hat nodded. "I had that once—CAT scan, I think they called it.''

"Of your head?''

"Yep.''

"They find anything?''

"No.''

"No surprise.''

"Doctors are a strange lot. Every time I go see my doctor, he wants to check my prostate. He's always sticking his finger up my ass. I think he likes it.''

"Maybe he's in love?"

"You gotta watch out. There are a lot of strange people in the world. You know, there are people who like to do that sort of thing to dead people?''

"Well, looking at you, maybe that's what it is.''

"So, did they find anything funny in the clown's head?"

"No broken bones. Just a little concussion, is what I heard.''

"She was lucky. She could have been killed.''

"Well, she's kind of broken up, I hear.''

Eleanor's interest perked up when she heard the word 'clown.' And the things they said after that gave her an uneasy feeling. She remembered what Betty had said about the warning Eugene had given to Alice. She leaned over to the two men. "Excuse me. Who are you talking about?''

"The clown—Alice.''

"Alice! What happened?" *Damn Eugene*, Eleanor thought.

"What we just heard was she got hit by a car this morning. The cops came by a few minutes ago to talk to Grace about it. Alice is in the hospital. Pretty badly beaten up, from what they were saying.''

When Peter and Eleanor got to the hospital, Walter, Charlie, Benny, and Caroline were already there. Though there were supposed to be only two visitors per room, they were all standing around the bed. Caroline had a large shopping bag with her. In it Peter could see the red wig from Alice's clown outfit. He assumed the rest of the outfit was inside.

"Alice, here comes two more visitors," Benny said.

"Just what I need—an audience to show off my new act." Alice's voice did not have the same spirit as her words. Her speech was slurred.

Eleanor and Peter stepped to her bedside.

"Alice," Peter said, "you look awful."

She chuckled. "Thanks for the kind words. How do you like my new costume? Think it'll be a hit with the kids?" Her head was bandaged, her face was bruised and one eye was swelling, her right leg was elevated in a cast, and there were various bandages over the parts of her body that were visible. There were signatures on the leg cast.

"It looks as if the hospital staff was practicing on you. Are you in pain?"

"Not with the juice they've been giving me. I feel like dancing." She moved her head and winced. "Well, not really up to dancing just yet."

"Most pain medication," Walter said, "can't get rid of the pain, just take the edge off."

"Somebody give these two a pen so they can sign the damn cast." Alice looked at the cast. "Just after I gave my walker away. Thought I wouldn't be needing it again, since I wasn't going to do any more somersaults."

"So, what's the damage?" Peter asked. Walter gave Peter a pen, and Peter put his signature on the cast.

"Lots of cuts and bruises. Some cracked bones, and a busted leg. So much for my clown act for a while. And my clown outfit . . ." She looked at the shopping bag Caroline was holding. "Tore the hell out of most of it."

"What happened?" Eleanor said, as she took the pen from Peter.

"Okay, everybody," Alice said. "Ready to hear the story again?"

Eleanor scribbled her name on the cast and gave the pen back to Walter.

"She knows it by heart." Walter grinned. "She's had to tell each of us separately."

"We stopped outside Sarasota News so I could pick up a newspaper for my act. Some car jumped the curb, and I didn't get out of the way fast enough. That's the short version.''

"Thank you for that." Walter smiled. He looked to Peter and Eleanor. "I was the first one here. I've heard the long, embellished version three times."

"What made the car jump the curb?" Peter said.

Alice shrugged, then winced from the movement. "We'll never know."

"Is the driver dead?" Eleanor asked.

Alice shook her head, and winced again. "I gotta learn to talk without moving. No. The guy drove off."

"You saw him, the driver?"

She was going to shake her head, but caught herself in time. "I don't know. I cracked my head on something, and don't really remember any of it. Bert really told me what happened. The last thing I remember was telling Bert I needed a dollar for the newspaper. Then I came to here in the hospital. Everything in between is gone."

"Bert?"

"The taxi driver. He saw everything. Told the cops the whole story. He saw the old guy who was driving the car. Even got the license number. Said the guy never even slowed down. Just knocked me aside and kept on driving. Just driving off like that. I mean, he had to see me. For God's sake I'm a clown, not your ordinary nondescript pedestrian."

"Betty told me that Eugene had warned you."

She shook her head, and grimaced at the sudden pain. "Can't talk without moving. It ain't natural. Yeah, he told me to look out for traffic. Some warning! He didn't say I should be looking on the sidewalk! What the hell kind of warning is that?"

CHAPTER
10

Alfred Temple sat in the chair and scowled at Ardley across the table. "I threw my passes away."

Ardley wrote this in his notebook alongside the other comments he'd written about Alfred Temple: "Alfred Temple. At Coral Sands less than two months. Thin, sixty-eight, looks like eighty. Large, old scar on left side of his neck, right shoulder lower than left and right hand not working correctly, severe limp—uses metal cane. Angry, aggressive, bitter."

"Where were you during the party?"

"I was in my apartment. I keep to myself. Don't much care for people. Getting old is bad enough without having to listen to the complaints of other old people. Got enough complaints of my own, as you can see. All of this."—he indicated his body—"from a damn auto accident years ago. Was stupid." He grunted. "And the damn tree I hit didn't have any insurance."

Ardley nodded and made more notes. "I think that will be all for now, Mr. Temple."

Alfred Temple nodded with a grunt, then stood, putting as much weight as he could on the cane, his right arm trembling as he placed his right hand on the table to brace himself. He sidled in tiny steps out from between the chair and the table, then with great difficulty walked out the door.

Ted Walden came slowly into the room and sat in the chair opposite Ardley. He took two orange passes from his pocket and laid them on the table. "I heard you were asking about these." His voice was listless. His shoulders hunched, as if they were too heavy to hold upright.

Word gets around fast, Ardley thought. "Thank you."

Ted Walden nodded heavily.

This was the seventh interview that Grace had arranged for the afternoon. So far, six interviews had led nowhere. "You didn't go to the party?"

"Haven't had the energy for that sort of stuff." Each word was spoken as if it was weighted.

Ardley's cell phone rang. "Excuse me," Ardley said to Ted, and reached for the phone. Ted Walden nodded listlessly. This guy Walden worried Ardley. The man seemed out of it, like he was in another world or on drugs, downers. Ardley picked up the phone and punched "send."

"Yeah?"

"Okay, Ralph." It was Fred Simmons, the young detective working with Ardley. "We got a name and address on the Phantom of the Opera."

"So who is he?"

Ardley could hear Fred flip through the pages in his notepad. "His name is Harry Benson. Lives over on Pineapple. 423. Apartment 3B."

Ardley wrote the name and address in his notebook. "What about the woman?"

"Nothing. She didn't rent the costume. She bought it, and she paid cash. No way to trace her."

"Can the guy who sold it to her ID her if we need it?"

"Yeah, I think so. He gave me a pretty good description of her."

Ardley nodded. "Where are you now?"

"I'm at the station. Just got back."

Ardley looked at his watch. Twenty to five. "Good. Let's see what we can find at the guy's apartment." He flipped his notebook closed. "Have somebody contact the manager of the place, and meet us there with a key. Also, get a forensic team out there."

"You got it. 'Bye."

Ardley turned his attention to Ted Walden. "Mr. Walden, I really don't have any more questions for you. I want to thank you for your cooperation."

Ted Walden stood. "Hope I helped you." He turned and walked out of the card room, a man carrying the weight of the world. Ardley made a mental note to talk to Grace about him.

Ardley turned back to the cell phone, punched in a number, and waited.

"Hello?" It was a woman's voice at the other end, a voice that was forever imprinted in his mind. He could picture her at the other end of the line.

"Amanda, it's me, Ralph." He could see her dark eyes narrow in suspicion. "I'm going to be a little late."

"But you . . ."

"I know, I know," he said before she could continue. He had put his hand up to stop her from speaking even though she couldn't see him. "It was a promise I shouldn't have made. There are some things I just can't control. People die."

"But there are others who can do this. You aren't the only one."

They'd gone over this ground a lot lately. He suddenly wondered why that was so. Why lately?

"You know the answer to that one. This particular dead body is assigned to me. I won't be long. Honest."

"What can I say?" There was surrender in her voice.

"That you love me?"

"If I didn't love you, I wouldn't want you home."

"I'll accept that."

"I'll wait up for you."

"Love you."

"It's the curse of my life, but I love you, too."

" 'Bye."

" 'Bye."

He disconnected the phone and slipped it in his pocket. Then he gathered up the notebook and pen, and left the card room. He walked across the lobby and stopped at the front desk, where Grace was talking to one of the residents.

"It's so awful. I just heard," the resident was saying.

"Yes." Grace nodded. "I wish I could tell you more, but that's all I know right now. Some people have gone to the hospital. When they get back, we should know more."

The resident shook her head sadly. "I hope everything is all right. There are some things worse than death, you know?"

"Excuse me," Grace said to the woman when she saw Ardley coming up to the desk.

"Hi, Grace," Ardley said. He turned to the woman for a moment. "I'm sorry to interrupt you." Then back to Grace. "Can I speak with you for a moment?" He indicated that he wanted to talk privately.

Grace guided Ardley off to the side, out of hearing range of others in the lobby.

"Two things," Ardley said. "One, cancel the rest of the interviews." He pulled out the list that was folded in his notebook, and looked at it. "There are just a few people remaining."

"All right, I'll let them know."

He handed her the list, then slipped the notebook into his back pocket. He leaned closer to Grace, and spoke in a low, serious tone. "That Mr. Walden. I don't know how you do things here, or what your responsibilities are, but I'd get him some medical help." He pointed to his temple. "He's either on a handful of depressants or he's depressed a handful worth, if you know what I mean."

Grace nodded seriously. "Yes. I've been worried about him, too. I'll give his daughter a call. Thanks."

Ardley patted her arm, and left.

Fifteen minutes later he was outside the door to Harry Benson's apartment. With him were Fred Simmons and an old man in shorts and slippers.

"You sure you got a right to do this?" He was a nervous old man, bald, unshaven, with skin so white it obviously had never seen the sun. His breath was sour with stale beer. "I don't want to get into trouble with the tenants. I could lose my job." He stood in front of the door, holding the key in his hand. "I mean, don't you need a warrant or anything?"

Ardley took the key from the man, moved him aside, and slipped the key into the lock. He turned the key and pushed the door open. Then he handed the key back to the old man.

"I don't want to get into any trouble. I don't think you can do this."

"Write your congressman," Ardley said, then turned his back on the old man. He shouldn't have done that. It wasn't like him. He knew better. But he had run out of patience. Maybe he was getting too old for this job. Maybe he just needed a good night's sleep. Lately he was lucky to get any sleep at all.

"You all right, Ralph?" Fred was standing next to him. They were putting on latex gloves before they entered the apartment. They didn't want to mess up the scene before the criminalists arrived.

"I don't know. Getting old, I guess." He stepped inside and turned on the lights. Actually, one light, a table lamp went on when he flipped the switch on the wall. The apartment was small and scruffy. "It's not the Waldorf."

The two men walked slowly and carefully through the

apartment, avoiding touching anything. Ardley checked the bedroom—the bed unmade, and looking as if it had never been made, dirty clothes on the floor, papers and pocket junk on the dresser. He opened the closet door. Clothes on hangers, shoes on the floor, some shoe boxes on the shelf. He turned to the dresser and pulled open the top drawer. Underwear and handkerchiefs.

"Ralph! Check this out!"

Ardley left the bedroom and joined Fred in the kitchen. Fred Simmons was pointing to the wine bottle and glass on the counter, and the note next to them. Ardley leaned over the note. It was machine-printed. Typed?

> To whoever finds this. I've had enough. Life isn't worth living anymore. Take what you want and dispose of the rest of my things.
>
>   Harry Benson

Ardley sniffed the glass, then the bottle. Nothing except the smell of wine.

"What the hell do you make of that?" Fred said.

"Well, off the top of my head, I'd say the man was going to kill himself. Possibly was going to poison himself, then decided to take the easy way out." Ardley straightened. "He stabbed himself in the back."

Fred Simmons chuckled. "Maybe his enemies beat him to it."

"I didn't see a typewriter around. Did you?"

"No."

"See if you can find one. And have this stuff analyzed." Ardley indicated the wine bottle and glass. "After the techs are finished here, get all the guy's papers and bring them down to the office." Suddenly, he wanted to be with Amanda.

"You're not going to hang around?"

Ardley started walking away. "No. I think I need to get home at a decent hour for a change."

• • •

"That whole thing with Eugene and Alice is spooky," Peter said.

"Eugene has done a lot of spooky things," Eleanor said. They were lying in Peter's bed. The room was dark except for the night light.

"I can't explain them, yet I don't want to believe in Eugene," said Peter.

"Why?"

"I don't know. Maybe it changes the world I've grown accustomed to. It puts me in a world I don't know. I don't want that."

"Sometimes you have no choice about such things." Then Eleanor added thoughtfully, "Like me and that note writer."

They lay for a moment in silence, then Eleanor suddenly got out of bed. "Maybe there's a connection," she said more to herself.

"What?"

She hurried across the bedroom. "I'll be right back."

Peter watched her leave. She sure looked great in those silk pajamas. Peter heard the door to his apartment open and close. He lay on his back and looked at the ceiling. He felt inadequate in this situation. He wanted to protect Eleanor, to be happy with her, to be carefree and just love the time they were together. But these notes had upset her, and tilted the happiness out of reach. And he felt powerless to do anything about it.

He heard the door open and close. Eleanor came back in the bedroom, to his side of the bed, and turned on the light on the nightstand. Peter blinked in the sudden brightness. Eleanor sat on the bed and opened the note.

"This is the note I got today with the candy: 'I know these are your favorites. Sweets for the Sweet. Friends will leave. But you and I will have each other to the end.' "

She looked at Peter. "You think it has anything to do with what happened to Alice?"

Peter looked curiously at Eleanor. "You think this guy ran down Alice?"

"Well, see what he says here—'Friends will leave.' "

Peter shook his head. "I think that's a bit of a stretch." He was worried. She was really very upset by this note business. Upset to the point of paranoia.

Eleanor looked at the note thoughtfully. "Yes, I guess you're right." He was right about it being a stretch, and that worried her. What the hell was happening to her that she'd let this get her so freaked out?

"I think we should see what the police can do about this guy."

"They can't help me."

"We won't know that until we ask them. Let's go see the police tomorrow."

Eleanor sighed. "All right. What can we lose?" She put the note on the night table, reached over, and turned off the light. Then she climbed over him, giggling as he grunted under her, and lay down next to him.

A few minutes later they were quiet. Eleanor lay on her back, looking at the ceiling but not seeing it. Carefully she was probing her memory for someone in her past who could have surfaced to cause her trouble. She had betrayed a number of people over the years. Could one of them be bent on revenge? Or was she just getting paranoid out of proportion to this silly note stuff? After all, it might be nothing more than what it appeared to be—some demented old man who was madly in love with her. "Might" was the operative word. She wasn't convinced.

"Flunitrazepam. Rohypnol. Roofies on the street," Pat Curtain said. Pat was a skinny man with dark hair that always needed combing, and that disheveled look of having been roused from bed and dressing quickly. He was seated at a desk in a small office. The office walls, of glass, overlooked the autopsy area. The blinds over the walls were down.

"You have the analysis of the wine already?" It was nine-thirty in the morning. Ardley was standing in the Medical Examiner's office. Curtain, the Medical Examiner, was holding a folder open before him, referring to the report it held.

Curtain looked up at Ardley. "Nope, but it's an educated guess."

Ardley still looked exhausted. "Since when are you in the guessing business?"

"Since we found that drug and a half dozen others in the man's body." He grinned. "I'm looking at the report I just got back from the lab on what we took from the body. Yesterday, when I heard the guy showed no reaction when he was stabbed, I asked the lab to do a quick and dirty drug analysis. Thought there might be some drug reason for his not reacting."

He put the folder on the desk and leaned back in the chair. "I know there are a lot of ways to kill a man quietly. There are branches of the military that specialize in training soldiers to do just that." He nodded in response to the unasked question on Ardley's face. "Even women soldiers. Now this knife wound was right on the mark with the training these people get in the military. The knife was long and slender. It was slipped in between the ribs in the back, and given a quick slice left and right. It sliced through the heart and arteries. Blood pressure would have dropped immediately, and the man would have been unconscious in seconds. But there's no such thing as an instant death. The man would have struggled, made some noises, even for just a moment." He shrugged. "So I thought maybe the guy was too drugged or liquored up to struggle."

He leaned forward and looked down at the open folder. "Anyway, the guy was loaded with flunitrazepam. There were close to twenty grams of it unabsorbed in his stomach. Plus a variety of other drugs. Let's see— acetylsalicylic acid, pseudoephedrine hydrochloride, triamcinolone acetonide, isopropyl alcohol." He looked over his glasses at Ardley. "What I'm reading to you is the contents of most medicine cabinets in the home. Aspirin, a decongestant, a steroid to treat nasal inflammation, rubbing alcohol." He nodded toward the report. "The list goes on. Looks like somebody emptied their medicine cabinet into this guy's stomach."

"Roofies aren't in medicine cabinets."

"Well, yes they are. In medicine cabinets throughout the world. People are bringing them into Florida all the time from Mexico and the Caribbean. It's only in the U.S. of A. that the drug is verboten. And it's used to treat sleep problems. It's actually a superpowerful drug in the family of drugs that includes Valium and Librium. You want to sleep, this drug will do it."

"How much to kill you?"

"Now, that's a different question. The normal prescribed dose is one to two grams. There have been cases of people ingesting forty or more grams and coming out of it"—he grinned—"with a good night's sleep." Then he looked more closely at Ardley. "Which is something you could use. You look terrible."

Ardley nodded. "Haven't been getting much sleep."

"You seen a doctor?"

Ardley shook his head. "No. I don't feel sick or anything." The "anything" was a lie. "Just can't shut down my mind."

"Been urinating a lot?"

"Couple times a night."

"Have your prostate checked. Could be a problem there." Curtain grinned. "Happens in you old folks."

Ardley smirked. "Thanks, but fifty isn't old."

Curtain grinned wider. "Not when you're fifty, it isn't. The age you are is never old."

"So what about the Roofies? Could they kill you?"

Curtain shook his head. "No valid info on that. The real danger is in combination with other drugs. Maybe that's why all the other drugs were fed to him—hoping for a deadly reaction. Some of the other drugs—isopropyl alcohol, even aspirin—can be deadly in large enough doses. Who knows what the effects would be in combination with flunitrazepam?''

"Was he dead from the drugs when he was stabbed?''

"No. But I'm sure he was in dreamland and didn't feel a thing.''

"Would he have died from the drugs?''

"Hard to tell. Treading on unfamiliar ground there. I think it's safe to say that if he didn't ingest this stuff himself, then somebody was trying to kill him.''

"Somebody did kill him.''

"Yeah. Well, the knife was a surer way.''

CHAPTER
11

It was ten in the morning when Peter and Eleanor came downstairs. Neither of them had slept very well, their minds too busy with problems without solutions. Jessie had set out some pastries next to the coffee carafes in the alcove. She was giving them to the construction crew, so why not the residents? Eleanor and Peter poured themselves coffee, and each took a pastry.

Eleanor looked through the glass doors and saw everyone out by the pool. Benny came around the corner of the building with Alex Conners, and directed him to a chair. Then Benny sat next to Caroline. "It looks like another beautiful day in Florida out there. The rest of the crowd is outside," Eleanor said. "Let's join them."

Peter nodded. "Sure." He was sullen. Eleanor had changed her mind about going to the police. She knew someone who could be more help than the police. There wasn't much Peter could do about it, but he felt the police were the best people to get involved. However, arguing with her would not accomplish anything, except to badly color their relationship. So he kept his mouth shut.

Peter slid open the glass door and stepped aside to let Eleanor go through first. He checked her over as she passed him. She was wearing a tan skirt and an orchid blouse with a gold chain and pendant. She sure looked terrific.

"I was so ugly when I was born, the doctor slapped my mother." Mr. Petersen, as Henny Youngman, was standing just outside the door, his back to them. He was entertaining the group, who, sitting at a poolside table, were giving Henny their attention. As usual, Benny, wearing his baseball cap, was laughing to split his sides. Caroline, sitting next to Benny, was smiling politely. *She's such a sweet lady,* Eleanor thought. Walter, in his usual array of colors and patterns, was stoic behind his blue reflector sunglasses, his hands resting on the handle of his cane. Charlie was chuckling. "Too bad Henri had to go out, he's missing this," he said to Walter. Betty was giggling behind her hand. Alex Conners was laughing big and loud. Even Frank, the bug man, who was standing off to the side, was laughing. *Looks like Henny is a big hit,* Eleanor thought.

"My son keeps complaining about headaches. I keep telling him, when he gets out of bed, it's feet first."

Peter followed Eleanor over to the table. She set her coffee and pastry down next to Betty, then pulled over a chair, and sat down. Peter pulled a chair over and sat next to Eleanor.

"In a congregation in a hillbilly county, the deacon was taking a census of the congregation. He asked the married men to stand up. They got up, and then sat down. Then he asked the married women to stand, which they did, and then sat down. Next he asked the single men to stand. They did, and sat down. Then he cried, 'Will the virgins of the congregation stand up?'

"Up got a fat dame with a tiny baby in her arms.

"The deacon gave her a fierce look, and yelled, 'I said virgins!'

"To which she replied, 'Listen, you dope, how do you

expect a two-month-old baby to stand up by herself?' ''

Benny was having trouble not falling out of his chair with laughter.

Betty, giggling, her eyes tearing, turned to Eleanor. ''He's so funny!''

Eleanor leaned over to Betty and said in a low voice, ''Betty, I wonder if you could do me a favor?''

''Sure,'' she said between giggles.

Eleanor looked around to make sure no one was listening. ''I'd like you to talk to Eugene for me.''

The giggles slipped away. Betty's expression became serious, worried. ''What is it, Eleanor? What's the matter?''

Eleanor again looked at the others as she spoke, hoping they were not able to hear what she was saying. ''Some guy is pestering me, and I don't know who it is.''

''You want me to ask Eugene who it is?''

''It must be wonderful to be a doctor. In what other job could you ask a girl to take her clothes off, look her over at your leisure, and then send the bill to her husband?''

Benny, laughing to choking, poked Walter on the arm. Even Walter had to smile at that one. He turned to Benny. ''I have said the profession has its rewards.''

''Yes. I need to know who it is,'' Eleanor said.

Betty thought a moment, then shook her head. ''Eugene never gives a straight answer, so you have to be careful how you ask the question.''

''I just want the man's name.''

''Well, he might tell me his name, but you may not know him.'' Betty shook her head. ''You have to really think about the questions.''

Betty was right, Eleanor thought. She was assuming that she knew the man, and all she needed was his name to identify him. But she might not know him. He could be somebody like the bartender at The Beach House. In which case the name would be little help.

"I know," Betty said, brightening, "why don't you ask Eugene yourself?"

Eleanor gave Betty a questioning look.

"Yes. That way you could ask all the questions you need. You come by at around eight tonight, and we'll contact Eugene together."

"Betty, I don't know."

"Oh, don't worry." She patted Eleanor on the arm reassuringly. "It'll be all right. I'll help you. It'll be fun to have someone with me."

"Have you noticed," Henny Youngman said, "that most people who give up smoking substitute something for it? Like irritability?"

There was a loud cry from the third floor balcony. The laughter stopped immediately, along with heart-beats, as they all looked up. They saw Warren in his wheelchair come racing out onto the balcony screaming, stop dead at the rail, and heave a large black plastic bag in the air. The bag, stuffed tight, landed with a loud thud a few feet from Mr. Petersen, who jumped back.

He peered down at the bag. "This is a tough crowd. I've had garbage thrown at my act, but never by the bagful."

"I was going through Harry Benson's papers while I was waiting for you. I think this is what we've been looking for," Fred Simmons said. He was standing by Ardley's desk. Moments ago Ardley had returned from the Medical Examiner's office. Fred laid a sheet of paper on the desk.

Ardley did not look at it.

"It's a P.I. report. Seems our Harry Benson had paid this Smith Investigations to find his long lost wife, Audrey Benson. According to the report, Mrs. Benson remarried a George Knitter back in seventy-eight. Seems she didn't go through the process of divorcing good old Harry before she did that. George Knitter died in ninety-four. And the report says that Audrey Benson, a.k.a. the widow Audrey Knitter, has been living off George's money at Coral Sands since ninety-five.''

Fred showed Ardley the two-page list of the residents of Coral Sands. He pointed to Audrey Knitter's name. ''Looks like we got our Cat Woman.''

''Okay,'' Ardley said. ''Get the papers we need right now. We'll invite Mrs. Knitter a.k.a. Benson to share our hospitality here for a while. Contact that costume place where she bought the outfit, and have someone come down to look at her. Might as well get a positive ID on her quickly.''

''Right on it.'' Fred left.

Ardley picked up the phone and dialed Coral Sands.

''Coral Sands Assisted Living. How may I help you?''

''Grace?''

''Yes.''

''This is Detective Ardley. Would you please arrange for me to interview''—he looked at the list of residents—''Audrey Knitter as soon as possible?''

''I think she's around. I saw her at breakfast. What time would you be here?''

He looked at the clock. ''Say twelve-thirty, one o'clock.''

''If I find her, I'll tell her you're coming.''

''If you don't find her, would you please call me back? I don't want to go out there if she's not around.''

After he hung up, he went through his notes of the interviews after the Halloween party. He wondered if Audrey Knitter had been one of the people he interviewed. He scanned through the pages—and what do you know, there was Audrey Knitter. According to his notes, she was wearing the Little Red Riding Hood costume. Hmm.

''Bernard is missing.'' The woman standing before Grace at the front desk was eighty-five and tiny, with white hair pulled back in a bun and soft blue eyes behind thick glasses. She was no more than four feet or so. She strained to look up at Grace. "I'm worried. He can't take care of himself, you know?" Her voice had the fragile quality that sometimes comes with age. She spoke carefully, as if afraid to tax her voice.

"Are you sure he's missing, Felicia?" Grace could see the woman was very concerned about Bernard.

It was after twelve-thirty, and most of the people were coming out of the dining room after lunch. Grace had just taken a piece of chocolate candy from the box Eleanor had left on the counter—only a half dozen pieces left on the top layer—*Grace, you're bad*, she thought, and put it in her mouth when Felicia had come out of the dining room and headed straight for her. Grace had hurriedly eaten the candy, feeling deprived of its full pleasure.

Felicia nodded with extreme seriousness. "It isn't easy for him to hide from me."

"When did you notice he was gone?"

"This morning. I woke up, and he wasn't anywhere in the apartment."

"But he was there last night?"

She nodded. "I just don't know where he could have gone."

"I'm sure he didn't go far."

"I feel better after that lunch," Peter said. "The pastry we had instead of breakfast didn't do much for me."

"I'm going to visit with Betty this evening," Eleanor said. They were walking from the dining room into the lobby area.

"Yes, I overheard your conversation this morning. You're going to talk to Eugene."

"I think he might be more help than the police. Maybe he could at least identify this jerk. Then we can go to the police and they'll have a target."

Peter shook his head. He could picture it now. Telling Ardley, or some other detective, that Eugene, Betty's dead husband, told Eleanor this was the guy bothering her. It was not a scene he relished being a part of.

"Anyway, you've got the poker game tonight. And I've never been to one of these, whatever you call them, with the Ouija board. Might be rather interesting, seeing the great Eugene at work."

"I'll see you after the game?"

"Of course." Eleanor took his arm in hers, and smiled. "I'll be waiting with bells on."

"No bells." He grinned at her. "They make too much noise."

She smiled, hugged his arm, and gave him a seductive look. "Okay. Quiet night, active night."

"With those thoughts on my mind, I don't stand a chance of winning at the poker game."

"You never win anyway."

"Alice usually takes us to the cleaners. I'll miss her."

"Yes. You might win for a change." She nudged him playfully.

He smiled. "I don't know. Henri's going to take her chair."

Incredulously she said, "You trying to tell me that Alice's *chair* may be lucky?"

"Any excuse in a storm." He grinned.

Audrey Knitter was sitting on a sofa in the lobby, waiting for the detective to show up. She was trying to tell herself there was nothing to worry about. He just wanted to talk to her some more about what she had seen at the party. That's all. What else could it be? She had covered herself well. She had taken care of every detail. Nothing could be traced to her. *Except,* she thought, *every criminal thinks the same thing. Until it's too late. Was it too late for her?* She took hold of herself. No sense making herself a nervous wreck. She still had options. If it smelled like this cop was getting suspicious, she'd hop a plane for Mexico in a flash. Simple as that.

The mouse scurried out on the arm of the sofa next

to Audrey, then stopped, sniffing and looking around to see where it was. Audrey caught the motion out of the corner of her eye. She looked toward it, and it took a moment to realize that she was looking at a mouse, who was looking back at her. She screamed!

The mouse, scared half to death, jumped off the arm of the sofa and ran for all it was worth. The other women in the lobby saw the mouse, and their frantic screaming followed the mouse where ever it ran, causing it to change course time and again—scurrying under a sofa, jumping on and over a plant, skittering across a cocktail table, and darting this way and that, blinded by its terror.

Felicia and Grace turned toward the screaming. "I think we've found Bernard," Grace said to Felicia. "Another prank of our Mad Joker, no doubt."

When Ardley and two uniformed policemen came into the lobby, everyone was shouting and running about, trying to corner and capture poor frightened Bernard, who, though small, had the energy of the desperate, and would not cooperate in his capture.

Ardley turned to Grace and Jessie. Jessie had just come out of her office to see what was going on. Felicia had left Grace and joined in the attempt to snare Bernard. "Is this a regular afternoon recreational activity?" he said.

"We try to see that everyone gets sufficient exercise." Grace, straight-faced, gave him a superior look. "We take our responsibilities to these people very seriously."

Jessie touched Grace on the arm. "What's happening?"

Grace looked at Jessie and smiled. "Felicia's pet mouse, Bernard, is on the loose. My guess is the Mad Joker snatched him from his cage this morning."

Shouts of triumph and relief rose from the crowd in the lobby. Then Felicia walked toward the elevator with Bernard in her hand, scolding him with every step. Among the crowd there was relieved laughter and excited talking and joking about the reactions and the fear.

"Which one is Audrey Knitter?" Ardley was speaking to Grace, but looking around the crowd.

"Over there." Grace pointed with her chin. "The dark-haired woman in the maroon dress."

Ardley nodded, and signaled the two officers to follow him.

Seeing the police, many of the people in the lobby stopped speaking and watched their progress across the lobby.

Audrey was standing off to the side. Flushed with fright, she was trying to compose herself, smoothing her dress and patting her hair.

"Audrey Knitter?" Ardley asked.

She turned to him. "Yes?" Then she saw the two police officers, and she swallowed the lump of fear that had suddenly grabbed her throat.

"I'm placing you under arrest for the murder of Harry Benson."

Everyone in the lobby stopped still and stared, unbelieving.

As Ardley spoke those words, the two cops came up on either side of Audrey, one of them taking out a pair of handcuffs. *They already know his name!* she thought. *That can't be!* The cops grabbed her arms and handcuffed them behind her back. While Ardley read her her rights, all Audrey could think of was how had she messed up? She had emptied Harry's pockets. No one knew who he was. She had been careful that no one knew who *she* was. She even bought the damn Cat Woman costume and used cash so there would be no way to trace it to her. And she had rented a car so anyone seeing them coming to the party would not recognize her by the car. It was perfect. Damn it! It was perfect! Had she screwed up at his apartment? No, couldn't be. She wore her gloves and costume. She left no fingerprints anywhere. Even the note she had typed, she handled with gloves on. What the hell happened! Where did she go wrong?

"Ms. Knitter?" Ardley had repeated her name three times.

Audrey snapped out of her thoughts. "Yes?" *This can't be happening!*

"Do you understand your rights as I have read them to you?"

"Huh? Oh, yes." She felt as if she were in a dream, the things happening a ghost of reality.

Ardley made a motion to the two cops. They took Audrey by the arms, and the four of them walked across the lobby to the front door. Ardley stopped at the desk while the two cops escorted Audrey to the waiting police car.

Grace, her mouth open, just stared at him, not knowing what to say. Jessie frowned.

Ardley took a folded paper from his back pocket, unfolded it, and laid it on the desk in front of Grace. "This is a search warrant for Audrey Knitter's apartment." Fred Simmons and three people carrying black cases of varying sizes came through the front door. "Please show us to Mrs. Knitter's apartment."

"I'll do it," Jessie said, and walked to the front of the counter. She wanted to say a lot more, but it all sounded trite. "Are you sure you have the right person, detective? Audrey could not be the killer, detective." Things like that. But she wisely kept her mouth shut.

She took them up to the second floor. Then she guided them down the corridor to Audrey's apartment, opened the door, and stepped aside.

"Thank you, Jessie," Ardley said.

For a moment Jessie Cummings was not sure it had been wise to let him call her by her first name. She felt like a collaborator in this, and she didn't like the feeling.

Ardley turned to the others. "All right, you know what we're looking for. I want everything dusted. Just one print of Harry Benson's is all I'd like to find. Also, I would be extremely grateful if we could locate the murder weapon. Put every knife in evidence bags for the lab. And empty the medicine cabinet. Everything that looks like a drug, I want back to the lab.''

The three people had put on latex gloves and entered the apartment. Ardley and Fred Simmons were putting on latex gloves. ''Now, what we've got to find is the typewriter and, if we're lucky, the Cat Woman outfit. Gather up all her papers. There might be something in there about Harry Benson or about the drugs.'' Fred Simmons went into the apartment.

Ardley turned to Jessie. ''I'm afraid this apartment will be off-limits to everyone for a while. No cleaning people, no utility people, no one. Can you lock this door?''

''No. All the apartments are kept unlocked. In case there's an emergency, there would be no delays because of a locked door.''

''All right. I'll have one of my people put a padlock on it for now.''

Jessie nodded.

''If you'll excuse me?'' Ardley said, then turned to go into the apartment. Jessie put a hand on his arm.

''Ralph,'' she said, ''old people get very upset by things like this. There's going to be all sorts of speculation and rumors going around. And they'll get wilder and wilder until some of these people sick with fear. Is there anything you can tell me that would keep the speculation down?'' Still holding his arm, she added with deep sincerity, ''Please, Ralph?''

Ardley took a deep breath. What he was about to do was not condoned, but he rationalized this by saying it was no more than he would give to the press. ''Harry Benson was the name of the guy who was stabbed. Audrey Knitter was married to him at one time. They broke up, and she married George Knitter, but neglected to get a divorce from Harry Benson.'' It was his turn with the sincere look. ''That's all I can give you.''

''Thanks.'' She smiled appreciatively, nodded, and took her hand from his arm.

"Now, if you'll excuse me?"

Giving him a warm, grateful smile, Jessie nodded.

Ardley no sooner stepped inside the apartment than Fred Simmons called to him from the bedroom. "In here, Ralph!"

Ardley walked into the bedroom. Fred Simmons, standing before the opened closet, was pointing at a plastic bag on the floor of the closet.

"Thought you'd like to see this," Fred said. He reached down, put his hand in the bag, and gently extracted the head piece of the Cat Woman outfit, holding it in the tips of his fingers. "Guess we didn't give her time to get rid of the outfit."

"She probably felt she had plenty of time."

"And there's that." Fred pointed to a portable typewriter on the dresser.

"If that matches the note, we may not need the knife. Have the ribbon checked. See if they can figure out what was typed last."

Ardley stepped into the bathroom, where one of the criminalists was carefully putting the contents of the medicine chest in individual plastic evidence bags. "How does it look in here?"

The young man reached down, grabbed an evidence bag, and held it up. In the bag were a number of foil bubble packs of pills. "So far, the only thing illegal are these Roofies. She's got a bunch of them. Everything else seems to be pretty normal stuff."

Ardley wanted to smile. "Well, so far she's got all the tools to be our star."

CHAPTER

12

"The guy was her first husband!" Betty squeaked excitedly. She fidgeted, her hands flitting around like little birds, her eyes wide with the wonder of it all.

Walter Innes, who had not witnessed the arrest, nor the Mad Joker mouse incident that preceded it, was sitting with Betty and the others in the coffee alcove. It had become rather warm outside, and the clouds were beginning to gather for the afternoon storm, so they had moved indoors. To Peter it seemed that Walter was not becoming excited enough for Betty. In truth, Walter was not becoming excited at all. Getting excited was not in Walter's vocabulary.

"Imagine, a cold-blooded murderess in Coral Sands!" Betty couldn't contain herself.

Peter looked at Eleanor and shrugged. She smiled knowingly. After all that he'd seen at Coral Sands, Peter didn't have to stretch his imagination much to include a murderess. In fact, he would probably have to stretch his imagination to exclude one.

"It's a good thing Henri wasn't here to see that, or

the Mad Joker incident with the mouse," Walter said. "Henri is upset enough about Coral Sands." He shrugged. "We must remember that murderers retire just like gangsters, thieves"—he smiled—"and clowns."

Benny and Peter exchanged glances when Walter mentioned gangsters and thieves. Peter knew that Benny had been involved with the mob years ago, had crossed one Bobby Dee, and for the past seventeen years, had been hiding from Bobby Dee. And Benny was the only one who knew of Peter's forays into the jewelry theft business.

"But she stabbed him right in front of everybody!" Betty said. Peter had to smile at Betty's persistence in trying to get Walter excited.

"Now that surprises me," Walter said, but he didn't look surprised. To Peter he looked to be in his lecturing mood. "It is true that the knife is not the woman's first choice of murder weapon. Though it does come in a close second, due to their proximity with the kitchen and a woman's domain. Women, trained in the art of cooking and the chemistry of the kitchen, most often use a man's mouth against him. Poison is weapon number one, usually disguised in food or drink." He shook his head sadly. "Men are too trusting of women."

Walter raised his head, and took on the pose of lecturer. "I remember a charming old woman who had gone through three husbands before they caught her. She had been slipping antifreeze into their beer. The sweet-tasting ethylene glycol does not break down in the body; it builds up over time. The husbands slowly became sick, and died of kidney or liver failure or whatever. And no one thought anything further of it."

Walter frowned. "It is puzzling that with all the chemicals we have around us, Audrey did not use one of them instead of the knife, with all its blood and possibly messy consequences. Also, there is the possibility that the physical attempt to kill might not succeed. And, considering where she purportedly did the deed, there is the likelihood of discovery.''

Peter admitted that Walter had a point. He wondered why she had chosen a knife over poison. He shrugged. But nobody said that criminals had to be smart. The smart ones were the ones who were never found out or caught. He was thinking of his own career. Only the stupid criminals got caught. Was Audrey so desperate she would take such a chance with a knife? And why not outside the party, in some lonely place, instead of in a room filled with people?

The hands, covered in latex gloves, searched patiently among the jars and bottles in the medicine cabinet and on the counter. Every so often the right hand began to tremble, and was brought under control by the severe grip of the left. The hands pulled two jars out from the others and set them in front on the bathroom counter. The first was a jar of Vaseline; the second, a jar of face cream. After a few moments, the hands replaced the Vaseline where it had been. Then they opened the jar of face cream and carefully laid the cover beside it. The left hand produced a small bottle, pulled off the top, and tilted it over the opened jar, drops of liquid falling onto the face cream. The bottle was recapped and put away. The index finger of the left hand carefully smoothed the liquid into the top inch of the face cream. The jar's lid was replaced, and the face cream returned to where it had stood at the rear of the counter.

As Ardley and Fred Simmons returned to the police station, Ardley was thinking the same thoughts as Peter. There were so many other ways this woman could have killed her husband. Why this crazy way? Why didn't she just let the drugs do their thing? Why resort to a knife? And in such a public place, where she could easily be discovered?

When they got inside the police station, they were

confronted by Audrey's attorney. *She didn't waste any time*, Ardley thought.

"Arthur Brownell," the man said as he extended his hand. "I'm Mrs. Knitter's attorney."

Ardley looked over Arthur Brownell, Esquire, and immediately he didn't like the man. Manicured, polished fingernails, coifed hair, expensive—from the way it fit—custom-made suit, and a brown leather briefcase. But he rarely liked the lawyers representing the criminals.

Ardley ignored the attorney's outstretched hand, and turned to Fred Simmons. "Get her ready."

Fred nodded, and left.

"Detective Ardley, may I speak with you before you interview Mrs. Knitter?" Brownell's diction was impeccable. Another reason for Ardley to dislike him.

"No." Ardley's voice was calm and his manner straightforward. "Mr. Brasswell, there is nothing you . . ."

"Brownell," the attorney corrected.

Ardley gave the man an annoyed look, and continued. "There is nothing you and I need discuss. You can talk to the District Attorney, and you and he probably have a lot to talk about. I have arrested a criminal. I intend to interview her, and you are there to represent her and advise her of her rights. There is nothing we need to talk about."

"Mrs. Knitter is in no emotional state to give a statement right now."

Ardley ignored the man. Fred Simmons came back, escorting Audrey Knitter. "Into the Interview Room," Ardley said. They called it the Interview Room, because Interrogation Room sounded too much like rubber hoses and sweating under bright lights. Of course, when they had a streetwise crook to interview, they called it the Interrogation Room for his benefit.

The room was windowless, with yellow walls, plain wood table, and six chairs. The yellow on the walls was chosen because some psychiatrist had said that color should not be used because it was too emotionally up-setting, which was just what they wanted. The table was heavily scarred. It had seen better days. Along one wall was a large two-way mirror. Behind it a video camera had begun recording as soon as they entered the room.

Fred Simmons set the tape recorder on the table. Audrey Knitter and Brownell sat on one side of the table; Ardley and Fred Simmons, on the other.

"Audrey Knitter," Ardley began, "we are going to record this session for your protection and ours. We will ask you some basic questions, such as your name and address, before we start talking about you and Mr. Benson. Do you understand?"

Audrey nodded. "Yes."

Fred Simmons started the tape recorder, then looked at his watch. "The time is four-fifteen P.M. The date is . . ." *Four-fifteen!* Ardley thought. *Where did the day go? This interview could take a while, and I still have reports to write. Amanda is not going to like my being late. And what is with Amanda, lately?*

"Please state your name."

"Audrey Knitter. Mrs. Audrey Knitter."

"This interview is being conducted in the presence of Arthur Brownell, Esquire, representing Mrs. Audrey Knitter."

Ardley nodded to Fred Simmons, then leaned his elbows on the table and looked directly at Audrey. "Were you at the Halloween party at Coral Sands on the evening of October thirty-first?"

Audrey swallowed hard. This was the real thing. "Yes. I was Little Red Riding Hood."

"You arrived at the party with one Harry Benson, the murder victim. Is that correct?"

"No."

Ardley let out a weary sigh, reached out and held his finger poised over the Pause button on the tape recorder. Then he changed his mind, and brought his hand back in front of him on the table. "Mrs. Knitter, we can save a lot of time here . . ."

"Why should I be concerned about saving your time?"

Ooops, Ardley thought. *She's got her sea legs back.* "Well, then perhaps it may make things easier for both of us if I tell you what we found in your apartment."

"You were in my apartment?" As quickly as she had gained her inner strength, it now slipped away. "What right did you have?"

"We had a search warrant issued by the court. And we *executed* it." He liked that word. Florida had the death penalty. Using the word "executed" always got the murderers nervous.

"We found the Cat Woman costume you wore to the Halloween party. We found a portable typewriter, which is being tested to see if it was used to type the phony suicide note we found in Harry Benson's apartment, and we found a large quantity of Roofies."

"Roofies, detective?" Brownell asked.

"Rohypnol, Mr. Boswell." Ardley didn't try pronouncing flunitrazepam. "An illegal drug. It's been called the date rape drug."

"It's Brownell."

"What?" Ardley gave Brownell an annoyed frown. Fred Simmons was trying to keep his grin under control.

"My name is Brownell, not Boswell."

"Oh." Ardley turned back to Audrey. "The same drug that was found in a large quantity in Harry Benson's stomach. Additionally, we came across evidence that you were once married to Harry Benson, and you were never divorced. So, you see, lying to us is absolutely useless." He took a deep breath. "Now let's start over again. Did you arrive at the party with Harry Benson? And let me also remind you that we have photographs, compliments of Jessie Cummings, of the two of you together at the party. So, did you and Harry Benson arrive together?"

She looked to Brownell for help.

"Mrs. Knitter, as I told you, you do not have to answer any questions. You are being charged with a capital crime, and you do not have to give testimony against yourself."

"That is correct, Mrs. Knitter. Mr. Boxwell is correct. You do not have to answer our questions."

"It's Brownell."

Ardley put on the annoyed frown again. "What?"

"My name is Brownell."

Ardley gave him a look that said: *Don't bother me with insignificant stuff*, then looked back at Audrey. He loved doing this. It so upset these wiseass attorneys when their name was mispronounced.

"But if you don't talk, we will have no idea what your side of the story is. And the jury will convict you without hearing from you. We have all the evidence, and it will speak for itself. You *do* want to be heard, don't you?"

Audrey sat looking at Ardley for what felt to Ardley like a long time. Finally, Audrey took a deep breath and, with her shoulders slumped, sighed in surrender. "I didn't kill him."

"You didn't kill who?"

"Harry. I didn't kill Harry Benson."

"I think it wise, detective, that we terminate this interview," Brownell said.

Ardley snapped a mean look at Brownell. "Mr. Baxswell, your client has to request that the interview be stopped."

"It's Brownell."

"What?"

Brownell gave a little wave of his hands, and sat back in his chair. "Never mind."

Ardley turned back to Audrey. "You went with him to the party?"

She turned to Brownell. "I have to tell them. Right now they have all sorts of evidence that points to me as the murderer. I didn't kill Harry. I've got to make them see that.'' Then she turned back to Ardley. "Yes. Yes. I picked up Harry at his apartment and drove him to the Halloween party.''

"Did you give him any drugs when you were in his apartment?"

She nodded. "I took his wine glass from him—we were drinking to a new beginning, the jerk—and when I put the glass on the table, I dropped a Rohypnol into the wine in his glass. I had it between my fingers. The glove hid it from view. The stuff dissolves quickly, and it doesn't take too long to take effect. Makes people feel and act drunk. By the time we reached the party, he was already feeling a little silly.''

"Where did you get the drug?"

"I spent a month in Panama. The heat was just unbearable. And the rain came down every day at four in the afternoon, and just poured until one or two in the morning. I don't know how anyone can sleep with that noise. I went to a doctor, and he prescribed the Rohypnol. It wasn't that expensive, so I asked the doctor to make it a large prescription, because I didn't want to keep coming back to him every month to have him write me another prescription. He wrote me a six month's supply, taking two grams a night. I brought most of it with me when I came home. The stuff really works. I slept like a baby in Panama after that. Bombs could go off, I don't think I would have heard them.''

Ardley was thinking that he could surely use something like that. "The Medical Examiner found an awful lot of Rohypnol and all sorts of other chemicals in Harry's stomach.''

Audrey nodded, and sighed. "I gave it all to him.'' She took a deep breath. "Look, I *was* trying to kill the bastard. I'll admit that. I was doing my best to poison the SOB. Oh, *was* I! I stuffed everything I could into good old rotten Harry. I was hoping some of the stuff would react with the Rohypnol, or maybe with something else. I kept going to my medicine cabinet and taking out whatever I could find. I dumped a lot of aspirin in him—hell, even rubbing alcohol. I heard that could kill you, the rubbing alcohol. The Rohypnol had him so dopey he'd swallow whatever I gave him. I kept it up until finally Harry passed out, and he couldn't swallow anything more.''

She slumped further in the chair. ''Then I went upstairs to my apartment and changed into the Little Red Riding Hood costume. I figured I'd get rid of the Cat Woman costume later. I went back down to the party, and the show was just beginning. I sat in the back with Charlie and some new guy—Henry, I think his name is? I made sure Charlie would recognize me in the Little Red Riding Hood costume.'' Then she shrugged. ''That was it.''

''You want us to believe that you didn't decide to put a knife in Harry's back to make sure he was dead?''

She shook her head in disbelief. ''I couldn't believe that he had been stabbed! I had planned everything to look like he killed himself. I just don't know what happened.''

''What did you do with the knife after you killed him?''

Audrey leaned forward, some of her inner strength back. ''Listen to the words.'' She pointed to her mouth. ''Watch my lips. I didn't stab him. Why would I do that after I went through all the trouble to make it look like he committed suicide? I'm not stupid.''

''You're trying to have us believe that someone else decided to kill Harry that same night?''

She shook her head. ''I don't know what to believe. All I know is somebody stabbed Harry and screwed up everything I planned.''

''Do you know anyone else who wanted Harry Benson dead? Who might have a motive to kill him?''

''No. I've got no idea who his friends were, if he had any. But I can tell you that everyone he met eventually became an enemy. Harry was not a nice guy—hell, he was a bastard. If he treated other women the way he treated me, then there's another woman out there with a knife." She thought a moment. "At first I was scared. Then I figured that maybe the police would find who stabbed Harry, and wouldn't even think about the suicide part."

"You forgot about the suicide note you left in Harry's apartment?"

"No. I just figured it wouldn't be considered, since he didn't kill himself. He was stabbed in the back. It's very difficult to kill yourself by stabbing yourself in the back, and then get rid of the knife before you die."

"Yes." Ardley sighed wearily. "I have to agree with you—very difficult." He reached over to the tape recorder. "End of interview." He pushed the stop button.

CHAPTER

13

It was five minutes to eight when Eleanor knocked on the door to Betty's apartment. She was carrying a red gift bag containing a bottle of Burgundy wine. What did you bring to a Ouija board session? For that matter, what did you wear to a Ouija session? She had visions of red silk robes with hoods and pendants with mysterious designs. What she had settled on was a red silk blouse and tan skirt and pumps. She did wear a pendant that had a gold sun with a silver quarter moon laid over it. That was the only thing she had approaching an exotic design.

She couldn't believe it, but she was nervous. There was the feeling that she was about to step out of the present world, into an unknown place filled with nothing she would understand. A place of misty creatures and smoky air, of strange music and mystifying surroundings.

As nervous as she felt, she also felt silly at being nervous. This was Betty she was going to see. Not some Wicked Witch of the West or some evil sorcerer. Betty, the flighty little woman who spoke with her departed husband. Harmless, fragile Betty. Maybe it was that fragileness that made Eleanor nervous. She was afraid she would embarrass Betty or in some unthinking way say something that would ridicule her and hurt her feelings. She didn't want that to happen. She liked Betty as one likes an innocent child, and she didn't want to hurt her in any way.

She was hoping Betty wouldn't greet her wearing something hokey and flowing and whimsically spiritual. How would she react to that? She mustn't laugh. Whatever happened, she must treat all this with the same seriousness that Betty treated it.

The door opened. Betty was there in a normal blue dress with a tiny white pattern. Thank God for that.

"Hi, Eleanor." Betty smiled brightly. Then she saw the gift bag, and her eyes lit up. "Oh, you brought something. You shouldn't have."

"It's just a bottle of wine. Burgundy. Thought we could use a little of the spirits when we're talking to the spirits."

Betty giggled. "Oh, Eleanor!" She stepped back from the door. "Come in, come in."

Eleanor stepped inside. Nothing mystical about the atmosphere. The lighting was pleasantly subdued. There were a few candles around. Nothing ritualistic or spiritual about the place. It looked normal.

"The corkscrew is in the drawer by the refrigerator. You open the wine, I'll get us a couple of glasses." Betty went into the living room, opened a small bar, and took out two stemmed glasses.

Eleanor stepped into the efficiency kitchen, opened the drawer by the refrigerator, and took out the corkscrew. She removed the lead foil over the cork and twisted the screw into the cork. She sniffed the air. There was a light, pleasant scent. She sniffed again, trying to recognize the aroma, but it eluded her.

"It's vanilla," Betty said with a smile as she came into the kitchen area. Eleanor sensed Betty was doing her best to control her excitement. "I put some vanilla-scented candles around. I like vanilla. I'm just a plain vanilla type of girl, Eugene always used to say."

Eleanor extracted the cork, and laid the corkscrew on the counter.

"I put the glasses on the cocktail table in the living room." Betty walked to the living room, and Eleanor followed with the bottle of wine.

Eleanor poured wine in each of the glasses, then set the bottle on the table. There was a platter of finger food on the table, with a couple of plates and some fancy blue napkins.

"I made some nibblies," Betty said as she sat on the sofa. "That's what Eugene called them—nibblies. I thought we could sit a while and chat."

Eleanor made herself comfortable in the armchair. She leaned forward, put some unidentifiable spread on a cracker, and settled back into the chair. She took a small bite of the cracker. Delicious, whatever it was. Then she noticed the round table in the corner of the room, next to the sliding glass doors that led to the balcony. The table was covered with a dark cloth, and there were two chairs pulled up to it. A fat candle burned lazily in the center of the table. On the table, Eleanor assumed, was the Ouija board. She couldn't be sure from that distance.

"The spiritual energy feels very strong tonight." Betty was clearly excited. Though she was seated, her body seemed to quiver with that energy. "We should have a good visit." She turned on the sofa to face Eleanor. "You know, there are nights when I get terrible reception. A lot of interference. You know, like a weak signal on the television?"

"Do you know what causes that?" Eleanor said, for want of saying something. She took another bite of the cracker, chewed, swallowed, then sipped the wine.

"Sometimes I don't clear the air of the bad energy. You have to surround yourself in good thoughts, happy thoughts. You can't be angry or sour or like that. That upsets the energy in the air, and things don't go right then.''

''So I should be thinking happy thoughts?'' She felt very relaxed. Betty knew how to set the mood.

''Oh, yes. That's why I thought we'd just sit for a while and let the good energy build around us.''

''Happy thoughts. You got it.'' The happy thought that Eleanor came up with was strangling the mystery note writer with her bare hands. That would make her very happy. ''How long do we have to do this, before everything is ready?''

Betty smiled sweetly. ''You're anxious to start, aren't you?''

Eleanor nodded. ''Well, yes, I am. This guy's been bothering me to where I want to strangle him''—her happy thought—''and I'd like to get him off my back. Get my life back to normal.''

''Well, I can't promise that you'll find out what you need. There are times when Eugene isn't very cooperative. And sometimes he isn't available. We may have to settle for my guardian spirit. Or yours.''

''Guardian spirit?'' Oh, boy. Now she was staring down that road toward misty creatures and smoky air.

''We each have a guardian spirit.'' Betty brought her head up and waved her hands defensively. ''Don't worry, it's not something you have to deal with right now.'' Betty stood, and picked up her wineglass. ''Let's go to the table. I have the board set up. We might as well do it now.''

Eleanor stood up and followed her to the round table. She carried her wineglass with her; she might need some fortification.

Betty moved the two chairs closer together, then sat in one, and indicated the other for Eleanor. Eleanor put her glass off to the side on the table, then sat in the chair and pulled it close to the table. There were two pads with pencils, one on either side of the board.

''I suggest you write down your questions and the

answers," Betty said. "It's so easy to forget what was said."

Eleanor nodded.

"Oh, my!" Betty said. "Your pendant! It has the same designs as on the Ouija board." She pointed to the top corners of the board.

Sure enough. Eleanor saw a full sun in one corner of the board and a quarter moon in the other. A tingle went up her spine.

"That's a very powerful sign." Betty was excited by this discovery. "The energy must be especially strong tonight."

Eleanor shrugged. "I just picked it out as something to wear."

Betty smiled. "*Why* you picked it out doesn't mean anything. *That* you picked it out is what's important."

Eleanor nodded. "I understand."

"Well, let's start, shall we?" Betty placed her fingertips on one side of the triangular pointer that sat on the board. The three short legs of the pointer had felt padding on the feet, making it easier for the pointer to slide on the slick surface of the board. "Lay your fingertips gently on the pointer."

Eleanor placed them as gently as she could, the tips barely touching the pointer. She took a deep breath. *Well, here goes nothing.*

Betty turned her attention to the center of the table, her eyes looking just above the candle. "Do you come in the name of light and love?"

Suddenly the pointer sprung to life, startling Eleanor. Rapidly it moved to the word YES. It was obvious to Eleanor that Betty was moving the pointer, because she was barely touching it, and exerting no pressure on it.

Betty looked at Eleanor in surprise. "Oh, my. The energy is extremely powerful tonight." Betty returned her attention to the space above the candle. "Are we guided and protected?"

Again the pointer dashed across the board to the word
YES.

"Do you have a message?"

The pointer raced around the board like a scurrying
insect, stopping momentarily at some of the letters of
the alphabet. It spelled out YOU ARE NOT ALONE
TONIGHT.

"Yes." Betty exchanged glances with Eleanor. "I
have Eleanor with me."

The pointer rushed around. WELCOME ELEANOR.

Betty looked at Eleanor. "Can you feel the energy?
It's really so strong."

"I don't know. I feel something in my arms. Like a
force pulling up from the fingertips." It felt to Eleanor
as if she were holding a very heavy weight.

"Yes, that's it. Sometimes I can't do much with my
arms after a session, they're so worn out from the force
of energy."

Unbelievable, Eleanor thought in wonder.

Betty turned back to the board. "Is Eugene there?"

The pointer moved to YES.

"Can he talk to me?"

Again the pointer scurried around the board. It spelled
out SWEET PEA.

Betty smiled, her eyes welling, and looked at Eleanor.
"He always called me that. It was his pet name for me."

"Do you have a message for me, Eugene?"

NOT TO WORRY.

"He always tells me that, because I'm such a worrier.
He tries to reassure me."

Betty said, "I have my friend Eleanor with me."

The pointer came to life. ELEANOR YOU ARE A
GOOD FRIEND.

Betty turned to Eleanor. "See, he knows you."

To Eugene, she said, "Eleanor is very worried."

The pointer spelled out WORRY IS NOT A CON-
STRUCTIVE ENDEAVOR.

"He's telling you not to worry."

Betty spoke to Eugene again.

"She'd like to ask you a few questions. Is that okay?"

The pointer moved to YES.

Eleanor was about to phrase a question when she became aware that in the few minutes they had been on
the board, she had come to accept all this as if it were
normal. She found that weird.

Eleanor looked at the space just above the candle in
the center of the table. "Do you know about the notes
I have been getting?"

A direct move to YES.

"Do I know the man?"

The pointer indicated?.

Betty said, "That means he doesn't understand the
question. You have to be specific. Which man are you
asking him about? And is it a man?"

Eleanor turned back to the space above the center of
the table. "Do I know the man who is sending the
notes?"

A quick YES.

"Who is he?"

The pointer got busy. THAT WILL BE REVEALED.

Great, Eleanor thought. "When?"

Eugene responded with SOON.

*Oh, boy. So you want to be evasive, Eugene. Well,
I'm not letting you off that easy.* "How?"

CHOCOLATE IS THE MESSENGER.

*It also keeps me awake and makes me fat. What the
hell does that mean? Maybe the answer is in the note
that came with the chocolates? Something in the note
I'm not seeing?*

"Does the note with the chocolates reveal who it is?"

YES.

*About time I got a straight answer from you, Eugene.
I'll have to reexamine that note.*

The pointer became active: I DO MY BEST.

Damn, he reads minds!

The pointer moved. YES.

"All right, all right. I get the message. What does the note writer want?"

YOU.

Duh. Betty is right, you're a pain in the ass at times, Eugene. "Why?"

HIS REASONS WILL BE CLEAR.

That's it, Eugene. Perfect. Keep that information coming. "What is his name?"

PEOPLE HAVE MANY NAMES.

"What name do I know him by?" She thought that was a clever question.

DARLING.

Darling? Peter? "First name or last?"

?

"What kind of answer is that? What word didn't you understand, Eugene?"

The pointer remained still.

Betty touched Eleanor's arm. "I know Eugene can be exasperating at times. But if you treat him badly, he'll go away."

He might as well go away. He's been no help. "Have I spoken with him?"

YOU HAVE SPOKEN WITH MANY.

"Have I spoken with the man who wrote the notes?"

YES.

Now that was a dumb question. If I know him as Darling, it's quite obvious I must have spoken to him.

"Recently?"

YES.

"Do I know him a long time?"

YES.

"When did I first meet him?"

TIME IS IRRELEVANT. THE PAST WRAPS AROUND THE PRESENT AND THE FUTURE.

"Do I know him intimately?"

INTIMACY IS RELATIVE.

Another pointed, informative answer by the wizard Eugene. Could it be Peter? "Is his name Peter?"

DARLING.

"How tall is he?"

HEIGHT RELATES TO TIME AND POSITION.

"Is he nearby?"

WE ARE NEARBY WHEN WE ARE FAR AWAY.

Now, that's an answer I should needlepoint into a sampler. Come on, Eugene, give me something!

"Does he live in the Home?"

EVERYONE LIVES SOMEPLACE.

Eleanor let out a frustrated sigh. "Betty, what sort of guy was Eugene besides being a pain in the ass?"

"Well," Betty said patiently, "there are certain rules about revealing things to us in the physical world. Eugene does his best without breaking those rules. Sometimes you must look into his answers to find the keys to the answer you're looking for." Betty took her hands off the pointer and began rubbing her arms. "Eugene, we're going to stop for a moment. My arms are hurting."

Eleanor took her fingers off the pointer. She realized her arms were aching, too. Strange. She picked up her wineglass and took a large swallow.

Betty took a sip of her wine. "Eugene is making you upset. Maybe you should try asking about something other than this man's name. I mean, are you afraid of him? Is that fear valid? There is a lot of information that Eugene can reveal. You have to think of the right questions."

Eleanor was respecting Betty more and more. She was not the sweet simpleton Eleanor had thought.

"I'm ready, Eleanor." Betty put her fingertips on the pointer.

Eleanor placed hers there as well. She formulated the question in her mind, but was afraid to ask it. No, not to ask it. She was afraid of the answer. Finally, she blurted it out. "Eugene, does the note writer want to hurt me?"

The pointer slipped around and spelled THERE ARE MANY KINDS OF PAIN.

Damn! "Eugene, you know if you were here I'd strangle you!"

YES.

Eleanor chuckled, and shook her head. Then she turned to Betty. "I don't know what other questions to ask."

"You have to think about the questions."

"Yes, you told me."

Betty looked at the space above the center of the table. "Eugene, it's Betty. Will Eleanor be all right?"

?

"Will she be safe?"

?

"Will Peter protect her from Darling?"

NO.

No? Eleanor thought. *So much for the constant vigil.*

"Will Eleanor meet Darling again?"

YES.

Eleanor jumped in quickly. "Is Peter this Darling person?"

YES.

His response took Eleanor off guard. *Peter? No! It couldn't be Peter! It just couldn't!*

"No. No," Betty said to Eleanor. "You have to be careful of the questions. That question can be taken a couple of ways. I mean, to you Peter is a darling person."

"Yes, I see what you mean." *But which way was Eugene answering it?* She turned back to Eugene. "Should I fear Peter?"

FEAR HAS MANY FORMS.

"Does Peter love me?"

YES.

"Does Darling love me?"

YES.

"In the same way as Peter?"

?

Betty sighed. "You see, that's another question with many interpretations. Do you mean physical love, and if so, at what particular time are you comparing? Do you mean emotional love? Again, you have to compare times. Love fluctuates with a lot of things, even during the day. You have to be very careful with your questions, or the answers may not mean what you think."

"All right, Eugene. Should I go to the police for help with this note writer?"

LOOK TO THE HEAVENS.

"I've had enough," Eleanor snapped at Betty. "Eugene is no help at all. All he's done is confuse the hell out of me, and play damn word games!" Then she looked back at the space above the table. "Tell me, Eugene, is it very hot where you are?"

"Oh, dear!" That upset Betty.

The pointer was on the move. It spelled COMFORT-ABLE.

Eleanor jerked her fingers off the pointer and slumped back in her chair. She was too angry to continue.

"Good night, Eugene," Betty said. She still had her fingers on the pointer.

The pointer moved among the letters I LOVE YOU. BYE.

Betty removed her fingers from the pointer and looked at Eleanor. "I'm sorry Eugene upset you so."

Eleanor sighed. "I'm the one who should be sorry. Eugene isn't responsible for my being upset. It's this situation with the note writer that's making me upset." She shook her head in despair. "I just don't know who to turn to for help."

"Well, Eugene did give you some information. Oh, you didn't write his answers down."

"No. He didn't say anything reasonable."

"You're going to find out who this person is soon. He did say that. And there was something about chocolate, I remember."

"Yes, chocolates!" Eleanor said with sudden revelation. ''That's right! Something about the note with the chocolates revealing who it is.'' She had to look at that note again. Eleanor stood up quickly. ''I've got to go, Betty. Thanks for all this. I really appreciate it.''

CHAPTER

14

Peter grabbed his small leather poker pouch from the dresser, unzipped it, and checked to see how much money was inside. Not much. He shook his head. Alice kept taking it from him at the games. She was either very lucky or a damn good poker player. He opened the top drawer of the dresser, took some money from beneath the underwear, and added it to the pouch. That should be enough. He put the pouch in his pocket and left his apartment.

He took the stairs down one flight. The elevator was classier, but too slow. As he approached Benny's apartment, he saw Benny coming from the other direction, carrying a plastic shopping bag. With him were Charlie and Henri. Peter waited at Benny's door.

"Sorry," Benny said. "Had to go out and get some beer. The cupboard was bare." He jerked his head toward the other two men. "Picked up my bodyguards downstairs."

Peter smiled and nodded to the two men, then opened the door. Benny went inside, followed by Charlie and

Henri. Peter went in last, and closed the door behind them.

"Well, it is certainly about time." Doc Innes was sitting at the table, his money piled in front of him, his cane hooked on the edge of the table. He was playing solitaire. "Been waiting for you almost ten minutes."

"That's what you get for being early," Benny said.

"I'm anxious to lose my money."

Peter took his seat at the table. "That may prove difficult with Alice not here."

Charlie sat down, pointed to Alice's chair for Henri, then put some money on the table in front of him. Henri took out some money, put it on the table, then sat in Alice's chair.

"Yeah," Walter said. "I'm not sure if I miss her. Losing gets to be tiring."

"And she takes our money so gracefully." Charlie chuckled. "Laughs while she scoops up every dime of it."

"I am not too good at this game of poker," Henri said.

"Uh-oh." Charlie mocked a serious face. "Last time I heard that, I went home in my underwear."

Walter nodded. "I'll watch him closely. I see him cheating, we'll dissect him here on Benny's table. And I'll use a very dull knife."

Henri made a wide-eyed face. "This is to be a very tough game."

Peter chuckled. He unzipped his poker pouch, took out some money, and arranged it on the table in front of him.

Benny came in with bowls of chips and pretzels, and placed them on the snack trays near the table. On the snack tray by Peter, he moved the can of peanuts aside and set down a bowl of potato chips. "Beers all around?"

"Coke for me," Walter Innes said.

Everyone else nodded for the beer.

"Find out who deals while I'm getting the drinks."
Benny went into the kitchen area.

Walter shuffled the cards, cut them, then dealt them
one at a time. "High card deals." The ace landed in
front of Charlie. "No need to go any further." Walter
handed the rest of the cards to Charlie.

"So what's the prognosis with Alice?" Peter said.

Walter shrugged. "Depends on how quickly she
heals. My guess is she'll be home on crutches in a week.
Right now the concussion is the major concern. They'll
be looking for internal bleeding."

Benny came in with the drinks, and set the cans on
the table in front of each man. Then he sat down in the
empty chair, took the coffee can from the snack tray near
him, opened it and spilled his money on the table.

"Ante a dime," Charlie said, threw in his own dime,
and started dealing out the cards. "Five card draw."

Peter took a sip of his beer, threw in his dime, and
picked up the cards one at a time as they were dealt to
him. The first two cards were jacks. *A good start,* he
thought.

"So what's happening with Eleanor's secret admirer?" Benny said, picking up his own cards.

Peter was taken back. "How did you know about
that?"

Walter, looking at his hand of cards, attempted a
smile. "Anything Grace knows, everyone knows."

"That is too much a general statement," Henri said.
"I do not know of this secret admirer."

It was Charlie's turn. "Heard she's pretty ticked at
this guy, whoever he is." He took a slug of his beer and
set the can back on the table.

Walter looked to Henri. "Eleanor, you know. Correct?"

Henri nodded. "A very handsome woman."

"I'm sure you also know that she is Peter's paramour.
Well, she has been receiving anonymous love notes from
some stranger."

"Ah." Henri raised an eyebrow, and looked at Peter. "That is a serious event, no?"

Looks like privacy is something you have to give up in a place like this, Peter thought. He didn't like that idea.

"Or is this a harmless incident?"

"Harmless or not, Eleanor is really upset by it," Peter said. "And that's what matters." *That's all that matters.*

"Anything we can do?" Benny said. "You know, if you need us, we're there for you."

"Thanks. I appreciate that. I don't know what's going to happen. Because Eleanor is so upset, I wanted her to go to the police, to see if there was anything they could do. She refused. She said the police can not help her. So we are left with waiting to see what develops." He didn't want to mention that Eleanor was going to see Betty this evening and speak with Eugene. He was afraid it would diminish her in their eyes that she preferred to speak with the spirit world than with the authorities.

Walter put his cards on the table and threw a dime in the pot. "I open." Then to Peter, "Do you think it's something serious?"

Peter shook his head. "I'm not sure." He pointed to his temple. "You know what happens to some men when they get old. It could be nothing more than that."

"Yes." Walter nodded. "But that something that happens does not necessarily make them harmless. Just because people are old doesn't mean they are not dangerous."

Just what Peter wanted to hear. He took a deep, tired breath, and looked at the pair of jacks in his hand. "I call," he said and threw in his dime. "Yes, there is that, as well. All I can do is keep a vigil over her." He shrugged. "I just don't want to see her getting paranoid over this."

"Well," Benny said, "if you want, we can help keep an eye on her, too."

Everybody called Walter's bet.

Walter threw one card on the table. "Women have it especially difficult in such situations. Men are apt to do violent and stupid things to women."

"Cards?" Charlie held the deck, waiting to deal.

"I'll let you know, Benny, if I need that support," Peter said.

Everyone drew three cards except Walter. He took one.

One. Probably Walter had two pair. Peter picked up his three cards and put them in his hand. "The other night she thought for a moment that the murder at the party was connected to the guy writing the notes."

"Well, Audrey Knitter's arrest should put her at ease in that regard." Walter threw a quarter in the pot. "Quarter." Henri raised a quarter; Charlie and Benny dropped.

Peter looked at his hand. There were now three jacks. At least things were looking up in poker. "I'll raise again." He threw in seventy-five cents.

Walter took the last raise. Henri called.

Peter looked once again at his three jacks. "I'm in." He threw in his quarter.

"Three tens." Walter laid his cards face up on the table.

Looks like my time has come, Peter thought.

Henri laid his cards on the table. "Three kings."

Ooops. So much for a change in luck. Peter shook his head, and threw his cards down. It *had* to be Alice's seat that was lucky.

Benny picked up the cards and started shuffling. "I'll keep my eyes and ears open. If I hear anything about who could be doing this, I'll let you know."

"I appreciate it." Peter took a sip of his beer, then reached over and picked up the can of peanuts on the snack tray next to him. He started to pry off the plastic lid.

"You didn't have to bring your own snacks," Benny

was saying to Peter as Peter removed the lid. Then the world exploded in Peter's face!

"What the . . . !" Peter jumped back in fright, knocking his beer can over on the table, the beer splashing over everything. His defensive reflexes in action, he tossed the peanut can onto the table. "Whoa!" Charlie, Henri, and Benny pulled back with a shout. The peanut can landed, bounced, and knocked Benny's can of beer off the table, into his lap. "Shit!" He jumped up and grappled with the foaming can. Charlie grabbed at Peter's beer can as it rolled and spilled foam across the table. Walter snatched some napkins from his snack tray and tossed them over the spreading beer. Henri sat wide-eyed in shock. Everyone's heart was dancing hysterically, blood pressure soaring, pulse racing. The three cloth-covered spring "snakes" that had been hidden in the can of peanuts, and exploded to life when Peter opened the can, were scattered about on the table.

"God damn!" Benny shouted, wiping a napkin at the beer on his pants. "That Mad Joker is really getting on my nerves!"

Walter calmly said, "I thought you found his trickery funny?"

Benny scowled at Walter.

Charlie was mopping the beer from the table. "He sure keeps the place jumping." Everyone laughed, that nervous laugh of relief. Charlie realized what he had said, and laughed as well. "No pun intended."

Peter, listening to his heart stumbling about in his chest, feeling the pulse pounding in his brain, was hoping the beta-blocker he took would do its job and restore the heart's beating to a regular rhythm. Always a worry.

Walter said, "Quite possibly the man works for a cardiologist, the way he keeps testing our hearts."

Henri shook his head slowly in wonder. "This is a very strange place."

•   •   •

Peter reached the door of his apartment about ten after eleven. They always ended the game at eleven, then they hung around a few minutes to help Benny clean up. He opened the door and stepped inside. He was pleasantly surprised to find Eleanor waiting for him. He had expected her to be there. The surprise was that she was fully dressed.

"Hi," he said, and closed the door behind him.

Eleanor gave him a smile.

He put his poker pouch on the counter as he passed the kitchen area, and stepped over to where Eleanor was seated at the small table against the wall in the living room. "Planning on going out?"

She gave him a questioning look.

"You're all dressed up. I thought you had someplace to go."

"No." She sighed. She looked tired, and she didn't look happy. "I came back here after the session with Betty and Eugene. Eugene said I would find who it was in the note in the chocolates. I left the note on the night table last night. So I came straight here."

"You actually talked to Eugene?"

"It was a very strange experience."

"All sorts of eerie sounds and strange music and crystal balls and candlelight?" He did not succeed in keeping the sarcasm from his voice.

She smiled. "That was what I thought I'd be involved in. But no, it was a perfectly normal scene. Except when we started using the Ouija board. Then it got strange. I mean, I actually felt as if I were talking to the spirits, as if they were there in the room. And while I was resting my hands on the pointer, there was this energy that was radiating up my arms, like I was holding a heavy weight. I'm telling you, Peter, there are things in life we do not understand."

"So the best you could get out of Eugene was that the man's name is in the note?" Peter grunted. "Sounds like Eugene was his old self."

"He was that, all right. I couldn't get a straight answer out of him, as hard as I tried. I don't know how Betty put up with him when he was alive. At one point I said to him, did he know that if he were there with us, I'd strangle him. And he pointed to YES. He got me so angry, I asked him if it was hot where he was. He spelled out COMFORTABLE.''

Peter grinned. ''Well, he has a sense of humor. So what did you find in the note?'' He looked over her shoulder. On the table, besides a half-filled glass of wine and an ashtray with three cigarette butts in it, there were pieces of paper scrawled with what looked like a code. Lying among the papers was a ballpoint pen.

''Let me tell you what I've done so far. Maybe you have some ideas on this.'' She picked up the note from the papers and laid it in front of her on the table. ''I first read the note a couple of times, trying to get some impression from the words. Maybe a picture in my mind that would give me a clue.''

Peter read the note over her shoulder to refresh his memory. ''I know these are your favorites. Sweets for the Sweet. Friends will leave. But you and I will have each other to the end.''

''When that didn't happen, I tried deciphering the note. I figured that maybe it was a code of some kind.'' She turned to the pieces of paper, picked one, and laid it next to the note. ''I tried simple stuff first. I tried the first letter of every word.''

Peter read the note paper:

IKTAYFSFTSFWLBYAIWHEOTTE.

''Made no sense.'' She pulled up another piece of paper and laid it on top of the first one. ''I tried one letter higher, then one letter lower, in the alphabet.''

(one letter higher) JLUBZGTGUTGXMCZBJXIPUUF
(one letter lower) HJSZXERESREVKAXZHVGDNSSD

''Nothing.'' She pointed to the other papers. ''I tried every other first letter without using I, the, to, and, but.

Then I tried one letter higher and one lower in the alphabet for that one. Still gibberish. I tried words with more than three letters, every other word. I tried them backward. I tried cryptograms on all of the gibberish I had to that point. I went back and tried them all two letters higher and lower, and then three letters higher and lower.'' She slumped in the chair. ''Nothing. I don't know what other combinations to try.''

She *had* been busy. He smiled with admiration. He would have never thought of all those combinations. ''Sounds to me like you're ready for a job with the C.I.A.''

She gave him a frustrated look. ''Not if I don't solve the code.''

''Maybe you need a break. Get your mind off it for a while. Then you can give it a fresh look.''

''Maybe you're right.'' She sighed. Then she looked up at him. ''So how did the poker game go? Was it Alice's chair that was lucky?''

He gave her a frown of phony annoyance. ''Yes. And Henri took us to the cleaners. All the while we thought Alice was a good poker player. Now we know it's the chair. Next time I'm sure we're going to be fighting over who sits in that chair.''

She chuckled. ''Poor Peter Poker Player.'' Then she giggled. ''Peter Poor Poker Player.''

He grinned. ''Both are correct. I'm poor Peter, and I'm a poor poker player. It would be more accurate to say Poor Peter Poor Poker Player.'' They both laughed.

''And on top of that, I was the victim of the Mad Joker.'' He told her about the snakes in the peanut can, and the beer going all over the place. That really got her laughing, and seeing her laugh pleased him. It made the annoying experience well worth it.

''I'll make some coffee,'' he said. ''Okay?''

Eleanor nodded with a smile. ''Okay.''

He made coffee while Eleanor opened the sliding glass doors to the lanai, wiped off the table out there, then brought out cups, spoons, sugar, and milk. She placed a stout candle in the center of the table, and lit it. Peter brought the coffeepot to the table, and they settled down to watch the lake in the moonlight, enjoy the cool evening, and drink coffee. In such an atmosphere, talk of the mysterious note writer faded, giving way to gentle conversation shared by two people who care for each other.

It was twelve-thirty when they slipped into Peter's bed. Eleanor did not go back to her apartment to change into her pajamas. She didn't want to break the intimate mood of the evening with mundane activity. She simply removed her clothes, folded them on the chair, and slipped between the cool sheets.

They lay awake, enjoying being with one another. Peter's thinking drifted around like a leaf on a gentle lake, and odd thoughts occasionally bubbled to the surface, seemingly from nowhere. In the quiet of the dark room Peter suddenly said, in a dreamy voice, "Maybe there's another note in the box of chocolates?"

15

"I think the box of chocolates is still downstairs on the front desk," Eleanor said. She was suddenly awake.

There was a moment of hesitant silence. Then Peter said, "Let's do it." He turned on the lamp, got out of bed, and went to the dresser.

"Okay." Eleanor rose from the bed and grabbed her clothes from the chair.

They dressed quickly. Peter pulled a pair of shorts and a T-shirt out of the drawer, and hurried into them, then went in search of his sneakers. Eleanor struggled into her clothes, but left the pendant on the dresser. They hurried through the living room, past the kitchen, and out the apartment door. They fought the urge to run down the corridor to the elevator, but they did walk rapidly.

"Why didn't I think there could be another note?" Eleanor was whispering as she walked down the corridor, trying to keep up with Peter.

"We don't know, yet, if there is one."

"There has to be. It's the only logical explanation."

"The only logical explanation to what—the fulfill-
ment of the Eugene prophecy?"

Eleanor did not respond. She knew when to keep her
mouth closed. If there was no note, she would take
enough ribbing from Peter without compounding it by a
vocal defense of her firm belief in Eugene. If there was
a note, then she could gloat as much as she wanted.

Peter pressed the button for the elevator. They heard
it groan to life, like an ancient man struggling to get out
of an easy chair. Then they waited for its slow rise from
the lobby floor, a rise that promised to take forever.
While they waited, they looked down into the lobby,
toward the front desk. There was no one around. Peter
wondered where Shirley Danzig, the night clerk, was.

"I don't see Shirley anywhere."

"That's it!" Eleanor whispered. She pointed to the
white box on the front desk. She was having trouble
controlling her excitement.

Peter sighed in exasperation. "This elevator is like a
'watched pot.' It never comes while you're looking at
it." Peter was excited, too. And he hoped there was a
revealing note in the candy box, if only for Eleanor's
sake. The quicker they put this mystery note writer behind them, the better she would feel, and the better he
would feel.

At long last the elevator appeared, and they patiently
watched as it brought its full height up to the floor, then
settled down. The doors slowly slid open. By that time
they were as excited as kids going off to a new adven-
ture. They got on the elevator. Peter hit the Lobby button, then both of them turned and stared through the
glass walls at the white box across the lobby. The doors
slowly pulled shut, and the elevator slowly, ever so
slowly, descended to the lobby. "Now I understand why
they tell you never to take the elevator when there's a
fire. You would be crispy by the time this thing made it
to the bottom," Peter said. He did not take his eyes off

the candy box. If it was a candy box. From this distance he couldn't be sure.

As the elevator approached the lobby floor, Peter saw Shirley in the coffee alcove having a cup of coffee. Shirley was a skinny woman whose wrinkles and hard lines made her look older than she was. Her short hair, in need of a combing, was a mix of blonde and gray, and she wore no makeup. She had heard the elevator, and was watching to see who was coming down. When she saw Peter, she smiled and gave him a little wave of her hand. Peter smiled and nodded in return.

The elevator gently came to a stop, and the doors opened with excruciating slowness, until Peter gave them a shove. They slipped out of the elevator before the doors opened fully, and headed across the lobby toward the front desk. As they approached the desk, Peter could see the box was indeed the chocolates.

"Have you thought about what you're going to do, once you find out who it is?"

"I decided to start with the police," Eleanor said. She was a little breathless from the excitement and the hurried anticipation. "If they can't do anything, then I'll have to think of something else. Any ideas?"

"No." But he did have some ideas. He thought of Benny's offer to help—that would be one option. He also saw himself confronting this guy—that was another option.

When they reached the desk, they stopped. Eleanor looked at Peter, then went straight for the box. Peter stood beside her. She took off the lid. The first layer of chocolates was gone except for two pieces. She carefully removed the two chocolates and set them aside. Then she lifted the cardboard that covered the second layer of chocolates.

There was a sheet of white paper almost covering the bottom layer of chocolates. The paper had what looked like a rust stain, and there were two words written on it. The handwriting was the same as the notes, but the second word became ragged toward its end, as if the writer was too overcome with violent emotion to control his hand. Eleanor read the two words, and they hit her as if she had just run into a stone wall: Sweet Butterfly. She froze with fright. My God! How could it be? How could it be? It wasn't possible! She had not expected something like this. Ghosts emerged from the gray fog in her mind, ghosts from another time, another world. Fear crept on chilled fingers up her spine, and the urge to run, to escape, surged out of the darkness of her mind. That urge collided with a confused barrage of desperate thoughts, panicked ideas.

"Are you all right?" Peter put his arm around her shoulders. He had seen her reaction, and it worried him. "Do you know who it is?"

With the strength of training long forgotten, she threw her arms around the panic in her mind, and dragged it out of the way. She took a deep breath, then looked Peter in the eye and lied to him. "No." She was well aware that he knew she was lying, but that couldn't change her answer.

Peter frowned at her for a few moments. It was an intense frown, as if his eyes were trying to pierce her thoughts. She was lying to him, and he didn't like it at all. He knew, in that moment, their relationship had changed. Something had wedged itself securely between them, something that, given the chance, would destroy the joy they had found in each other.

He looked back down at the sheet of paper. If Peter could have gotten his hands on the mystery note writer at that moment, he would have strangled him with his bare hands for what he had just done to them.

He took his arm away from Eleanor's shoulders, and reached for the paper. He carefully pulled up one end of the sheet. If Eleanor took this to the police, he didn't want his fingerprints all over it. He lifted the note off the bottom layer. With that act, hideous insanity charged like a snarling animal into their world. He heard Eleanor catch her breath. There was something among the chocolates on the bottom layer. What they both stared at was a knife. A long, slender knife with dried blood on the blade.

"You guys are that hung up on chocolate you had to come down in the middle of the night?" Shirley, smiling, was coming across the lobby toward them.

"All I ask is that you go see a doctor," Amanda said. Amanda, short and slender with dark hair and dark eyes, was one of those women who, without working at it, would always retain her beauty. The beauty would grow old, would mature, take on a softer power with time, but never disappear.

"I don't need a doctor." Ardley was adamant. It was after one in the morning, and they were sitting in the kitchen, Amanda in her silky nightgown, Ardley in his underwear. Ardley had a cup of coffee in front of him. He had slept for a little more than an hour, only to wake up and not be able to get back to sleep. Finally, he had gotten up and made himself a cup of decaf. Amanda had awakened and come out to see where he was. She was doing that a lot lately, waking up when he was not in bed.

"Will you look at yourself?" She was losing her temper.

Ardley knew that things were in danger of deteriorating into a shouting match. That was another thing that was happening a lot lately.

"Look, calm down. We can talk about this." He tried the soft, easy approach.

"Don't you tell me to calm down!"

So much for the soft, easy approach. "I'm not sick. I don't need to see a doctor."

"How can you say that! You're up half the night. You're dragging around all day with your eyes half closed. What is that—chicken liver? That's something wrong!"

He waved away her concern. "It's just a phase of some kind. It'll pass."

"Yeah, it'll pass when they put you in the ground. Why don't you want to go to the doctor?"

She just wouldn't let up. He was too tired to deal with her. "Because I'm not sick."

She ignored his answer. "You afraid he might find something?"

"That is not the case." But it was the case. Every time he lay down to sleep, his heart started pounding erratically. It was all right at first, but after a few minutes it suddenly began with a large, noticeable beat, and then a quieting, followed by another large beat. At times he was afraid it wouldn't beat again. It gave one large, pounding beat, then stopped. During the day, everything was fine. It was at night, in the quiet of the bedroom, that the damn thing started. And when it did, he was not able to sleep. All he did was lie there listening to his heart, wondering what the hell could be going on? Amanda was definitely right—he *was* afraid of what a doctor would find. He was in that age group where open-heart surgery was too damn common. The thought of some guy cutting open his chest and snipping away at his heart was enough to make him sick to his stomach. Not knowing meant not having to face the collapse of his career and his life, and he could maintain the hope that it was nothing serious and would pass with time. What the hell would he do without his job—sit around in a rocker all day? Sometimes not knowing was better.

"Then do it for me! You say you love me. Well, prove it. Do this for me. Go to the doctor."

Why did she always pull that 'if you love me' bit? It wasn't a fair way to settle a disagreement. It took all his personal freedom away from him, robbed him of his right to his own views and values.

At that moment the phone rang. *Saved by the gods*, he thought.

Amanda knew, too, that he had been saved. The only

calls he received in the middle of the night had to do with his job, which meant he would be leaving to tend to some dead body.

As he reached for the phone, she said, "I want you to think about retiring." Then she turned and headed back to the bedroom.

Whoa! Where did that come from? He held the phone in his hand and watched her walk away. He pressed the Talk button on the cordless phone.

"Do you have the other notes?" Ardley was sitting at a table in the coffee alcove, his notebook opened in front of him on the table. He held a pen in his hand, ready to write the answer. Opposite him were Eleanor and Peter. The candy box and the knife had been carefully placed in plastic evidence bags and removed by the criminalists. Shirley was sitting at the front desk, talking to Jessie Cummings on the phone, telling her what was happening.

"Yes." There was a distance in Eleanor's voice, as if she were talking from far off, her attention somewhere else.

Her demeanor reminded Ardley of Ted Walden: removed, in another world. In her case he attributed that to shock.

"Can you get them for me?" He kept his tone soft and gentle. Being tired helped him with that.

Eleanor nodded, and stood. "It will be a few moments."

"Okay."

She walked to the elevator. Ardley watched her go. She walked as if she were carrying a heavy burden on her shoulders, just the way Ted Walden had walked. As the elevator started to rise, he turned to Peter. "You have any idea who this guy is that's writing the notes?"

Peter shook his head. "No." He wished he did.

What Ardley saw in Peter was not shock, but determined anger. "If you find out anything about him, I want you to call me."

Peter nodded.

"Don't try anything on your own, you hear me?" Ardley put some force behind the words.

Peter frowned at Ardley.

"I know you and your buddy Benny, and I don't want any complications, you understand? I don't want to have to put you or him in jail for assault or whatever. This is a matter for the police to handle, for me to handle. Not you. So don't get any ideas that'll make trouble for either of you."

"I understand."

Yeah, but do you believe? Ardley thought. He was not convinced Peter would back off. It saddened him how some people let their emotions screw up their lives.

"Is that the knife that killed the man at the Halloween party?" Peter changed the subject. He didn't feel like being lectured to.

"We feel it is. That's why they called me in the middle of the night. That murder is my case."

"You mean Audrey Knitter is involved with this note writer?"

Ardley shook his head. "I find that hard to believe. It just doesn't compute."

Now Peter was puzzled. "But you arrested her for that man's murder?"

Ardley sighed heavily. "What it looks like is she was trying to poison Harry Benson—that's the name of the murdered man—and somebody else killed him before she finished."

Peter gave Ardley an incredulous look. "That sounds highly unlikely."

"If you remember, Harry Benson was sitting off in the back, right near the sliding glass doors to the outside. If someone was looking to kill just anyone at the party, they could have slipped through those doors when the room was darkened for the show, and Harry, drugged and alone, would have been the ideal target. All Audrey did was set Harry up in the right spot, and anesthetize him in her attempt to poison him.''

"You're suggesting a drive-by stabbing?" Peter said in disbelief. "Or in this case, it would be a walk-by stabbing. Besides, I would have heard the sliding doors being opened. We were sitting near enough to the man that I heard his death sigh."

Ardley frowned. A walk-by stabbing. He must be getting old. He wrote "someone else at the party—accomplice?" on his notepad.

They heard the sound of the elevator starting down. Peter returned his attention to Ardley. "Maybe she is clever enough to divert your attention from her."

"I find, in practice, that for the most part, murderers are never clever enough. After talking to Audrey Knitter, I think she falls into the 'most part' category."

"People still often get away with murder."

"That's simply because of the limited manpower and resources of the police. There is just so much time and money that can be spent on investigating a murder. Especially in the big cities, like New York, where the murder rate overwhelms the police capabilities. Given unlimited resources, there would be few, if any, that are not solved."

Except those deaths you don't know are murder, Peter thought.

Eleanor came up to the table and sat down in her chair. She handed Ardley three slips of paper. He carefully grabbed them by the corner, and laid them on the table. "The one on the top came with the chocolates."

Ardley took some small plastic evidence bags from his pocket. Holding the top note by a corner, he slipped it into a bag and zipped it close. He laid the bag down where he could read the note, and wrote what it said in his notebook, along with the fact that it came with the chocolates. "And this one?" He pointed to the note on top. "That says, 'Dearest, I desire your full attention?' "

"That was the first one I received. The one under it came with the flowers the day of the party."

Ardley put the two remaining notes in individual plastic bags, then wrote what they said in his notebook, along with when they had arrived. Then he looked at what he had written in his notebook for the note they had found inside the box of chocolates, before the technicians had taken the note and chocolates away.

"Sweet Butterfly," Ardley read. He looked at Eleanor. "All of these notes were directed to you. The others were clear statements. This one, which reads 'Sweet Butterfly,' implies that you would know what it meant."

Eleanor shook her head. "Well, I don't."

"No idea at all? Something somebody may have called you at one time? Or someone you know was called that? Or a name for a pet? Or a piece of art, a painting or sculpture? A song title? Or words from a song? Possibly words from a play or a book?"

Eleanor looked Ardley in the eye and shook her head. "No idea."

A sound went off in Ardley's mind like the hum of a tiny insect. Eleanor was suddenly not in that detached state. What he felt, instead, was that she was guarded. Not a good feeling.

"You sure about that?" He watched her closely.

"I don't know what it means." She kept her eyes on his eyes.

Now Ardley was sure she did. He looked at Peter, and wondered if he knew she was lying.

CHAPTER
16

P eter and Eleanor sat in the coffee alcove and watched Ardley leave through the front door. Shirley was at the front desk. She had finished talking on the phone with Jessie Cummings.

"Let's go," Peter said, "before Shirley comes over to extract information from us. Her dull routine has been broken, and she'll be looking to talk." He wanted to get Eleanor alone; then she might open up to him about the sender of the note.

Eleanor nodded.

As they began to stand, Shirley was coming around the side of the desk.

Peter held up his hand as he and Eleanor walked to the elevator. "Not now, Shirley. It's been a terribly long evening."

"Oh, okay," she said, the disappointment in her voice. "Good night. I hope you can sleep after all this."

"Thanks. We're going to try our best." But it wouldn't be easy.

They got on the elevator and suffered through its agonizing climb to the third floor. The doors opened, and they got off. As Peter headed down the corridor to his apartment, Eleanor stopped him with a hand on his arm.

"Peter, I'm going to my own place."

He looked into her eyes. She didn't explain why she wanted to go back to her place; it was delivered as a simple statement. He knew her well enough to know that trying to persuade her to come back to his apartment would be futile. He didn't like it, but he didn't see what he could do about it. He ached desperately to comfort her, to hold her in his arms and shield her from the world outside. It was a real pain, and it grabbed his heart. He sighed, pushing the ache down, and gave her a warm, sincere smile. "The door is always open, if you change your mind."

"I know." Eleanor gave him a weary smile. It would be nice to lie in the comfort of his arms, especially tonight. But she needed time alone to think. Her world had been turned upside down, and there was a lot she had to sort out.

Peter kissed her gently on the cheek. "Good night, my love," he whispered, then turned away and headed down the corridor to his apartment.

Eleanor stepped inside her own apartment, turned on the lights, and shut the door. "Sweet Butterfly"—her mind was still numb from the impact of those two words.

She felt so very tired, as if life was suddenly too difficult to bear. In the bedroom she stripped off her clothes, laid them on a chair, and went into the bathroom. She cleaned the makeup off her face with Vaseline, followed by soap and water, then rubbed in facial cream to moisturize her skin overnight. Though she thought cleaning her face would make her feel a little better, it failed to do that. She was still tired to the bone. All she craved was a long time in the peaceful world of sleep, where troubles and sweet butterflies did not live. She came out of the bathroom, turned off the lights, and slipped between the sheets. Tomorrow. She'd worry about all that stuff tomorrow.

But sleep escaped her. Eleanor stared into the darkness for a long time, her thoughts restless wanderers in a haze of conflicting emotions and fears. Everything had been going so well for her. Meeting Peter had brought her all the happiness she could ever ask out of her life. If she had met him when she was young, there was no doubt in her mind she would have married him and had his children and settled down to a wonderful life with him. And she knew in her heart it would have been a wonderful life. That did not happen but, thanks to the powers that run life, she had met him before her life was over. How many, though they spend their lives with wonderful people, go to their graves without ever meeting someone they fit so perfectly with? To have met that person, then . . . Sweet Butterfly. Damn! It just wasn't fair.

With all the troubled thoughts occupying her attention, and her mind sluggish from the need for sleep, Eleanor hadn't noticed when the darkness first moved. She wasn't sure, even then, that it was really moving. It was more like it had become a liquid in which she was immersed. Things wriggled ever so slightly. At least that's what she thought she was seeing. The darkness was like a smoke that obscured the shadows of the objects around her. Solid objects decided to become flexible, stretching themselves like sleepers slowly coming awake. She blinked, trying to straighten out reality. The only thing that did was to make her realize how heavy her eyelids felt, and how very tired she was. And the shadows continued to move.

Eleanor frowned. Were they moving, or were they changing? The shape of the dresser against the wall now appeared to be taller and narrower. She turned her head to look at the side chair, and found turning her head to be difficult to control, like a drunk trying to keep the room steady. Was that it? Was she drunk? She couldn't remember if she'd had anything to drink. She realized she couldn't remember anything clearly. Was this a dream? Or was she waking from a dream?

The darkness in the room began to change, to lighten. Eleanor saw candles on the windowsill. The light from the candles brightened, and now there were other candles, placed strategically around the room to make the lighting warm and seductive. She saw the antique armoire, the sturdy yet ornate wood furniture. Old furniture, well cared for. Paintings on the walls. Portraits of hounds and hunters and royalty. Scenes of rustic countrysides. And the fixtures on the door, the handles on the multi-paned windows were brass, polished to a shine that showed points of candle flame reflected in them like jewels. There was snow falling outside the window. Snow?

She heard someone come in the front door. She was in bed, in a filmy, flowing nightgown, and the door to the bedroom was opened wide. She was expectant, smiling. An arm outside the bedroom door tossed in a bouquet of flowers that landed at her feet on the bed.

"André? Is that you?" She smiled, knowing full well it was. The arm tossed in a dark jacket and tie. "Or are you a thief, come to have your way with me?"

André, in a white shirt opened at the throat, and dark trousers, stepped into the doorway. He was tall, with dark hair. He smiled at her. "Would you fight fiercely if I were a thief?"

"If you were the thief, I would resist terribly." She laughed playfully.

André jumped onto the bed, his laughing face near hers. "You are a wicked woman, to toy so with a man's pride."

She caressed his face and kissed him warmly. "Would you sacrifice your pride for me?"

"In an instant." He kissed her, his lips searching. When he pulled away, they were both a little breathless.

"How long do we have together?" Eleanor said.

"Forever." He smiled and touched her lips lightly with his.

"Does that mean until Monday?"

"Monday is forever. Three days are forever."

"Three days is not forever."

"We will make them forever, my sweet butterfly."

She softly caressed his face, and looked longingly into his dark eyes. Beautiful eyes. "My darling, with you, forever is not long enough."

They kissed with a tenderness and longing that reached deep inside to touch them both as if they were joined by electricity. They broke, breathing hard from the experience, and lay back, André with his head on her shoulder. She stroked his hair. "Where does your wife think you are?"

"Doing my duty. Serving the government by attending a boring conference in a far-off place." He rolled over and buried his face in her neck, his lips softly kissing her flesh.

She held her hand behind his neck, gently caressing him. Then the figure appeared in the doorway, and the shock of terror was a blast of lightning in her mind. Before she could react, before she could do anything, André rolled over and looked at the man. Pointing to him, he frowned at Eleanor. "Who is he?"

"I can't leave you alone," Peter said.

"I don't know him!" she cried. But she did know him. What was he doing here!

"Who is he!" André demanded. He sat up in the bed, and looked at Peter. "Who are you! I demand to know!"

"Go away," Eleanor shouted. She struggled to get out of the bed, but she was tangled in the sheet. "Go away!"

"I'm not going anywhere. I intend to stay with you, to protect you. It was a mistake to leave you."

"Protect her from what!" André was shouting, and he stood up.

"Get out of here!" Eleanor screamed. She got out of

the bed, ran to Peter, and pushed against him. Peter grabbed her by the arms, and stood where he was. She kept trying to push him away, but she had no strength. "Leave now! You don't understand. You don't know what you're doing. You're ruining everything!"

"I will leave only if you come with me."

"Come with you! Who the devil are you?" André reached to the drawer in the night table beside the bed.

"Please, Peter," Eleanor pleaded helplessly. "You must go. You've stepped into something that is none of your business. Go, now, before you get hurt. He's got a gun in there. Please, please go."

André had opened the drawer, and pulled out a gun. A while back he had given the gun to her for protection.

"He will kill you! Don't you understand? He will kill you!" She was crying, the tears in flowing streams down her face.

"Maybe. But I'd rather die protecting you, than leave you."

André stood straight and raised the pistol. Anger and the pain of betrayal were in his voice. "Get out of the way, my sweet butterfly, or I will kill you both!"

"No, André!" She turned to face him, putting herself squarely in front of Peter, the world a blur through her tears. "Don't!" She made to run at André, but she couldn't move; she was being held back by Peter.

"I'm sorry, my sweet butterfly." The words dripped with his hate. He aimed the pistol at her. Even as he did, he began stretching and expanding, growing like a balloon being inflated. Startled and frightened, Eleanor watched André transform into a giant hovering over them with a pistol the size of a cannon. "You cannot stop me." His face had become evil, the words boomed with power.

Peter grabbed her around the waist and pulled her back. She knew she was moving backward, yet they did not move farther from André. "Peter, go away! I love you! I don't want to see you hurt because of me. Go, please!'' She cried this with all that was in her soul.

She looked at André. "Please, André!" It was a desperate plea. "I'll do anything you want. Don't shoot him!" The barrel of the gun exploded in a huge belch of smoke. *But there was no sound*, she thought, as she screamed, and dropped like a stone into a deep, dark well.

CHAPTER

17

"It looks like she's all right." Walter Innes, leaning heavily on his cane, was struggling to his feet. Peter grabbed him beneath the arms and helped him up. Eleanor was lying unconscious on the floor of her bedroom. Peter had thrown a blanket over her, and propped a pillow under her head. "All vital signs are normal. She'll just have to sleep it off."

"Sleep what off?" Peter's mind was a jumble of worried thoughts. God, he didn't want anything to happen to Eleanor, yet here she was passed out on the floor, and he was helpless to do anything about it.

"Well, my guess is she took something to make her sleep." Walter's red striped pajama top was partially tucked into his trousers. "Because she's 'out like a light,' as they say. But there doesn't seem to be anything going on that's life threatening."

"What about a hospital?"

Walter shook his head. "They won't do anything more for her than simply let her sleep, check her vital signs, and wait and see what happens. It is best to leave her where she is until morning."

"But the way she was acting—how do you explain that?" He could see her all crazy, shouting at him, and struggling to get him out of the bedroom.

"My boy, with all the chemical compounds out there today that bombard the brain, it is difficult-to-impossible to predict how they will react in some people. But there is a common side effect for many of those drugs, and that's hallucinations." He looked down at Eleanor. "It seems that the worst is over for that. When she wakes in the morning, she'll tell us all about it, if she remembers. Right now, there is nothing to do."

He looked at Peter. "But it was fortunate that you found her before she could hurt herself. Hallucinations are real to the person experiencing them, and there have been cases where people have been crippled or killed by the things they did while hallucinating." He started toward the living room and the front door. "Now, if it is all right with you, I'd like to continue my beauty nap. At my age it takes a lot of napping to keep one's beauty."

Peter walked him to the door. "Thanks, Doc. I really appreciate it." He wasn't less worried; he was simply resigned to the fact that there was nothing he could do until later in the morning.

As Walter went through the door, he said over his shoulder, "If you really appreciate it, you'll let me have Alice's chair at the next poker game."

Peter chuckled. "It's a deal."

"Now get some sleep yourself. You'll be no good to her tomorrow if you can't see straight."

Peter closed the door and went back into the bedroom. He looked down at Eleanor with a feeling of aching helplessness. Doc was right, he'd better get some sleep. *If* he could get some sleep. He went over to the side chair and pulled it closer to the bed. He grabbed a pillow from the bed, sat down in the chair, took off his shoes, and put his feet up on the bed. He propped the pillow behind his head, folded his arms, and tried to make himself as comfortable as possible. The bed would have been more comfortable, but he didn't feel right leaving Eleanor on the floor while he took the bed. If he had been younger and stronger, he would have been able to pick her up and put her in the bed. Those days were long gone.

The pain dragged Eleanor from the depths of her sleep. It was a nagging, persistent pain that resisted the hunger to remain sleeping. The dream she was having faded into a gray haze as she slowly opened her eyes. She turned, trying to relieve the aching pain, and then the dozens of other small cramps and aches that showed themselves. Sunlight filled the room, hurting her eyes. She squinted against it. Her eyes brought in a blurry picture that her mind refused to decipher. The haze of sleep drifted slowly away, and she stretched aching muscles as she struggled to figure out just where she was.

She was in her bedroom, on the floor. That fact bubbled around in her thoughts for a few moments as she brought herself more fully awake. What was she doing on the floor? She sat up and looked around. Peter was asleep in what certainly looked to her like a very uncomfortable position in the chair next to the bed.

Eleanor reached back into the darkness, looking for the memories of what had happened. Her mouth was dry and gummy, and had a nasty metallic taste. She didn't feel rested. Her head felt like it was stuffed with that plastic popcorn they used in boxes to cushion things. It allowed her thoughts to move about, but they moved about on weighted feet. Vague scenes of last night slowly found their way to the surface of her thinking. What came through was confusing. She had to wake up.

She twisted her neck around, freeing it from the stiff aches, then, wincing from the other pains in her body, she slowly and heavily got to her feet. There were pains in her back, her legs, and her arms. She twisted her body and stretched her arms, trying to ease those aches. God, she was thirsty. A glass of cold orange juice was what she craved. She walked unsteadily to the kitchen. Every step brought with it more fragments of last night. She opened the door of the refrigerator, took out the container of orange juice, got a glass from the cabinet, and filled it. She put the glass to her lips and gulped the cold juice. God, it was heavenly going down. She glanced at the clock. Eleven-thirty. It had been a late night. She poured another glass, put the container back in the refrigerator, and went to sit in the living room near the glass doors.

She looked outside at the lake. *Another beautiful day in Florida.* The view always lifted her spirits, and made her feel good to be alive.

She was feeling better. Her head was clearing, and last night was coming back in huge wads of memory. What was emerging was a confused picture. She remembered the dream with André and Peter. But it seemed more than a dream. And with Peter sleeping in the chair in the bedroom and her on the floor, there must have been more to it than mere dreaming.

Her mind shifted into the gears of planning, purpose, and action. It was time for her to get moving. This whole André thing had to be dealt with. She was still sure it couldn't be André. André had to be dead. Someone with a twisted mind had to be doing this, and she was going to find out who that was. She reached way back in her memory, quietly sifting through old files, looking for the phone number she had to call.

Peter came out of a painful sleep to a painful wakefulness. His body ached as if it had been the object of severe torture. Sleeping in that chair was not the smartest thing he had ever done. He hadn't gotten to sleep right away. For a long time he had sat there in the dark, struggling with the ache to protect Eleanor, being helpless to do anything for her. He wanted her to confide in him, take him in as part of her life, let him share her problems and help her deal with them.

He saw that she was no longer on the floor. That was a good sign. She was up and conscious. He tried to move, to get out of the chair, and the pains shot through him like knives. His back, most of all, felt like it would never be the same. Once he was able to stand, he took a few moments to stretch his body to take some of the stiffness from his muscles and joints. Some of the pain eased, but his back would not cooperate. On limbs of wood he headed toward the living room. His mouth was gummy and tasted foul.

His first reaction, when he saw Eleanor curled in the chair, was aching joy. God, he wanted to love and protect this woman.

She looked up as she heard Peter come out of the bedroom. He stepped stiffly into the living room and walked over to her. His hair was tousled and standing up in places. Sleep was in his eyes, and his chin was a white stubble of whiskers. She smiled to herself. *He looks cute,* she thought. He leaned down and kissed her affectionately on the forehead. "Are you all right?"

She nodded.

"You put up quite a struggle last night."

So it was more than a dream. "Sorry."

His shrug said he'd live.

She remembered hitting out at him. "Did I hurt you?"

He shook his head. "No." Then he said, "I'm sorry I had to leave you on the floor. I wasn't strong enough to get you into the bed. I guess I'll have to get back to working out at the gym."

She smiled. "Don't worry. I don't plan on doing that again."

"So what did you take?"

She frowned at him.

"Walter said you must have taken some drug to put you to sleep. You were really out of it."

She shook her head, not understanding what he was getting at.

"He said the hallucinations sometimes came from such drugs."

It was the word "hallucinations" that shook loose something from the back of her mind, and opened old doors to dusty memories long forgotten. *André, you bastard!* She thought over what she had done before getting into bed. As she went through the steps, it came to her— the face cream. That was it! He, or whoever was posing as André, had drugged the face cream. Trying to show her how accessible she was to him. Damn!

Peter was waiting for an answer.

"I don't remember."

Lying to him again. He couldn't help her if she didn't tell him what was going on. "I didn't know you spoke Russian?" Peter said it innocently, but it was a loaded question.

"Why do you think I speak Russian?"

"When I came into your room . . ."

"Why did you come into my room?" she interrupted with a frown.

He shrugged, and smiled. "How could I keep a constant vigil otherwise?"

She smiled her understanding and approval.

"Anyway, when I came into your bedroom, you were speaking Russian to someone only you could see. I'm fairly good with languages, and I could clearly hear it was Russian. I know a few words, too, and you used them."

She gave him a teasing smile. "The words you know have to do with romance, no doubt."

He grinned. She was right. "And who is André?"

She sighed deeply. This was going to be difficult. She spoke in a soft voice. "A nightmare from my past."

"Want to tell me about him?"

She shook her head. "I can't."

"Does he have anything to do with 'Sweet Butter-fly'?"

She looked deep into his eyes, and spoke with a sincerity he had to accept as honest. "Peter, I can't talk about it now. I'll tell you everything when I can. You have to trust me on this."

He nodded. He understood, but he was not pleased. "When you're ready. But no more going off alone."

She shook her head. "There's something I must do today, and you can't be with me. I have to do it alone." When she saw the reluctance in his eyes, she added, "Promise me you won't try to follow me. I need to do this by myself. It's very important."

He sighed. He didn't really want to do that, but what choice did he have? "All right. I promise." Then he smiled. "Well, I did learn a few things last night."

She frowned, not knowing what to expect, and not sure she wanted to know. "Like what?"

He smiled warmly. "That you love me, and you don't want me to get hurt."

She smiled.

He leaned down and kissed her gently on the lips. She kissed him back.

Jessie Cummings was in a snit. What the hell did he think he was doing! "Damn it, Warren! You're going to break your neck!"

She was outside, along with almost everyone in Coral Sands. About five minutes before, everyone had been inside. Then Betty came running up to Grace at the front desk, and told her that Warren Styck was outside, climbing all over the building. With that announcement, everyone immediately left the air conditioning to view the event of Warren breaking his neck. Jessie had immediately called 911, and then had run outside to try getting control of the situation. In that she had no luck. Warren paid no attention to her.

Peter had come outside just after Jessie. Eleanor had left to do what she said she had to do alone. He joined Walter, Charlie, Benny, Betty, and Henri, who were all standing in a group, looking up. "What's going on?"

he said as he joined them. Then he looked where they were all looking. He wasn't surprised at what he saw. After all that had happened while he'd been at Coral Sands, he was past being surprised.

"Some more of the excitement of Coral Sands," Henri said.

Warren was dangling from the balcony outside one of the apartments on the third floor, his long gray hair blowing softly in the breeze. He was wearing a white T-shirt, tan shorts, and new sneakers. His sneakers were always new, because they never received any wear. Hand over hand he moved along the balcony to its end, his legs swaying uselessly. Peter could see the huge muscles in the man's arms working hard, making his movements appear effortless. Warren reached the end of the balcony, then, in a large swing, he flew into space, catching hold of the rail on the next balcony. And giving everybody down below a heart attack.

"Is being retired as you expected it?" Walter said to Henri.

"This is not being retired, this is being committed." Henri shook his head. "I keep thinking over my life to discover what it is I did that I am being so punished for."

Frank, the bug man, came up to them. "What's with that guy? He crazy or something?"

"You think it's a suicide attempt?" Charlie said to Walter.

"If it is, it isn't a very good one."

"How long has he been up there?" Peter asked.

Walter shrugged. "I don't know. It was Betty who saw him first. We were outside by the pool a few minutes ago, talking about the discovery of the knife last night, when she suddenly screamed and pointed up." He nodded toward Warren. "And ran inside to alert everyone, so they wouldn't miss the action."

"I went inside to get help for him," Betty huffed.

"And what returned was an audience." Benny grinned.

Peter frowned. "Why is he doing this?"

"Ask him," Benny said. "And he'll probably say 'Why not?' The man's not playing with a full deck, is my guess."

"A challenge can bring a person alive," Walter said.

"Yeah, and doing something this stupid can make a person dead."

"What kind of a place you run here?" Alex Conners came up alongside Jessie.

"I'm thinking of changing the name of the place from Coral Sands Assisted Living to Coral Sands Zoo." Her face was hard.

It was clear to Alex that Jessie was not happy. He stepped back, away from her line of fire.

Sailor Hat and Gray Hair, Tweedledee and Tweedledum, were standing in front of Jessie, calmly looking up at Warren. *Only something like this could get those two guys away from the gazebo*, she thought.

Sailor Hat was wearing a T-shirt that read NOW THAT THEY HAVE THE SEXUAL REVOLUTION, I'M ALL OUT OF BULLETS.

"Guess he ain't afraid of falling," Gray Hair said.

"Me neither. Never had a fear of falling," Sailor Hat said.

"It always terrified me."

"I was only afraid of the sudden stop after you fall. That's what kills you every time."

"Warren!" Jessie yelled. "Just what are you trying to prove?" Sometimes she felt like she was managing a mental institution.

" 'Trying' is the incorrect word, my dear Jessie," he yelled back, as he continued to move hand over hand across the balcony. "For you see, I am *proving* that I can do this."

"For what purpose?"

"Self-fulfillment!" he shouted back, then went into a

swing, sailing across the empty space to grab on the rail of the next balcony. "And I am being self-fulfilled! Gloriously so! It is great to be alive! To soar above mere mortals, to reach for the sky—that is life and that is living!"

"Me, I prefer a good glass of wine," Sailor Hat said.

"And a sexually active woman," Gray Hair said.

"Sexually active woman? Are you testing my memory?"

"I told you, the guy's a bedbug." Benny looked at Frank. "Maybe you should use a stronger bug killer. They're still moving around."

"I'll get my shotgun."

"Where's he going?" In some respects Peter could understand Warren. He'd taken some risks in the past, and he remembered how he felt afterward—more alive, more powerful, more in control, and less afraid of life. Not a bad trade.

"His wheelchair is on the last balcony down that end." Walter pointed to the far end of the building. "I assume he came from there and is now going back."

The firemen, followed by Grace, came running around the side of the building with a net that looked like a folded trampoline. Grace pointed up to Warren. The firemen positioned themselves under him, flipped open the net, and, holding it, six of them spaced themselves around it. A seventh fireman held a bullhorn to his mouth and said, "It's okay, sir. Don't worry, now. Just let yourself go and we'll catch you." The words boomed out into the air.

"God! You scared the living bejesus out of me!" Warren looked down at the firemen holding the net. "Oh, lads, you take the fun out of living. What is the value of a risk when someone will catch you if you fall?"

CHAPTER
18

"It's all right, sir. It's all right. Just calm down. Everything is okay." The bullhorn exploded the words toward Warren.

"It isn't all right, lad!" Warren kept moving hand over hand as he spoke, not looking down. "You're here to ruin a perfectly valid life experience! Man against himself, against his limitations! What greater challenge is there? It is why men climb mountains, soar into space, dive out of airplanes!" He reached the end of the balcony, and started swinging. "And work without a net!" He leaped across the empty space and caught the rail on the next balcony.

'C'mon, Warren!" Jessie shouted. "It's all over now. You've proven yourself. Let these firemen go home."

Warren stopped moving and looked down at Jessie. He shook his head sadly. "Ah, Jessie. You have a way of deflating a man's ambitions." He took a deep breath in surrender. "All right, lads. Hang on tight to your rigging. I'm coming your way."

He pulled himself up until his waist was resting

against the top of the balcony, then with a huge push he shoved himself backward into the air, dropped his hands, bent his upper body forward, and grabbed his legs. His body sailed down in a somersault that landed him on his back in the net, his legs held tight to his body.

Everybody cheered and applauded and whistled.

"Was that a half gainer with a double twist?" Gray Hair said.

"Looked more like a cannonball to me," Sailor Hat said.

"Ah, but what style. I give him an 8."

"Considering the degree of difficulty, I'd give him a 9."

Jessie, the concern gone, only the anger remaining, turned away from the scene and headed back inside Coral Sands. She didn't want to confront Warren in his moment of glory and yell at him like a mother berating her child. But she would definitely have a talk with him later.

Eleanor, dressed in a white blouse and tan slacks, had left with a large handbag. She drove to downtown Sarasota, parked the car, then walked two blocks, looking around as she did so, before she hailed a taxi.

"The Beach House on Anna Maria," she told the driver after she was in the cab. Throughout the drive she avoided conversation with the driver, and kept checking the cars behind them. She spotted none that appeared to be following her. When the taxi pulled up in front of the restaurant, Eleanor leaned forward, and handed the guy forty dollars. He looked at her as if she were crazy. "I want you to drive north along this road for exactly a quarter mile, park the cab and wait for me. You do that, and they'll be fifty more for you."

He looked her up and down, then looked again at the money. "What is this all about?"

"The fifty that's coming is so you don't ask questions."

He nodded his understanding. "A quarter of a mile. How long you gonna be?"

"No longer than a half hour. I'm not there by then, you can leave."

He considered this once more. "Half an hour." He thought some more, then said, "Okay. You're on."

Eleanor left the cab and went into the restaurant. Inside, she went to the ladies room. Five minutes later, a woman came out of the ladies room wearing a silky blue and pink shirt over her blue bathing suit. She had dark glasses but no makeup, her hair was tucked under a white visor, and there were blue beach sandals on her feet. On her arm was a large white tote bag with "Florida" in blue script on its side.

She walked to the restaurant deck outside, stepped off the deck onto the sand, and began a slow trek up the beach. The woman appeared to be enjoying the walk, the thrill of being alive. She would turn every so often and take deep breaths as she admired the bright world around her, a world filled with the soothing sounds of waves stroking the beach, gulls crying out above her, and the blue sky spotted with clouds that were too white to be real. The dark glasses hid the movement of her eyes searching for someone following her.

When she approached the taxi, the driver was listening to the radio. She opened the rear door.

He turned around. "Sorry, lady. I'm taken."

She reached in her bag, pulled out a fifty-dollar bill, and handed it to him.

"Oops." He took the fifty and looked her over. "I never would have known it was you."

"That's the idea." She settled into the back seat. "The Holiday Inn on Lido Beach."

"You got it." He started the cab, and pulled away from the curb.

When the taxi dropped her in front of the Holiday Inn, she gave him another fifty, then got out and went inside the hotel. The lobby was air-conditioned. The de-cor was Florida pastels with fish and tropical plants. She walked toward the rest rooms and stopped at the bank of telephones. She put the tote bag on the floor at her feet. Before she dialed, she rehearsed the telephone number in her head. She looked around to see if anyone was watching her. Then, using her phone card, she called the number that she had resurrected from those dusty memories. She hoped she had it right.

It rang three times before it was picked up.

"Off Shore Enterprises," a woman said.

"I have a message from Rose." She could hear the woman punching the keys of her computer, and pictured her eyes scanning the entries on the screen.

"I'm sorry, madam. I don't understand." Her tone had become guarded and cold.

Eleanor had hoped for more than this. "I gave you the code. What's the problem?" She was annoyed.

"I can't help you, madam, if you won't tell me what you want."

"I'm looking for Gerald Oberlin. I heard that he worked there." Eleanor could hear the keys of the computer again. She hoped he still worked there. It had been a long time ago. In fact, considering he was older than she, he was probably retired by now. Not good.

"I do not have that person on the list of employees."

"Then give me someone who has a better list."

"I could let you speak with our personnel manager."

"Fine."

There was some ringing on the other end, and then the receiver was picked up. "Tom Cannon."

"I'm trying to reach Gerald Oberlin. He worked the Russian desk at one time."

"Who is this, please?"

"Rose."

She heard him tapping the keys of his computer.

After a few moments he said, "I'm sorry, but we have no record of Mr. Oberlin."

"Listen, I haven't been an employee for many years.

But now there's a ghost from the past who is threatening my life. I need to know if he's for real. I need to speak with someone who can help me.''

''I wish there was something I could do for you, madam.'' She could feel him shaking his head.

''So you're going to leave me swinging in the wind. What happened to the old Company spirit? I'm facing this situation because I worked for the Company. I expect some cooperation here. I think it's time I spoke to someone with more authority than you.''

''Where are you calling from?''

She read off the number on the telephone.

''If you wait there, I'll call you back in a few minutes. I'll check the branches to see if they have Mr. Oberlin listed.''

''Fine.'' She hung up.

She left her tote bag on the floor by the phone, and sat in a stuffed chair where she could see the phones.

The telephone conversation had not gone as she had planned or expected. She didn't know what she would do if they didn't help her. But she did know that innocent people were going to get involved, and that angered her. She wished she had a cigarette. Like Peter, she was an occasional smoker. A heavy day of smoking might include a half-dozen cigarettes. But right then she could have become a chain smoker with no encouragement.

The time ticked by slowly. She looked at her watch repeatedly, only to find the time had barely changed. When you're conscious of the time, it taunts you by dragging its feet. The phone finally rang. She jumped up and lifted the receiver.

''Hello?''

''Rose?''

''Yes.''

''I've checked our archived employee records. You were an employee a very long time ago. I have been advised that our obligation to you no longer exists. Do you understand?''

"Yes." Damn them!

"However, I did come across Mr. Oberlin's name in one of our branch offices. I can give you his telephone number."

"Hold it." She leaned down, dug into the tote bag, pushed aside the folded clothing, and pulled out her purse. She searched in her purse for a pen and something to write on. She found the pen, and took a dollar bill from her wallet. "Okay."

He read her the telephone number, and she wrote it on the dollar bill. A Florida number, that was a break. Then he said, "That's all I am able to do for you. Do not call here again for assistance." He hung up.

Bastard! She put the receiver back on the hook.

She looked at the phone number on the dollar bill. There was still a chance that George could help her. If he had hung around until retirement, he might still have contacts and credibility with the Company.

She dialed the phone number. It rang twice.

"Hello?" A woman's voice.

"I'd like to speak with George Oberlin, please."

"That's not possible. Who is this?" The woman spoke slowly, as if she had to concentrate to bring every word forward.

"Kathy? Is that you?" So George was retired. They had given her his home phone number. She could picture a woman in her forties, dark hair, dark eyes, pleasant and friendly. But that was almost twenty years ago.

"Yes?"

"It's Rita. Rita Stanley. I used to work for George."

"Rita? I'm sorry, I don't remember any Rita."

Not good. "C'mon, Kathy. I was at your son's wedding. George used to bring me to the house because you were such a good cook. And I was single and a lousy cook. He was always worried I'd poison myself with my own cooking."

"Oh, yes, Rita. I remember. My, that was a long time ago. I wasn't thinking that far back. How are you?"

"Old."

"Aren't we all."

"Kathy, I really do need to speak with George."

There was a long pause. "I'm sorry, Rita. George is no longer with us. He had a heart attack last year." Eleanor was no longer listening. Her mind tumbled with panicky thoughts. She was on her own in this nightmare. On her own! What the hell was she going to do? She hadn't expected to be abandoned like this. When she had left the Company, they had given her all that rah rah about support no matter what. Except, it seemed, when push came to shove. She had believed it, had depended on that support being there. She had been confident that this situation with André would be calmly taken care of. That confidence had kept her from panicking last night when she saw "Sweet Butterfly" in that candy box.

"Rita? Are you still there?"

"Oh, yes. Sorry, Kathy." She pulled herself back to the conversation. "I just didn't know about George. It comes as a shock."

"Yes. It was a shock to us, too. He seemed in perfect health. Jogging, exercising, tennis. No one expected it."

"Life's not fair," Eleanor said. *And people don't make it any better.*

"No, it isn't." Kathy paused a moment, considering that. "Is there something I can do for you?"

"No. Thanks."

"Do call if you're ever in the area. It would be nice to sit and talk with you again."

"I'll do that, Kathy." She said it, but she knew it would never happen. "But I really must go now. And I'm really sorry to hear about George."

"Yes." There was a sad sigh on the other end of the phone. "Nothing and no one lasts forever."

"Good-bye, Kathy."

"Good-bye. And take care of yourself."

"I'll try." She hung up the phone. *But it isn't going to be easy.*

• • •

Ardley came up to Grace at the front desk. "Is Ms. Cummings in?" He looked like he'd slept in his clothes. He had a large brown envelope under his arm.

"I'm here, Grace." Jessie's voice came from her office, behind Grace.

Grace shrugged, and smiled. She indicated Ardley should go into the office.

"Thanks," Ardley said. He walked around the counter and entered Jessie's office.

"Seems neither of us is getting any sleep," she said. "Heard you had a busy night."

"Better than watching television."

"Was the knife the one that killed that man at the party?"

He nodded absently. "Seems so. The blood type's the same. No fingerprints on the knife. The prints we got off the box match Eleanor Carter's. But most of the prints were Grace's. Guess she has a sweet tooth." When Jessie gave him a questioning look, he added, "I still have the fingerprints we took of all the residents last spring when that woman was murdered. Had them checked against the prints of the people I knew had handled the box."

Among the papers on Jessie's desk there was a coffee cup, and next to it a bottle of pills. Ardley looked at her and raised a questioning eyebrow at the pill bottle.

She noticed where he was looking, and sighed. "Something to calm my nerves. These crises don't make my job easier."

He laid the envelope on the desk in front of Jessie, then pulled the chair up to her desk and sat down. "I've gone through the photographs and my notes, and matched up costumes to the people who wore them. There was someone at the party I couldn't identify." He indicated the envelope. "Possibly you know who it was."

Jessie opened the envelope and pulled out an eight-by-ten photograph. It was one she had taken at the Halloween party when everyone was coming in the door. "Looks like the Crypt Keeper."

"I've got people checking with the costume places again. But I suspect we won't find him that way."

"Or her," Jessie said, challenging him.

"Or her," he added. That was true. It could be another woman. What was happening to his thinking? He'd been making some stupid assumptions lately. It was going without sleep that was doing it. Had to be.

Jessie looked at the photograph more closely. Then she shook her head. "No, I have no idea who this is." She slipped the photograph back in the envelope.

"You mind if I have Grace go around and ask the residents?"

"Grace?"

"They might be more honest with her. The police make some old people very nervous." Then he smiled sheepishly. "Besides, I'm a bit shorthanded right now."

"And a bit exhausted, from the look of you."

He wished people would stop telling him that.

She pushed the chair out and stood up. "C'mon. I'll tell Grace."

CHAPTER
19

"I thought you were keeping an eye on Eleanor?" Benny said.

"Yes, so did I." Peter sighed. "But she refused to let me go with her. She simply said she had something she must do alone." He didn't want to say that he was really worried about her out there alone.

"You mean finding the knife last night didn't scare her?" Charlie asked. They were seated in the coffee alcove. After the excitement of Warren's stunt, Frank had chased them inside while he sprayed around the swimming pool area.

"Oh, I think it frightened her. And what she had to do alone today had something to do with that." He just hoped what she had to do wasn't dangerous or reckless. He didn't know Eleanor well enough to be sure what she was capable of doing. But he suspected she was more courageous than he.

"It is unbelievable, this killing and everything." Henri just came back to the table with another cup of coffee. "It is like I am in a television mystery program."

"Reality is more complicated than television programs," Walter said. "And things rarely turn out fine in the end."

"What does it all mean?" Betty asked. "This knife and the chocolates and the notes?"

"I wish I knew." Peter felt it would make things a lot easier if he did know. Things were more terrifying when unknown. The monster stepping out of the shadows into the light, might be ugly, but it was then a known quantity, and certainly less terrifying. "Whatever it means, it isn't good."

"Obviously, something sinister is directed squarely at Eleanor." Walter had both hands folded across the handle of his cane, the cane upright between his legs. "And it implies that the killing at the party was also directed at her. Why else would the knife appear in the box of chocolates meant for Eleanor?"

"Unless it was put in the box afterward." Charlie sipped his coffee, and made a face. Since his heart attack he had been drinking decaf coffee, and he could swear he tasted a difference he didn't like.

Put in the box afterward? Peter hadn't thought of that. It was possible the note and the knife were not related.

"Hmm." Walter looked to the ceiling in thought. "That's true." Having digested this new thought, he returned his gaze to them. "The box had been out on the counter for a whole day. Someone could have taken the opportunity that was presented, and slipped the knife into the box."

"Yeah." Benny was eating a pastry. Jessie had put some pastries out by the coffee carafes again this morning. "Turning attention away from the real killer and the real motive for the killing."

Betty leaned forward, intensely interested. She found all this very exciting. "You mean that Audrey maybe did kill her husband, and planted the knife in the chocolates?"

"Well, that is a possibility," Walter said. "The box

had been open on the counter for more than a day before she was arrested. She could very easily have planted the knife.''

Benny licked the sugar glaze off his fingers. ''You know, maybe Audrey had somebody helping her kill this guy. Maybe somebody else at the party was working with her.''

Peter wondered if Ardley had thought of that.

''I don't know. It sounds too complicated.'' Charlie grimaced at his coffee again. ''There are simpler ways of killing somebody.''

''Ah,'' Henri said, suddenly understanding. ''But not for an Agatha Christie mystery.''

Frank, his tank of insecticide strapped to his back, the spray nozzle in his left hand, came in the front door, carrying a gift box that obviously contained wine or liquor. It was wrapped in gold foil and there was a gold ribbon on the top. An envelope was attached by tape to the side of the box. He came over to the front desk.

''Hi, Grace.'' He put the box on the counter next to the photograph of the Crypt Keeper taken at the Halloween party. He noticed the photograph and looked closely at it. ''Hey! What's this? Pictures from the party?''

''Yes. One of them,'' Grace said. It was the photograph Ardley had left her. She had put it on the counter, and was asking everyone passing by if they knew who it was.

''Is that you?''

Grace made a face. ''C'mon, Frank, I've got more class than that. I went as Minnie Mouse.''

Frank chuckled. Then he put on a mock serious expression. ''I would think you were better suited for Sleeping Beauty.''

''Get off it, Frank.'' But she smiled at the flattery. ''Nobody seems to know who the guy in that outfit is.''

''A party crasher?''

''Yeah, sure.'' She gave him a look that said the

thought was ridiculous. "Somebody anxious to get their hands on our superb cuisine and flavored punch." She shook her head. "We haven't figured out who it is. Jessie wanted to put the names on each picture from the party. So I have to try and find out who this guy is." She thought that was a good cover story.

"Where are the rest of the pictures?"

"Well, Jessie's holding off putting them up, considering what happened. You know what I mean?"

Frank nodded. "I hope she puts them up soon. I got only a couple days of spraying here before I go to the next job. I'd sure like to see them."

"I'll tell her. You're not the only one asking for them."

He was about to turn away, then stopped. "Oh, yeah. Some old guy came by in a car while I was outside, and asked me to bring this inside for him." He nodded at the box wrapped in gold foil standing on the counter. "The note says it's for Eleanor Carter."

Oh, God! "Thanks," Grace said. But she didn't dare touch the box. And she didn't know what to do.

Eleanor came in the front door, and stopped. Benny, Peter, Betty, Charlie, Walter, and Henri were seated on the sofas nearest the front desk. A large group of people was standing in the background. God, even the antisocial Alfred Temple was there, leaning on his cane. And they were all looking at her. It was as if everyone was waiting for her. She was still in her bathing suit outfit, and felt self-conscious with everyone watching her. No one was talking. Then she noticed that Detective Ardley was there! Puzzled, she asked, "What's going on?"

Peter and Ardley got up and walked over to her. "It seems"—Ardley pointed to the gold package on the counter—"that another gift has come for you."

She went cold inside. On the drive back she had struggled with what she would do, and whether she would tell the police and Peter. She had gone over the few options open to her. Now, it seemed, all of that was beyond her control.

"I'd like you to open the note, please."

Eleanor looked at him a moment, then stepped over to the counter and looked at the package. There were dusty smudges over the surface of the package and the envelope.

"Don't mind the black smudges. I had the package dusted for fingerprints."

She looked at him hopefully.

He shook his head. "We just found prints belonging to the exterminator." He nodded in the direction of Frank, who was standing off to the side. "He was handed the package by someone to bring inside."

She nodded, turned back to the note taped to the side of the box, and placed her tote bag on the floor. She did not want to do this. She did not want any part of this. All that was on her mind at that moment was to leave, to turn and walk out the door. That was one of the options she had mulled over in the car. Just move away. She could get lost where even André couldn't find her. But she didn't want to go alone. She had intended to talk to Peter, was ready to tell him everything, and then try to convince him to come with her. They could be happy anywhere they were together, she was sure of that. There didn't seem any point to leaving without him, not after having found the one person she felt truly comfortable with. She took a deep breath, then carefully eased the envelope off the package as if it were connected to a bomb, turned it over, and lifted the flap.

"Please, let me." Ardley held up a pair of tweezers. "I'd like to have the note dusted for fingerprints."

She frowned at him, convinced he was being overly cautious. "You think he would be that careless?"

Ardley shrugged. "It's been known to happen more times than not."

He pinched the edge of the note with the tweezers and worked it out while she held the envelope. He then laid the note carefully on the counter, took his pen out of his shirt pocket, and deftly unfolded the paper, using the tweezers and the edge of the pen.

She leaned over the note and read: "Sweet Butterfly— Some champagne to celebrate our reunion. It is time for you to leave your friends and join me. As it once was, it will again be the two of us alone, against the world. I suggest you hurry to depart. I am sure that you do not want any more of your friends to be hurt." The handwriting was worse, the lines shaky and at times wandering off.

Ardley had read the note over her shoulder. Using the tweezers, he picked up the paper and slipped it into a plastic evidence bag. He turned to Frank. "If you'll wait a few minutes, I'll take you down to the station, where you can work with the artist to come up with a sketch of the guy you saw."

Frank nodded. "Sure."

Then Ardley turned to Eleanor. "I think it's time we talked."

CHAPTER
20

They were seated at a table in the card room. Ardley had retrieved a blue nylon case from his car that he now placed on the table between them. He sat on one side of the table; Eleanor and Peter were facing him. Each had a cup of coffee. Ardley unzipped the case and took out a small tape recorder, his cellular phone, and a letter-size yellow pad. He set the tape recorder in front of Eleanor, placed the phone to one side, and put the yellow pad in front of him, beside the note in the plastic bag. He took his pen from his shirt pocket, then reached out to the tape recorder and pressed the Record button. A tiny red light went on, and in the little window, the tape could be seen spinning slowly.

He asked Eleanor to state her name, her address, the date, where the recording was taking place, and who was present.

"Are you sure you want Peter Benington present at this interview?"

Peter looked at Eleanor. He was glad she had asked that he be with her.

"Yes." She had thought that over carefully, and felt it was the best way for Peter to learn what she had to say. She didn't know how he would react, but hearing it all in front of Ardley, where he wouldn't express his feelings, would give Peter a chance to digest the information before they spoke privately.

"All right. Now why don't you tell me all you know about this person who is sending you the notes. You know who it is, don't you?"

She sighed. "I know who he's pretending to be. I'm not sure the man himself is still alive." She shook her head. "No, I'm convinced he can't be alive." But even as she said it, she knew she wasn't convinced. It was something she desperately wanted to believe.

"How about giving us the man's name?"

"André Aleskov."

Ardley waited for her to continue.

She let out a long sigh. It was time to tell it all. "All right. I met him in Moscow. He was a low-level official in the KGB. My assignment was to get close to him."

"Assignment?" Ardley interrupted.

"Today I contacted the Company, and they told me I was on my own. So, here goes nothing. I worked for the C.I.A."

Ardley listened impassively. He had his doubts up front, but would wait before reaching any judgment. It was the nature of his training. He'd heard some fantastic tales in his career, and some of them turned out to be absolutely true.

Peter was not surprised. He had known from the beginning there was more depth to this woman.

"I spoke fluent Russian, and was eager to do my job. So I was instructed to get close to André Aleskov. The information we had on him said he was unhappy in his marriage—he had a dull, dumpy wife and two dull children. At that time he was thirty years old, and had been married for nine years.

"He wasn't a very important figure in the KGB when

he was targeted, but we felt he was a comer. Once he had achieved a significant status, he would be especially wary of anyone trying to get near him. It was decided to compromise him early in his career, and ride along with him as he climbed the ladder.''

"So you became his mistress," Ardley said.

At the sound of the word, Eleanor looked at Peter's reaction. She had never before been that worried about anyone's reaction to who she was or what she had been.

Peter's expression was attentive, but nothing of what he was thinking was visible there. It did not trouble him. Hell, he'd been with more women than he could remember. The important thing to him was that he was now with one woman he truly cared for and wanted to be with.

She looked at Ardley. "Yes. The plan worked beautifully. For ten years he and I maintained that relationship, and during those years he moved up and up until he was in just the right position to give us the information we wanted about the operations of the KGB. André spoke freely to me about his work—the aggravations, the impossible assignments, the mundane tasks—because we had built a mutual trust over the years. His wife didn't want to hear what he had to say, so who better to talk to than a trusted lover who had witnessed and even assisted in his rise to power?''

Ardley nodded.

"We obtained some excellent information. Some lives were saved." She shook her head and waved her hand. "No need to go into that. I'm not sure it's important here."

Ardley interrupted. "From this last note"—his eyes momentarily looked down at the plastic evidence bag— "it appears this André wants to hurt your friends. Why do you think that's so?"

Eleanor was hit with a sudden realization. Until now she was not sure what was going on with André. "You think he tried to run down Alice?"

Ardley looked at her and nodded his head thoughtfully. "It would fit some things, wouldn't it? We checked the license plate number the cab driver gave us. The owner had reported his car stolen that morning. The next day the car was found abandoned in the parking area by Café On The Beach in Manatee County. The car had been wiped clean of fingerprints. It certainly looks like it was an intentional hit-and-run. We had been checking into Alice's background for someone who might want to harm her. This note gives us another avenue of investigation."

Damn, Peter thought. *This was getting to be very serious. An addled old man stalking a woman had now become a demented killer.*

"And killing the man at the party—Audrey's husband? You think André might have done that?"

"I'm not sure there. We still like Audrey Knitter for that one. But we were looking for an accomplice at the party. Now, however, because of this"—he tapped the plastic bag holding the note—"I'm reconsidering." He leaned forward on his elbows. "You haven't mentioned why this André would be doing all this."

"If it is André, I think he wants me to suffer." She pointed to the note in the plastic bag. "He was alienated from all his friends, his family, his life, everything. I think he wants the same for me." She pressed her fingers to her forehead just above the eyes, and rubbed at the dull ache there. It wasn't a physical pain, but more an ache brought on by stress and frustration. "Then I think he intends to kill me."

Peter reacted to that—his eyes widened, and his expression went cold—but Eleanor was not looking at him, and did not see that change. He felt angry and at the same time inadequate. Could he really protect her?

"Why would he want to do that?"

Eleanor turned to Peter. "Do you have a cigarette?"

Peter took the pack of Benson & Hedges from his shirt pocket, pulled out a cigarette, and handed it to her.

Then he produced a lighter and put the flame to the
cigarette while she puffed it to life. She removed the
cigarette from her mouth, and exhaled smoke.

"Thanks. If this keeps up, I could become addicted
to these things." She turned wearily back to Ardley. "I
did a terrible thing to him. The day after we celebrated
being together ten years, my contact and another man
came to my door. I was being pulled out immediately.
Something had happened, and I was in danger. There
wasn't time to pack. I asked Boris—he was my contact;
I never knew him by any other name—if he was getting
André out, too. You see, I had an agreement with the
Company that André would not be thrown to the wolves.
He would be given the opportunity to defect. Boris told
me everything had been arranged, and I left with them."
She took a deep drag on the cigarette, and let out the
smoke in a heavy sigh. "Two days later I was being
debriefed in Berlin, and I found out that André had been
arrested in Moscow. They had done nothing to try and
bring him out." There were tears in her eyes as she
remembered the pain she had felt. "Nothing." She swallowed the aching knot in her throat. "They told me it
would be more effective to have André tried and con-
victed. They hoped such publicity, even if it never
reached the Russian population, would cause the KGB
internal confusion for awhile."

"The pawns of war," Ardley said absently.

"Detective, there is something you must understand."
She was angry and hurt by his flippant remark. "I lived
with the man for ten years." She hesitated. The tears
slowly tracked down her face. It was difficult to say
aloud what she had admitted to herself a very long time
ago. "We lived for each other. I loved him. And he
loved me. He trusted me, and every day I betrayed that
trust. The only hope I had was that someday we would
be spirited away to the United States, and openly share
a life together in a free world. I prayed that when that
happened, he would love me enough to forgive my be-

traying him for my country." She took a puff of the cigarette. "Instead, I was betrayed by my own people."

"And you think he has found you?"

"I don't think he has found me." She kept saying this because she didn't want to believe it. It was the past, it was over with, she had come to terms with the events, it was no longer what her life was about. It had no place in her life now. But she couldn't deny the events, couldn't deny the notes, couldn't deny Sweet Butterfly.

"The man was tried for collaborating with the enemies of his own country, in a land where human rights and human life meant nothing. I think, because of his position of importance, they did not try him as a traitor. He probably knew things about them to hold over their heads. The last I heard, he had been sent to the outer reaches of Siberia to spend twenty years in a prison there. They were really condemning him to death. The guards did not distinguish between an unwitting collaborator and a traitor. Traitors were not treated kindly by prison guards and officials. The guards blamed a traitor for the terrible state of their own lives. Without the betrayal, Russia might have succeeded in taking over the world sooner, and they would not be forced to live in hovels and poverty. Any sort of sadistic torture was tolerated and encouraged. He could not have survived that. No one did, that I know of."

"I heard that a lot of the political prisoners were released when the Russian government collapsed," Peter said. "He might have been among them." He felt she was denying what seemed was apparent—André was among them.

Eleanor looked at Peter, and shook her head. "By that time he would have been in prison for fifteen, sixteen years. André was not a strong individual. I doubt he would have survived more than a year or two."

"Unless he had something worth living for," Ardley said. "Something strong enough to make him want to survive—like an all-consuming hate. And the lust for revenge rooted in his very soul.'' *Heaven has no rage like love to hatred turned.* The quote popped in Ardley's head from God knew where. He shrugged to himself. *Something I had to memorize in high school, no doubt.*

For a moment no one spoke. Eleanor could no longer avoid facing what had happened, and what would happen. She knew that. The pleasant, carefree time with Peter was over. Life was not going to be a happy experience anymore. She was back in the trenches with the enemy, and fighting was the norm of the day. Twenty years had passed since that was the order of the day. She had left the Agency four years after they pulled her from Moscow. What they had allowed to happen to André had soured her allegiance to the Agency, made her feel dirty, made her feel no better than the animals she had considered the enemy to be. But that very vigilance against the enemy would be all that would protect her now.

Peter spoke first to Ardley. ''Maybe you can have someone watch the place for a while.''

''Watch for who?'' Eleanor said to Peter. She tried to keep the desperation from her voice. ''They don't know what he looks like. I don't know what he looks like. It's been over twenty years since I last saw André. It's possible I might not be able to recognize him even if he had aged normally, but what sort of disfigurement had he suffered in prison? He could have been changed so drastically that his own mother wouldn't recognize him. He could even be living right here in Coral Sands. I could have talked to him, stood next to him, and not recognized him.''

He could be here. Interesting thought. Ardley made a note to think about that later. ''What else can you tell me about André?''

She put the stub of her cigarette out in the cup of coffee. She sat back in the chair and took a deep breath. Her mind looked back through the long stretch of time to the man she had loved for ten years. ''He spoke four languages fluently. His American was flawless, thanks to the extensive training the Russians give such people. He was skilled with a variety of weapons, in hand-to-hand fighting. He liked Mozart and Tchaikovsky. He was a weekend artist, an avid reader, a very strong chess player, and he had the heart of a romantic.'' *And a look of innocent awe in his eyes when they made love, a little boy in a world of his dreams.*

Ardley reached over and shut off the tape recorder. He looked at Eleanor. ''I'd like you to come down to the station with me and work with the artist on coming up with a likeness. He may not have changed severely, and with a little creative aging by the computer, we may come up with something we can use. It would be interesting to see how close a likeness you and the exterminator come up with. It's possible the man who gave him the package was André.''

''I'll go with you,'' Peter said to Eleanor. It was the only way he could let her know he was staying by her side.

She knew that, and it made all the difference. She wiped at her tears, then nodded, and gave him a weak smile.

CHAPTER
21

It was nearing six in the evening when Eleanor and Peter came through the front door of Coral Sands on returning from the police station. Eleanor was wearing a blouse and slacks. Frank was right behind them, looking as beat as only a bent old man can look. Grace felt sorry for him.

"Thanks, Frank," Eleanor said. "I'm sorry you got involved in this."

Frank shrugged. "If people don't help each other, who will?" He went over to the corner of the lobby next to the front door. His tank of insecticide was standing there, where he had left it.

"You're coming into the dining room, aren't you?"

Frank nodded. "Just want to put this out in the truck before I'm too tired to lift it."

"Let me give you a hand with that." Peter went over, and with a grunt of effort, picked up the tank. "Damn, Frank, how do you carry this thing? It's pretty heavy."

"You get used to it," Frank said.

"So, how did it go?" Grace asked. Grace knew where

they had gone and why. At Coral Sands everybody knew, and Grace kept everyone up to date.

Eleanor stepped up to the front desk. She, too, knew that nothing like this could remain a secret at Coral Sands. Gossip was all that some of the people lived for, and the juicier the better. Might as well spread the truth along with the fantasies.

Frank held the front door open while Peter struggled to carry the tank outside.

"Tiring. We sat there and studied the pictures the policemen created on the computer, then made some suggestions and watched it change. I was working with one policeman; Frank with another. After doing that for a while, looking at eyes and noses and chins, my mind was turning to mush. I can't imagine what Frank was feeling, but he didn't complain." Eleanor nodded in Frank's direction. "We invited him to join us for dinner. He really has been caught up in this. We felt buying him dinner was the least we could do."

Frank followed Peter outside and left the door to close behind him.

"Well, looking at him, I think you'll be lucky he doesn't fall asleep in his food. He looks really beat."

"Yes."

"Did you come up with a drawing of the guy?"

Eleanor nodded. "Two of them. Frank's is a lot different from mine. Ardley thinks André has an accomplice, or maybe hired somebody to deliver the gifts."

"So what happens now?"

"Detective Ardley is posting a policeman here for the night. He said he'd make sure there was one around all the time until this situation clears up. The policeman should be here any minute. He's bringing the pictures with him. They were having copies made when we left the station. He'll probably want to post them where everyone can see them."

"You think it'll help—having a policeman here?"

"Detective Ardley said it couldn't hurt. And if André

sees a policeman, he may think twice about doing something else.'' Eleanor shrugged. ''It was all he could do right now.''

''Well,'' Grace said, ''at least he'll be company for Shirley. It gets lonely here in the wee hours of the morning.'' She thought back to the last time they had a patrolman guarding the place at night. She wondered if Policeman Blue Eyes would be assigned here again. She no sooner finished the thought than Patrolman Jerry Otis came through the front door. Tall, dark hair, a build like Sylvester Stallone, and the brightest blue eyes Grace had ever seen. *God is a nasty tease*, she thought with a sad smile.

He came up to the desk, and gave Grace a smile that melted her heart. Where did they hide the men like this lovely creature when she was young? ''Hi. I'm Patrolman Jerry Otis.'' Then he frowned at Grace. ''You look familiar. Didn't we meet the last time I was here?''

''Yes.'' She smiled. *But we didn't get to know each other the way I would have liked.*

''I'm to spend the night here.''

In my bedroom, I wish. ''Yes. I was told to expect you.'' She was having trouble keeping her thoughts in order. She had to concentrate on speaking, or the words wouldn't come out. *God, that a man could do this to me!*

Frank and Peter came back through the front door.

''I'll see you later, Grace.'' Eleanor smiled. She saw the way Grace was looking at the patrolman. ''We'll be in the dining room.''

Grace, looking as if she were in a trance, turned to Eleanor. ''Oh. Yes. Okay.''

Eleanor turned away, still grinning. As she walked toward Peter and Frank, she heard the patrolman say, ''I've got these pictures I'd like you to put up where everyone can see them.''

•   •   •

They were seated in the dining room and half through with dinner—Frank seemed to be the only one with an appetite—when the ambulance, sirens screaming and lights flashing, pulled up in front of Coral Sands.

On hearing the sirens, Peter and Eleanor exchanged worried glances, then they got up to see what was happening. Frank remained at the table, working on his meal. As they reached the lobby, they saw the emergency personnel come rushing in the front door. Grace and Shirley were by the front door and, clearly, were expecting them. Shirley hurried with them across the lobby, past Peter and Eleanor and the others who had come to see what the commotion was about, and took the medics to an apartment at the rear of the building.

Grace hurried to Peter and Eleanor. Peter had taken Eleanor's hand. "It's Gary Emerson, Gladys's husband. He's taken a turn for the worse." She saw the look on Eleanor's face, and knew immediately what Eleanor was thinking. Grace shook her head. "It has nothing to do with you. Gary's been dying for over a month now. Lots of internal bleeding and, well, you know. Gladys has been doing her best to keep him alive. He's her third husband. Guess she doesn't want to lose him."

Eleanor was relieved. She didn't notice that the news brought expressions of relief on the faces of the others in the crowd. Peter squeezed her hand in reassurance. They turned to go back to the dining room.

When Eleanor and Peter got to the table, Frank was finishing his dinner. They sat down with him.

"It sure is nice to come here to Coral Sands. I've had this account only a year, but there's so much excitement here." Frank put the last forkful of food in his mouth. "And the food is great."

"I hope you won't be bothered anymore by the police."

"Hey." He shrugged to say it wasn't a bother. "At my age, excitement is good. Most of the time passes with nothing happening."

"Well, the food must be good." Peter smiled. "You didn't get up to see what was happening."

"If they're not coming for me, I pay no attention to sirens." Frank put his napkin on the plate. Struggling, he pushed his chair back, then stood. "I want to thank you for dinner. It was very nice of you. But I have to get home. If I don't do it now, I'll be too tired to drive, if you know what I mean."

They both nodded and smiled.

"Thanks again." Frank nodded, then walked—the careful, unsteady walk of an old man—out of the dining room.

"I don't think I can eat any more." Eleanor pushed her plate away. The food had hardly been touched.

"Me neither," Peter said. "I have no appetite. I came in here only because we promised Frank a dinner."

"Me, too." She turned to him. "I don't want to face anybody right now." With all she had brought on their heads, she didn't know if she could ever face them again. She was thinking of poor Alice laid up in the hospital. Who would be next, if she didn't give in to André and leave?

"Let's spend the evening in my apartment," Peter said. He gave her a coaxing grin. "I have plenty to drink. We could drive away the evil spirits with evil spirits."

She smiled, but her heart wasn't in it. "All right." She didn't want to be alone. She moved the chair back and stood up. Peter did the same. "Let's stop at my place first, so I can get some pajamas."

The shrill noise pierced the confused images of Eleanor's dream. It was a dream of menacing shadows and monsters and fear. It made no sense at all except in the world of dreams, where all things make sense. The noise sent the images stumbling in a new direction, a direction that somehow explained the presence of the noise, and included it in the unfolding drama of fear.

But the noise was persistent and demanding, until it finally disrupted the dreamy images, chasing them into a swirling well of gray haze, and brought her out of the deep sleep, a sleep made deeper by the alcohol she had consumed prior to going to bed. It took a few moments for her mind to clear away the vestiges of the dream and orient itself to being awake. She opened her eyes, but there was nothing to see but blackness.

In the muddle of her mind, the first thought she had was that she had drunk too much brandy, which she had. She and Peter had spent the evening drinking and talking quietly, and listening to soft, gentle music. Peter had not once mentioned anything about André and her past. There were no questions, no accusations, no probing for more lurid details, no laying blame for what had been done. Nothing at all. Just comforting closeness and soothing words, and the pleasant peace of being together. Thank God for him.

Her sleepy mind struggled with trying to make sense of that shrill noise. She heard Peter grunt, and felt him stir next to her. She realized then where she was. The night light in Peter's bedroom must have burned out, because it was too dark to see anything.

Peter, too, had been dreaming, but his dream was of anger and loss. The noise came into his dream like a bright spear, disrupting the dream, and that made him angrier. He tried to find the noise, to stop it, to stamp it out of existence. The more it persisted, the angrier he got, and the more he thrashed about in his search. He screamed at it to stop, to leave him alone, and he ran around in a rage, trying to find it. What he found, suddenly, was the darkness of the bedroom, his anger a hot flame in his mind.

"What's that noise?" Eleanor was frowning into the darkness, the noise piercing and annoying, making her grimace.

There was a moment's silence. "Damn!" Peter said. "It's the fire alarm!"

CHAPTER
22

Peter quickly reached up, fumbled with the light switch, and turned on the lamp next to the bed. The bright light was like a sharp knife in their eyes, forcing them to squint. "At least the electricity is still on," he said through a mouth thick and foul-tasting from the alcohol he'd consumed. He tossed off the sheet and put his feet on the floor. Eleanor got out of bed quickly, and stood there looking at Peter. He pulled on a pair of shorts and a T-shirt, and slipped his feet into his sneakers. Eleanor was wearing her red silk pajamas.

"Okay," he said, hurrying to her. "Are you ready for this?"

She nodded. "Let's get out of here."

With Peter leading the way, they rushed through the living room to the door leading to the corridor. There they stopped short, and Peter slowly pressed his hand to the door. "No heat," he said. He took her hand and then carefully opened the door. The smell of smoke swept past them into the apartment, accompanied by the louder sound of the alarm, and a thin haze of smoke.

They could hear the sounds of people talking, some loud, some anxious and frightened. When they stepped into the hall, the corridor lights glowed an eerie yellow in the smoky air. Peter turned right, Eleanor following, holding tight to his hand, and walked quickly in the direction of the stairwell.

Warren Styck, in his wheelchair, was blocking the door. "The fire's gotten into the stairwell!" he shouted over the noise of the alarm. They could see smoke seeping from around the door. "You can't go down here. Use the stairway at the rear of the corridor."

Peter looked at Warren. "What about you? How are you going to get down?"

He gave them a superior smile. "I've got my own fire escape. No need to worry. I'll be downstairs before you."

"Are you sure there's no way we can help you?" Eleanor asked.

"Dear lady, you'll have trouble enough getting down yourself. Wait until you see what's happening at the stairway back there." He jerked his head toward the end of the corridor.

"All right," Peter said. He didn't want to stand there arguing with Warren while the building burned around them. They hurried through the haze to the rear of the hall. There they found a crowd of people at the entrance to the stairwell—women, many in cotton nightgowns that covered them throat to toes, and men in all varieties of night and day attire. They were huddled anxiously together and shuffling in tiny steps toward the doorway to the stairs. Some of the people remained calm and quiet; among others there was excited twittering and nervous talk; and from some they heard frightened whining. The constant piercing cry of the fire alarm dug into the mind and shouted fear and urgency, making it difficult to stay calm.

"What's going on?" Eleanor's voice betrayed her fear.

"Looks like the downward progress is regulated by the speed of the slowest." Peter shrugged helplessly. "I don't know what we can do to move them faster. Looks like we'll just have to wait our turn." Then he added, "Or wait to be rescued by the firemen."

The anxious crowd moved inch by agonizing inch toward the stairs, while Peter and Eleanor grew more nervous as the smoky haze whirled around them in the draft coming up from the stairs. When the two of them finally reached the stairs, the smoke had grown thicker and acrid. It burned their nostrils and throats, and scratched at their eyes, spilling tears down their faces.

"Maybe we should have taken the elevator," Peter said, coughing out some of the words. "Couldn't be slower than this."

"Yes," Eleanor said. "And after we're broiled to death, they could bury us in it."

By the time they made it halfway down the first set of stairs, Peter was wishing somebody would shut off that damn fire alarm. It was driving him crazy.

The smoke was thinner and less irritating when they reached the landing for the second floor. Just then one of the women on the next set of stairs down misplaced the tip of her cane and, with a cry of fear, fell, taking three others with her.

Peter released Eleanor's hand and shoved his way through to the fallen women. Fortunately the people were all too old to panic physically and throw each other around. Peter helped the woman with the cane to stand up. She seemed to be more frightened than injured. Two other women stood by themselves. But the third woman, the one the lady with the cane had fallen on, was moaning in pain and grabbing at her hip. Eleanor had pushed her way to Peter's side. "Undoubtedly something is broken," he said to Eleanor. He looked at the woman with the cane. "What's your name?"

"Evelyn Chambers," she said in a trembling voice.

"Can you manage without the cane?"

"No."

"Eleanor, will you help this woman down the stairs? I need her cane."

"Yes, of course."

He reached for the cane, and Evelyn pulled it back. "Eleanor will help you the rest of the way down. I need the cane." Evelyn looked terrified. He grabbed the cane and forcibly pried it from her hand.

"C'mon, Evelyn." Eleanor took her arm. "We don't want to stay here any longer than necessary, do we?" She guided her down the next flight of stairs.

"What's your name?" he asked the woman moaning on the landing. Peter pulled off his T-shirt, and tore it in two.

"Melissa," was all she could mutter through the pain.

He laid the cane along the hip, from waist to thigh. "Well, Melissa, we're going to do a little thing here with the cane to keep that hip joint from moving around too much. We don't want it to become more damaged." He wrapped one piece of the shirt around her waist and the cane, tying it to secure the cane to her side. Her moaning grew louder once he tied the piece of shirt tightly. The second piece he wrapped around her thighs and the other end of the cane, binding the thighs together, the cane acting as a splint to secure the hip joint. "This is not going to be a painless descent, Melissa. Of that I can assure you. If it makes you feel better to shout and cry out, you go right ahead." *It couldn't be worse than that damn alarm noise.* He bent down, put one arm under her arms and the other under her knees and, with a grunt of effort, carefully lifted her up. She stifled a scream, forcing it down to a pitiful moan. Thank God she was on the short side of eighty pounds, but his back and muscles were complaining nonetheless.

By now many of the people had moved down the rest of the stairs. The others had stopped to let him go in front of them, so the stairway was open below him. He took the steps one at a time. With each careful step he

tried to block out the panicky vision of losing his balance and both of them taking another tumble down the
stairs. It seemed forever before he reached the next landing, which was halfway between the second and first
floors, and the way his body was complaining, he wasn't
sure he could make it to the bottom.

Just then two firemen came running up from the first
floor. *Thank God*, Peter thought. They quickly took Melissa from him, handling her more confidently and more
easily than Peter had been able to manage. With the
release of the weight, Peter had difficulty walking, on
legs trembling and weak from the strain, down the remaining steps to the door on the first floor that led to
the outside. He was breathing heavily, and his heart, his
pulse pounding in his head, was trying to get a grip on
the right rhythm. He now knew what they meant when
they said "breathing like an old warhorse."

When he stepped outside, the night air smelled fresh
and cool, even though it was laced with the aroma of
smoke. The people were standing around on the grass,
watching the fire shooting large gouts of flame and roil-
ing smoke from the three windows of the other stairwell.
The fire was a living thing that growled in its ferocity,
lighting up the night and throwing heat at their faces.

Eleanor came over to him. "Are you all right?"

He nodded, too breathless to speak. He rubbed at the
muscles in the small of his back.

"When you didn't come out right away, I sent the
firemen in after you."

"Thanks," he said, still gasping. "I've got to get back
to the gym."

She gave him a playful grin. "I don't give you enough
exercise?"

He returned the grin. "Obviously not."

The crowd milled about and worried in fretful whispers. Change did not come easily to them in that stage
of their lives. To have their possessions, their home
threatened was a devastation.

Warren Styck came rolling over to them. Peter thought it had to be really difficult pushing that wheelchair over the thick mat of grass. He secretly envied Warren's muscular development. "So you made it out okay."

Peter nodded, still working on getting his breath. "How did you get down?"

Warren pointed to the balcony on the third floor.

Peter and Eleanor looked up. There was a rope hanging from the balcony.

"Simple. I lowered the wheelchair, then climbed down the rope."

Peter didn't find anything simple about it.

"So what does one do now, besides stand around and watch the place burn to the ground?"

Warren shook his head. "Not going to burn to the ground. The fire was confined to that stairwell."

"What could burn in the stairwell?"

"Paint on the walls, and mostly the vinyl floor covering. But when that goes up, it's deadly. And the stairwell acts like a chimney—the air is sucked in at the bottom and feeds the fire, pushing it out the windows going up to the top."

Eleanor leaned over to whisper in Peter's ear. "You're never going to believe this. Look over your shoulder."

Peter turned around. Right behind them were Tweedledee and Tweedledum. And Sailor Hat was wearing not only his sailor hat, he also had on a T-shirt that read DON'T TAKE LIFE SERIOUSLY. IT'S ONLY A TEMPORARY SITUATION.

Peter chuckled to Eleanor and Warren. "The T-shirt is certainly appropriate."

"Ever see such smoke?" Sailor Hat said.

"Reminds me of a barbecue I was at once."

"What were they barbecuing to make smoke like that?"

"Christians."

"You know, most fires are caused by smoking in bed."

"Yeah. Probably some guy upstairs lit up a cigarette after sex. Very common."

"Do you smoke after sex?"

"I don't know. I never looked."

Eleanor chuckled. "Those guys should be on the stage."

"Yeah." Warren grinned. "The next one leaving town."

Smiling, Peter groaned. "Not you, too?"

The flames twisting out the bottom window of the stairwell suddenly were blotted out by a white plume of smoke. First the flames were there, defiant and angry, then they were gone, the soft white smoke a blanket that calmly enveloped the fire, taming its ferocity.

"Looks like the firemen are on the job," Warren said.

That extinguishing of the first flames was the signal for everyone to relax. Peter could feel the relief settle over the crowd. Everything was under control, order was being restored, and their possessions and environment were saved.

"How do you think a fire like that got started?" Peter asked. He watched as the outside door to the burning stairwell was suddenly thrown open. A fireman came out and secured the door to keep it open. Water was pouring out the door onto the concrete pad and into the lawn.

Warren shook his head. "Nothing in the stairwell. No open flame, no exposed electrical wiring. Hard to say."

It was clear to Eleanor that it might have been hard to say, but it was definitely being thought by a lot of the people, and she was sure it was being spread on vicious whispers among the crowd. She could feel their eyes on her, accusing, hateful. She had brought this on their heads—she, with her affair with that Communist. *They're blaming this fire on André, whether or not it was his doing.* But Eleanor's gut said that André was behind it, and, with the image of the injured woman in her mind, that made her feel more guilty. Not an easy burden to carry.

Peter had the same suspicion: that André had started the fire. He remembered Eleanor's words—that André could be right there among them. He scanned the crowd for someone suspicious, picking up, among others, Edmund Stanton, his hands trembling uncontrollably, looking very angry, and Alfred Temple, who always looked annoyed. He'd put those two at the top of his list of suspects just because they were both nasty people. He kept looking from one face to another, each one not a happy camper, everyone throwing angry glances in Eleanor's direction. After a few minutes he gave that up. Every damn one of them looked suspicious to Peter, even the women.

CHAPTER
23

The world was quieting down. The residents, in their assorted nightclothes and fire-escaping attire, were scattered about the lobby, the coffee alcove, and the dining room. Jessie Cummings had arrived while the fire was in full swing. Once the fire had been extinguished and the firemen had gone, she and Shirley had brought out pastries and made gallons of coffee. Now the conversations were dying down; there was just so much to be said about the experience, and people were slowing slipping back to their rooms.

There was cleaning up to do, but most of the damage was in the one stairwell: the vinyl tile flooring was gone or charred, the walls were blackened with smoke and burned paint, and the windows were gone, leaving shards of glass everywhere. The carpeted area in front of the first floor door to the stairwell was soaked through with water; the rest of the water that had been hosed on the fire had run to the grounds outside. The worst damage was to the air. The sour smell of smoke was on the walls and furniture and people. It would be a long time before the smell would be gone.

Any attempts at cleaning up, however, would have to wait until the police and the fire investigators had done their thing. The firemen found evidence of a planted incendiary device, which put the fire in the category of a crime. Jerry Otis had placed yellow Crime Scene tape around the area to keep people away.

Detective Ardley had shown up, looking like he had been pulled from sleep and thrown out of his house with barely enough time to dress. He and Jerry Otis had checked the stairwell.

"Definitely no accident," Ardley said. He was seated in Jessie Cummings's office, having a cup of coffee with her. She looked as sleepy and as bedraggled as he felt. "From the pieces that survived the fire, I'd say it was a timer attached to a gallon of something like gasoline in a plastic container. The timer goes off, the gallon jug explodes, and you've got an instant fire." He took a sip of coffee. "No attempt to hide that it was a set fire."

"The talk circulating around is this has something to do with Eleanor's note writer." Jessie was thinking she would talk with Jacobson in the morning about hiring some security people.

Ardley nodded. "It could be. But there are other possibilities. Possibly—what's his name?—Jacobson has some enemies that want to put him out of business."

Jessie shrugged. "You'd have to talk to him about that. Wouldn't be the first time that's been attempted."

"What do you know about him?"

"Jacobson?"

"Yeah."

"Not much. I've worked for him for ten years, but all I know is he's got a quick temper, and pays a fair wage."

"I've met him before. You have his address?"

Jessie flipped through the Rolodex on her desk, stopped, and scribbled the information on a sheet of paper. She handed the paper to Ardley. "This fire being intentionally set is going to screw up the insurance coverage, no doubt.''

Ardley folded the paper and put it in his shirt pocket. ''That *will* be a problem.''

''I wish you luck when you talk to him.'' Jessie gave him a look that said *Better you than me.*

''One more thing. I'd like a list of employees who have been fired over the past six months. Could be some disgruntled employee out for retribution.''

''You think this is the Post Office?'' Jessie grinned.

The gang was seated around a table in the coffee alcove. Peter had left them for a few minutes. He'd gone outside, then came in the front door and stopped at the desk to talk to Shirley Danzig before rejoining the group at the table.

''Well, it wasn't as exciting as in the movies,'' Walter said.

''It is one experience that I must add to the crazy house scenario.'' Henri was looking carefully at his coffee before he took a sip.

Benny chuckled. ''It ain't like this all the time.''

''No?'' Henri gave him a mock expression of surprise. ''You mean this is the good time? And there are the moments when it becomes much worse?''

Benny smiled and shook his head.

Peter grimaced. ''The coffee tastes like smoke.''

''Is that an improvement?'' Walter asked. He was wearing his red striped pajamas.

Benny looked at Peter. ''So, what did you find out from Shirley?''

''Nothing much. Except that the fire definitely was started on purpose. She said the police found something that was used to start the fire.''

Henri shook his head in despair. ''Now it is an arsonist. What is coming next?''

''Eugene never mentioned this fire to me.'' Betty was annoyed.

"It might have spoiled the experience. After all, you did survive."

Eleanor was seated with them, but she was silent. Her thoughts were on André. She was afraid to say anything, for fear everyone would turn on her.

"Well, when I get upstairs, I'm going to talk to Eugene, and give him a piece of my mind."

Then Benny turned to Eleanor and said what was on everyone's mind. "Don't you worry about this. I know what some of the old ladies are saying. But I can only talk for myself, and I'm here if you need anything. You can't be blamed for the actions of some nutcase."

"Well," Walter said, "I'd like to add my own support there."

"Me, too." Betty smiled.

"And me," Charlie added. "So just remember we're here for you."

"I am a stranger to this group." Henri shrugged. "But I am also a fool for a lady in need."

Peter looked at Eleanor and gave her an encouraging smile.

Eleanor sighed, and smiled. "Thanks. You don't know how good it is to hear that." But she knew she would never call on them for help, she would never put them in any danger on her account. She would do what she had to do to keep them all out of it.

The metal cane supported the weak steps of the man who moved quietly down the hall. His progress was slow and deliberate, and on the hall rug, silent. He stopped in front of the door to Peter's apartment, leaned down, and slipped a folded piece of paper beneath the door.

Peter woke up to find Eleanor not in bed with him. His brain felt as if it had been stepped on by a giant in muddy boots. He and Eleanor had finally gotten to bed near four in the morning. The bedside phone was ringing angrily. He looked at the clock—nine-thirty. Clumsily he reached for the phone, fumbling with the receiver before getting it to his ear.

"Hello?"

"Peter, this is Grace. Shirley left me a message to call you."

Peter snapped awake, and sat upright in the bed. "Yes. Thanks, Grace." His mind in full gear, he hung up the phone, jumped out of bed, threw on shorts and a T-shirt, slipped on his sneakers, and, as he was moving toward the door, saw the note on the counter. He grabbed the note, and read it. IT'S TIME YOUR GIRL-FRIEND LEFT AND TOOK HER TROUBLES WITH HER.

"Damn!" He bolted out of the apartment.

"What the hell went on here last night!" Frank was outside by the pool. Walter, Benny, Charlie, and Henri were nursing coffees poolside, looking terrible after the night's ordeal. Frank, his spray tank on his back, had just come up to them.

"Just another wild party," Charlie said.

"Yeah," Benny grunted. "You missed out. We had a real hot time."

With that they all chuckled.

Walter nodded. "Yes. We old-timers know how to get a party moving, to put a fire under it, so to speak."

Groans and more chuckles.

Henri, trying to keep a straight face, added, "As the young people say, we know how to make a party smoke."

More groans and chuckles.

Peter came through the sliding glass doors and rushed to them. "Guys, I need your help. There is a problem."

"Don't tell me." Alex Conners grinned. "You had another party last night—a housewarming."

Grace made a face. "And you expect coffee and pastry after that remark?"

Eleanor came through the front door and walked up to the desk. "Hi, Alex." No cheer in the greeting.

"Eleanor."

She turned to Grace. "Grace, could you call me a taxi? I can't wait for the auto club. I'm in a hurry."

Grace shrugged, and reached for the phone. "It'll probably take the taxi as long to get here. Triple A said it would be fifteen, twenty minutes." She looked at the clock. "Should be here any minute." Movement at the back of the lobby caught her eye, and she turned her head in that direction as the six men came in through the sliding glass doors from the swimming pool deck. *It's about time,* she thought.

Eleanor turned to see what had attracted Grace's attention. She groaned and shook her head in despair. Peter was leading the group that was coming toward her. She didn't want to believe what she was seeing. No, she didn't want this, she didn't want to face him. It wasn't supposed to happen.

Grace watched as the group of men stepped up to the desk and surrounded Eleanor.

Peter stepped forward. "Eleanor, I know what you're trying to do, but we can't let you do it."

"Can't?" Annoyed, she looked over the group. "A bit sexist, isn't it? I don't think you can stop me."

"I'm sorry." Peter shook his head. " 'Can't' was a poor choice of words. We don't think you should go." He held up the note, his words angry. "Don't let some jackass troublemaker drive you away." Peter crumpled the note and tossed it on the counter near Grace.

Eleanor sighed with the weight of the world on her shoulders. "I can't stand by and watch all of you get hurt on my account."

Walter spoke up. "We don't think it is wise or just for you to run from this psychotic individual."

"Don't you understand!" Her voice raised with anger and frustration. "He's going to keep hurting my friends until I do what he wants! I don't want to see that happen.

He's not interested in you. He wants me!''

"I want you, too," Peter said.

Benny jumped in. "Me, too. Not the way that Peter does. But I like having you around. You're a good friend, and I don't want to lose a friend just yet."

"Do you want to be hurt?"

Benny shrugged. "I'll take my chances. This is a free country, and I ain't going to let some jackass bully run things, and hurt my friends."

"Look"—Charlie's voice was soft and sincere—"I fought in a war against the jerks in the world that wanted to control people, like this guy is trying to do to you. I'm not going to stop that fight now."

Henri said, "And I, too, fought in such a war, and paid a dear price for that fight. When someone like this can come along and do such a thing to you, and I permit it to happen, I suffered for nothing. I am willing to suffer it all over again to stop him."

"We are your friends, dear lady," Walter said. "And as friends we cannot stand by and watch you suffer."

"None of you is afraid of being hurt by André?" It was a plea for sanity rather than a question.

Walter shrugged. "We have walked down streets in fear of being hurt. We have lived each day of our lives with fear. Nothing has changed. Fear is still with us. Maybe more so with age. Only here, to suffer hurt to protect you, would have a higher meaning." He looked around the group. "We've all lived a very long time; being hurt in a noble cause is more than any of us could ask for, and a lot better than the mewling, puking future that some of us will face and all of us fear."

"That sounds like a lot of romantic crap, Walter."

"Do not confuse idealism with unrealistic romantic notions. There are principles for which many, including myself, have faced death. Friendship is one of those principles."

She stared in disbelief at Frank, who was standing back from the group. "Frank? You, too?"

"There's no way that I know all that's going on. But it seems very wrong for you to desert friends such as these. I would give a lot to have such friends."

"My reasons are more personal." Peter stepped closer. "I don't want to lose you. I have searched all my life for you, and I don't intend to have you walk out on me in order to keep me from harm. Losing you would be more harm than I could bear."

The sentiments were more than Eleanor could bear, and tears welled in her eyes. She looked suspiciously at Peter. "Did you give me a flat tire?"

He gave her a sheepish look. "Yes, before we went upstairs after the fire. I was afraid you'd try to leave like this. I had to do something to stop you until we could at least talk."

She turned to Grace. "Were you in on this?"

Grace shrugged. There were tears in her eyes. *Men were such heroic, romantic fools, God bless them.*

"I had asked that she call me when you tried to leave." He reached out and put his hands on her arms. "We want to face this thing with you. We're willing to take the risk. We've all been exposed to risks before, we know what we're getting into, and we're prepared."

"Me, too," Grace said, her voice breaking, at the edge of sobbing. "Don't go."

Eleanor's eyes were tearing. She turned to Frank and struggled to speak over the swell of her emotions. "You're right. I would be mad to leave friends like these."

"Besides, you could not go," Henri said. "They do not let the inmates leave the crazy house."

CHAPTER
24

Jessie Cummings was not in a good humor. She had had little sleep—her eyes kept drifting over the paperwork. The first thing she had to deal with was the TV news crews that had showed up at first light. She had spent the rest of the morning on the phone with the insurance company, who gave her a hard time, then had to listen to Jacobson shouting at her over the phone about the insurance company being a bunch of crooks, and he wanted to know what kind of place she was running that someone tried to burn it down. She had finished the morning with the smell of smoke still in her nose, and one huge, pounding headache.

The telephone at the front desk rang six times before Jessie, annoyed, punched down the extension number on the telephone on her desk and picked up the call. Where the hell was Grace? She took a deep breath so she wouldn't snarl at whoever was on the other end of the line. "Coral Sands."

"Could I please speak to Grace?" The voice was raspy and hoarse.

"Hold on while I see if I can find her." And find out why she wasn't at the front desk.

Jessie put the receiver down on the desk, got up, and walked out of her office. The front desk was unattended, and there was no one in the lobby. She spotted the envelope taped to the inside edge of the counter. "Jessie" was hand-printed on the outside of the envelope. She pulled it away from the counter, lifted the flap, took out the paper, and unfolded it. Her eyes widened as she read: "I will telephone at precisely 2:30. Grace is in my custody and her life is in my hands. I will speak only with police detective Ardley."

Jessie read the note three times, because she didn't believe what she was reading. She looked at the clock—12:47. Then she looked at the telephone on Grace's desk and saw the button for the extension was not lit. Whoever had called had hung up. Her headache was suddenly much worse.

"So, what do you think this is all about?" Ardley was pointing to his notebook, where he had written down the contents of the note. The note itself was at the lab, getting fingerprints lifted from it. This time there were fingerprints all over the envelope and the paper. He was hoping they didn't all belong to Jessie Cummings.

Jessie was hoping she didn't look half as bad as Ardley. By all standards the man was running on fumes. He kept yawning, and his eyes moved with sleepy sluggishness, unable to settle on anything for long. She had gotten him a cup of coffee, which sat on the table in front of him. The way he looked, a gallon of coffee wouldn't help.

They were seated in the card room. Two tables had been pulled together. Besides Jessie, there were Eleanor, Peter, and, at Eleanor's insistence, Walter, Benny, Henri, and Betty. Betty had spent much of the night fruitlessly complaining to Eugene. Consequently, she had not awakened until nearly noon. Sitting next to Ardley was a policeman in uniform.

Peter, his elbows on the table, leaned toward Ardley. His expression was intense. "It is clear that André wants Eleanor to leave here alone. I think that's what he's going to ask in return for Grace."

"I'll do whatever he asks in order to get Grace back unharmed."

Peter turned to Eleanor. He was holding back on his temper. "We've gone over that, and you're staying here."

"I can't let him hurt Grace." Eleanor was determined.

"You can't stop him from hurting her. If you leave, there's no guarantee he won't hurt her. After all, she must know who he is, and that is information this guy doesn't want to let out. You said he doesn't want anyone but you. If you refuse to leave, even with Grace's life in the balance, then it makes no sense to hurt her. What we've got to do is try to get him to come to you."

Eleanor looked to Ardley. "What do you think, detective?"

Ardley was taking a gulp of coffee. He swallowed, shrugged, and stifled a yawn. "It's a gamble." His thoughts were wandering around as if they had heavy weights attached to them. *Got to get some sleep,* he thought. "The normal police procedure is to buy as much time as possible, which increases the chances of the guy making a mistake." He touched his fingers to his chest. His heart was beating hard and hesitantly. This was the first time he had noticed it during the day.

"Well, he hasn't made any yet." Peter turned to Eleanor. "We have to get him to come here. If he wants to hurt you, he's going to have to come and get you. It's the only chance we have of stopping the guy."

Ardley shifted his weight in the chair, moving around, trying to keep alert. "We can protect you, if you decide not to give in to his demands. I'll have policemen all over you, following you so he can't get his hands on you."

Eleanor shook her head. "I'm sorry, but I can't trust that would work. Too many times people protected by the police have been killed. And André would definitely be planning for that."

"Would the C.I.A. do it any differently?"

Eleanor didn't reply, but her mind went into overdrive. She would have to make this decision herself, regardless of the support of friends. Their gestures were warm and sincere. But she had given in to them like a weak woman looking for protection. No more. This would require things she had been trained to do, skills she was taught a long time ago.

"You told me that he wants to kill you."

"He wants me to suffer, then kill me. Yes, that's what I believe." She was completely convinced of that. He was blindly driven for revenge, and that might be André's weakness, what she could use against him.

"Well, if we convince him that you won't leave, then he must come after you. He's not going to walk away from this after hungering for it so long."

"Yes."

"He could simply shoot you from a distance."

"C'mon, detective. From his handwriting, he can't hold a pen steady. A long shot would be impossible. Besides, I'm sure he wants to talk to me before he kills me. Make sure I know it's him and what he has suffered because of me. That much hate won't be satisfied with simply shooting me."

Ardley sat there a moment, thinking about what Eleanor had just said. Specifically, about André's handwriting. Why hadn't he registered that his hand wasn't steady? He shook his head. Damn, he was really slipping. "You said André had children?"

"Yes. A boy and a girl."

"How old would they be now?"

Peter jumped in. "You think it's the son behind all this?"

"Or the daughter." Ardley wished he had thought of

this sooner. It had popped uninvited into his head just a moment ago. "Obviously, they suffered as much from their father's betrayal as their father did. There could be a lot of hateful resentment that has to be satisfied."

"The son was ten when I met André. That would make him forty-four or so."

"The daughter?" Ardley, stifling another yawn, wrote in his notebook.

"Two years younger. She'd be forty-two."

"Do you remember their names?"

"The boy was named Alexei. The girl's name was Bogdana."

"And there's the wife. She's a possibility as well."

Eleanor frowned. "I'm not sure of her name. André and I always referred to her simply as his wife."

"It's all right. I really don't think she's behind this. I'd rule out the daughter as well. This doesn't have a woman's flavor." But he was feeling more strongly about the son. He thought of the construction work going on outside. They had been looking for an old man, while the note writer could have been walking in and out of the place unnoticed.

Ardley sighed. "Well, when he calls, I'll tell him what you've decided. And I'll get some police protection for you. I can't have people guarding you indefinitely, but I can get some coverage for a few days, maybe a week or more. If he decides to wait it out, there'll come a time when you will have no protection. Meanwhile, we'll see what the lab has turned up on the fingerprints."

Walter leaned forward, both hands on his cane. "Until you have adequate protection for Eleanor, we"—he looked around the table—"will stay with her." The others at the table nodded.

Ardley put his hand over a yawn. "It shouldn't take too long to get a few more men over here. Meanwhile, Carl Jackson—he indicated the policeman in uniform—"will stay with you, for now." He turned to Carl. "Nobody comes in this place unless Jessie Cummings gives her approval." Ardley looked at Jessie. "That means you'll have to remain near the door."

Jessie nodded. "I'll stay until Shirley comes on duty. I called her, she'll be in around six. She can vouch for the people then."

"Good."

"But what about someone coming around the side and through the swimming pool area, or the rear door?"

"Until I can get more help, there's not much I can do. Hopefully these gentlemen"—Ardley indicated Peter and the others—"will stay close to Eleanor until then."

"On another note," Ardley said to Jessie, "you've had time to think. Are you sure you didn't recognize the voice on the phone?"

"No. Sounded like the man had a cold or was disguising his voice."

Ardley nodded. He looked at the clock—2:10. "Well, now it's just a matter of waiting. I've got the phone company alerted. They'll be recording telephone numbers of all calls received here after two. With the equipment they have now, we don't even have to pick up the phone to get the number where the call originates. And there are three cars roaming the streets. As soon as we locate the phone, they'll be on it." He looked at the cup of coffee, and his stomach turned. He was getting sick of coffee, and it didn't seem to be helping him stay awake.

"I would think he'd call from a public phone," Walter said.

"Probably. Then we stand a better chance of getting some prints. A man would draw attention to himself wearing gloves while using a public phone. Especially in the heat of Florida. Also, someone might see him, or notice his car. Public phones mean people around."

Peter wasn't convinced. He felt Ardley was saying things more with a hope and a prayer than with conviction.

At 2:25 Ardley was standing by the telephone at the
front desk. He could have sat down, but standing helped
him stay awake and focused. Eleanor was standing outside Jessie's office. She was ready to go in the office
and pick up the phone. Ardley had asked her to listen
in on the call, to see if she could tell if the caller was
André or someone else. Jessie was standing near the
front door with Carl Jackson. He had Ardley's cell
phone, and the line was open to the phone company.
Everyone else, except Henri, who had left after the meeting in the card room, was hovering around the desk. The
tension was like a taut spring binding them all together.

They all watched the clock tick toward 2:30. After an
interminable time it finally reached 2:30, then ticked on
past. At 2:32 the phone rang, and everyone stiffened.
Ardley let it ring three times before he picked it up.

"Coral Sands," he said.

"Is that you, Detective Ardley?" The man's voice
was distorted, like it was coming through a machine.
Ardley waved to Patrolman Jackson, who started speaking into the cell phone. Eleanor went into Jessie's office,
carefully picked up the receiver of the phone, and placed
it to her ear.

"Yes."

"I want you to see that Eleanor Carter leaves Coral
Sands in her car within the hour. She is to go alone. She
is to head out to I75, then north. No police following
her, by car or by air. I have Grace wired with explosives.
If Eleanor is followed in any way, I will detonate those
explosives. Once I join her and we are safely away, I
will telephone you at this same number and tell you
where you can find Grace. Is that understood?" The
man's voice was hard but calm.

"I would like to speak with Grace."

"You can talk to her after Eleanor has left."

"She has refused to leave."

"If she doesn't leave, I will execute Grace very pain-
fully."

"Well, she said even if you kill everyone she knows, she will not leave to meet you."

Eleanor replaced the receiver and came out to the front desk. Ardley placed his hand over the receiver and looked questioningly at her.

Eleanor shook her head. "I don't know," she said. "It's too distorted."

"She is crazy! Are you going to permit her to sacrifice her friends? You are a policeman. You have a responsibility to prevent death! You must make her do it!" The man's anger was an exploding bomb, his voice trembling with rage. *This was a man on the edge,* Ardley thought. *He was dangerous and erratic.*

Ardley removed his hand from the mouthpiece. He was not going to do anything to calm the man down. If anything, he wanted to get him angrier. With anger comes talk, and Ardley wanted to keep the man on the line for as long as possible. He put a firm edge on his voice. "She's not the one doing the sacrificing, pal. You are, and I've taken that personally. You . . ."

"Ha," he interrupted. "You are a fool! I want to talk to Eleanor."

Ardley put his hand over the phone and looked at Eleanor. "He wants to talk to you."

She gave him a hard frown and shook her head. "No."

Ardley removed his hand from the mouthpiece. "She says she's got nothing to say to you, and she is not interested in what you have to say to her."

The connection was broken immediately.

Ardley shrugged. "He hung up. I was hoping to keep him talking for a while longer." He hung up the phone and looked at Carl Jackson. "Everything okay?"

Jackson nodded. "They nailed down the location. A public phone at Denny's on the Trail. They're on the way."

Ardley nodded. "All we can do now is wait." Then

he turned to Eleanor. "Why didn't you want to talk to him?"

"I didn't want to give him the opportunity to ease his anger. This way I think he will be in a sufficient rage to come after me."

Ardley gave Eleanor an appraising look. What he saw was a woman who had become hard as steel. "You're not afraid of him?"

"Of course I am."

CHAPTER
25

It was going on four-thirty. Walter, Benny, Charlie, Peter, Eleanor, and Betty were outside by the swimming pool. Henri had gone out earlier in the day and had not returned. No one was looking good. The tension of the day, the fire last night, and little sleep were taking their toll on them all. Peter had whipped up a large batch of pina coladas for everyone. Ardley had just joined them. He had been inside, on and off the phone, for the past half-hour.

"Okay," Ardley said. "Two more uniforms are on their way here. I've arranged to have three men on the premises around the clock for the next three days. If things don't come to a head by then, I'm sure I can extend that."

Peter was seated in a lounge chair next to Eleanor. "Did they find anything at the public phone?"

Ardley shook his head. "No witnesses. They lifted a ton of prints. It'll take a while to sort them out."

"I thought fingerprints were useless unless the person's prints are on file somewhere."

"True. But if this guy is who we think, there's a good chance his prints are on file with Immigration, for a start. That would give us a name, a picture, and maybe a valid address."

"I've got a question," Peter said.

"Okay. Shoot."

"Why do you think André disguised his voice on the phone?"

"Because it might be recognized. Why else?"

"So it's someone whose voice we'd know. Even Jessie would know it."

"Possibly. Or maybe just Jessie would know it."

"It's possible that he's here among us."

"Possible. But it's just one possible among many. So be alert." Then he shrugged. "I'm heading home. You guys stick close to Eleanor until the uniforms arrive. If anything happens, one of the uniforms will be able to reach me."

Ardley left them sitting there, went back inside the building, and crossed the lobby to the front entrance. Carl Jackson was seated on a chair by the door. Jessie was seated at the front desk.

"Help is on the way," he said to Jessie. "There'll be two more men here shortly. I'm signing out for the day."

"Well, try to get some sleep. You look absolutely awful."

"I wish people would stop telling me that."

Ardley pushed through the front door and stepped outside. The weather was beautiful, the air pleasant, the temperature comfortable. Even though he was very tired, he noticed it all, and that felt good. He took his car keys from his pocket, walked across the parking lot, bypassing the deserted construction, and headed for his car. Thoughts had been coming to his exhausted mind in strange ways lately. Like bubbles in a stagnant pool, they just suddenly drifted up to where he could see them. Like the idea of it possibly being André's children at the root of this trouble. It just came out of nowhere, as if somewhere back deep in his brain some thinking was going on without his knowledge, and the resulting ideas were sent to drift up at their own speed to his consciousness. *There was no one working on the construction site out front.* He stopped and turned to look at the site—the large hole and the forms to pour concrete for the fountain pool. What was that project manager's name, again? Alex Conners. Yes. André's son was named Alexie. Alex, Alexie? Hmm. Coincidence? The man looked to be the right age for André's son. And he had complete access to Coral Sands. It wouldn't be hard for him to do all the things that have been happening, including the fire and the kidnapping. Grace had been friendly with him and would go with him unwittingly. What did they know about him? Where was he now?

Ardley looked off at the distant construction where they were putting in another lake behind the new extension to be built to Coral Sands. He could see some of the heavy equipment. Nothing seemed to be moving. He looked at it a long moment before he decided to walk over and take a closer look. He thought about getting the gun out of the glove compartment of the car, then changed his mind. He didn't think he'd really need it. He was just going to look around.

He put his keys back in his pocket and started walking across the parking lot toward the lake site. Being in construction, this Alex Conners could get his hands on explosives. He was thinking about André's threat to use explosives on Grace. Would there be a place on the site where Grace could be hidden? She might even be dead. They'd had no verification she was alive, or even that she was with the man who called. For all anyone knew, she could be on a shopping spree somewhere.

He left the parking lot and stepped onto the grass. It was like walking on a thick mat. He was feeling guilty about not thinking of this sooner. It was his job, and it was what he was good at. Yet this time he didn't perform. This time he'd let everyone down, including himself. He let out a long yawn. Amanda was right, he should see a doctor. There was no way he could continue to do his job with his mind feeling like cotton had been stuffed in his head. He had to get a decent night's sleep. Maybe a sleeping pill of some sort might do the job.

Halfway along the side of Coral Sands he saw Frank, toting his insecticide sprayer, walking along the side of the building heading toward the rear. Maybe he'd seen something. "Frank!"

Frank stopped, and turned toward Ardley.

Ardley slowly walked over, while Frank waited patiently. Ardley was thinking that he'd have to go over everything about this case again. So much had happened and so quickly that he was sure there were things he had missed. Especially with a sleep-deprived brain that was moving like a glacier. Maybe this evening, after dinner, he'd carefully go over everything in his notes. See if something jumps out at him, something he should have noticed.

He stepped up to Frank. Frank was wearing the heavy workman's vest under the insecticide tank strapped to his back.

"What is it, detective?"

"I was just wondering if you had seen that construction foreman around the grounds?"

"That guy with the white hat?"

"Yeah. I was surprised to see the construction crew wasn't working."

"Haven't seen him. They could have knocked off early, with all that's been going on around here."

Ardley nodded in thought. "All right. Thanks. I see *you're* working late."

Frank shrugged. "Trying to get done so I can move on to the next job. Didn't make much progress the last couple of days."

Ardley remembered Frank spending a couple of hours at the police station coming up with a picture of the guy

who handed him the box containing the champagne.
"Yeah. I understand." He sighed. "Well, I'll let you
get back to work." Ardley turned and was about to walk
away when another of those thoughts bubbled to the
surface. The box of champagne had only Frank's fingerprints on it. Only Frank's. Yet Frank had said some
old guy gave it to him to bring inside. He didn't mention
anything about the old guy wearing gloves, or handling
the box strangely. "Frank," he said, moving to turn
around and face him, "there's something . . ." It felt as
if the building fell on his head, and the world blew up
in a flash of light brighter than the sun.

"So how do we do this?" Charlie said. "Do we circle
the wagons and bring the horses inside?"

"You think we need some plan of action?" Walter
said. They were still out at the pool area. Walter and
Charlie were now in the lounge chairs; the rest of them
were at a table.

"Some strategy might be good."

"Look, everyone," Eleanor said, "I don't want to put
you all out. I think the police can handle this bodyguard
business."

"Nonsense, dear lady, we consider ourselves the pal-
ace guard. The last and best line of defense."

Eleanor grinned. "Stuff it, Walter."

"Besides, the police are not good drinking compan-
ions." Walter raised his pina colada. "That's it! We'll
move our drinks in a circle, and stay happily in the bag
until this is all over."

"I think Walter has had a few above his limit." Betty
smiled at Benny.

"It's getting so little sleep that's doing it." Benny
said. "We're all getting punchy."

"Oh. I hadn't noticed any change in you." Betty giggled daintily.

Benny gave her a look.

Peter got up from the table. He was restless. He

wanted something to happen to end all this, so they could get back to normal.

"Where're you going, Slick?"

"Just to stretch my legs." He needed to think. He walked along the outside bar, past Charlie and Walter in the lounge chairs, to the end of the building. He saw Tweedledee and Tweedledum in the gazebo by the lake. Maybe he'd walk down there for a little comedy relief. He gazed around, not sure if he wanted to make that walk. Frank was coming toward him alongside the building. The spray tank was hung on his right shoulder, the sprayer in his right hand. Peter thought about how he had helped Frank load that tank in the pickup truck. The tank was damn heavy. That man was a lot stronger than he looked.

"So, Frank," Peter said, "how's the spraying coming?"

A serious expression on his face, Frank leaned close to Peter. "I have just seen something I must tell you all about. I don't want to alarm Eleanor." Frank's voice was just a whisper. "Quickly." He motioned for Peter to follow, and he headed for Walter and Charlie.

Puzzled, Peter followed.

Frank stopped in front of Walter and Charlie. Peter came up alongside. Frank raised the sprayer and sent a blast of liquid into Peter's face.

"Jesus!" Peter jumped back, throwing his hands reflexively over his face, his eyes on fire, the foul smell of insecticide burning in his throat and nostrils. He stumbled around blindly, moaning at the pain.

Before Charlie and Walter could react, they, too, were treated to a dose of insecticide, and were clutching their faces and moaning against the burning liquid in their eyes and throats.

Everyone had been watching this exchange—at first friendly and nonthreatening, then suddenly not, and now they were frozen in shock. There is that moment when things change suddenly and unexpectedly, where the body freezes while the mind rapidly assesses the situation before it sends the body into action. In that moment, while they all looked on, Frank dropped the spray tank; it hit the deck with a clank then tipped over into the swimming pool, and he pulled a gun from beneath the work vest.

Benny was on his feet, when Frank turned the gun in his direction and fired, the loud explosion once again froze everyone. The bullet snapped off the concrete deck near Benny's feet. "Just stay right there, Benny."

The shock of the shooting was compounded by the identity of the person doing the shooting. Eleanor frowned in disbelief. "André?"

Frank walked toward the table, the old man's walk gone. "Yes, Tatiana."

"My God! How could that be? Your face, your . . . ?"

"My countrymen know how to treat the disloyal." Anger and bitterness were in his voice. He stopped by the table. He pulled a small device from his pocket, and with the help of his gun hand, extracted a long antenna. "One press of the button on this detonator, and Grace will be gone in a spectacular explosion. So don't do anything rash.

"Get up, Tatiana." He spat the words as if they had been fighting desperately with each other to get out. "We are leaving. I have much to tell you about pain and betrayal, about the years of torment and loneliness I suffered because of you." His hand was trembling with emotion, the barrel of the gun wavering. "About the terrible loneliness when my country, my friends, my own family turned against me."

Eleanor stood, her mind rapidly assessing the situation, looking for options, for courses of action. "I thought they had killed you." Beyond her control, tears welled in her eyes.

"They kill traitors. I wasn't a traitor, I was a fool. Fools they torture and beat and work to death." He held

up his right hand holding the detonator. The hand was
jerking around in an uncontrollable spasm. "I caressed
you with this hand. It transmitted my love to you in so
many ways, and now I can not keep it still." He dropped
the hand to his side. "I do not know this face. Nothing
of what I was physically survived your betrayal of that
love. The surgeons pieced together what was left. But
the surgeons could not mend my heart, my soul. My
hate. My life was destroyed. It is only just that I destroy
yours." His face softened, his voice suddenly gentle. "I
would have betrayed my country for you, had you only
asked. I would have gone anywhere with you." Then
his face hardened, his voice demanding. "Now you will
go away with me." He waved the gun, signaling her to
move.

Betty suddenly pushed her chair back and stood up.
"You leave her alone!" Betty shouted. Her voice didn't
have much volume, but the effect was clear.

"Shut up!" He pointed the gun at her.

"You want to kill us all! Is that it! Big deal! It doesn't
take a brain to do that. Any jerk can get a gun and pull
the trigger! So, go ahead! Shoot us all! But Eleanor is
not leaving here!"

Benny and Eleanor were shocked at Betty's reaction.
They'd never seen her so angry. Frank was taken back
by this onslaught from Betty, who had seemed to be a
spineless, whimpering old lady.

Betty grabbed Eleanor by the arm and yanked her
away from the table, toward the sliding doors leading to
the inside of the building. Eleanor was too flabbergasted
to resist, and stumbled after her. Frank regained his com-
posure and rushed quickly to stand in their way.
"Enough of this!" he shouted. They stopped before
him. Benny had jumped up from the chair and was moving after them. Frank looked at him. "Not another
step!" He raised the detonator in his trembling right
hand.

Benny froze a few feet from them. Benny could see

some movement inside the building. *Where the hell was that cop?*

"YAAAAAAH!" The scream came from above. Frank jerked his head up. A large black bag came sailing over the railing of the balcony and headed toward him. He jumped back as the bag hit the deck almost where he had been standing. Eleanor made her move. She jerked free of Betty and threw herself at Frank, reaching for the hand with the detonator. Frank stumbled under the impact and twisted, hitting Eleanor ineffectively with the gun, the blow bouncing off her shoulder. She grabbed the hand with the detonator and sank her teeth in his wrist. Frank screamed, dropped the detonator to the deck, then gained his footing and hit Eleanor on the head with the gun, forcing her to release her grip and stumble backward, blood spilling from the cut in her scalp. Betty screamed for help. During the quick scuffle, Benny made his move. Frank quickly turned to reach down and retrieve the detonator, but Benny was standing there. He kicked the detonator into the pool. "Think it's waterproof?" Then he punched Frank in the face as hard as he could, the impact sending a knifing pain up his hand and arm. Frank stumbled backward from the blow, lost his balance, and fell into the swimming pool.

Carl Jackson came running out of the building as Frank hit the water. He looked around, puzzled.

"He's all yours." Benny pointed to Frank floundering in the water, blood running from his nose and mouth. Jessie came outside right behind Carl. "Call 911," Benny said as he moved toward his fallen friends. "Walter and Charlie and Peter got a faceful of bug killer." Without missing a step, Jessie turned around and ran inside to make the call.

CHAPTER
26

It was a busy evening in the emergency room of the hospital, made busier by the group from Coral Sands. Benny came out of one of the treatment rooms, his hand bandaged past the wrist. The X-rays showed nothing was broken, but he had torn the skin over a couple of knuckles, and had done some weird things to the ligaments and tendons in his hand and wrist. He joined Betty and Jessie in the waiting area, waiting to hear something about Detective Ardley and the others. Jessie told Benny that Ardley had been found unconscious on the far side of Coral Sands by one of the policemen, and had been brought to the hospital after they arrived. At that moment Henri showed up.

He sat down next to them. "I heard about all the terrible things that happened."

"Yeah," Benny said, "it was like the shoot-out at the O.K. Corral."

"The what?"

"Never mind."

"It was awful," Betty said.

"What of the others? Do you have any news?" Henri asked.

Benny grunted and shook his head.

Eleanor came out next. She had a thick swath of bandage along one side of her head. Blood had spotted her clothing. Benny and Betty rushed to her and guided her back to where they were sitting.

"My God!" Henri said.

Eleanor waved away his concern and sat down. "Took a few stitches, that's all. Nothing broken or cracked. My father always did say I had a hard head. I'm glad he was right."

"Did you see the others back there?" Benny asked.

"Yes. They should be out soon. The doctor was washing out their eyes and swabbing their throats. Not much else he can do, it seems."

"They brought in Detective Ardley."

"What happened?"

"They found him out like a light, lying on the grounds somewhere. Probably ran into Frank's bad mood."

Then Eleanor turned to Betty. "Betty, why did you do what you did? You could have been hurt."

Matter-of-factly, Betty said, "Eugene told me to do what I felt I had to do, and everything would be all right. So I did. And he was right."

Peter came out. He was walking a little unsteadily. Benny went over to him. "How you doing, Slick?" He took Peter's arm and guided him back to the others.

"Well, for one, I have the cleanest eyes in town, but they're not working too well right now, with all the stuff they put in them. And my throat feels like I swallowed an awful lot of sandpaper. The other two blind mice should be out in a minute."

"They brought Ardley in a little while ago."

"Ardley?"

"We figure Frank knocked him over the head before he got around to us."

Peter saw Eleanor, and his heart ached for her suffering. He smiled at her, and she at him, and he sat down next to her.

Shortly after, Charlie and Walter carefully walked out. Betty and Jessie went to them, to guide them.

"Damn it, woman!" Walter said to Jessie, who had grabbed his arm to help him. "The world is a little blurred, not black. I can manage on my own."

"The only thing you can manage to do on your own is be a smartass." Jessie did not release Walter's arm while she brought him to sit with the others.

The doctor who had been working on them came over. He had three prescriptions in his hand. He handed them to Jessie. "Have these filled. They're eye drops to help ease their discomfort for the next few days. Their eyes'll be a bit sensitive to light for a while. Dark glasses would help."

"Will they be all right?"

"Other than discomfort, I think they'll be okay. It isn't as if they swallowed a glass of insecticide. Then they would be in real danger."

"What about Detective Ardley?" Peter asked.

"The policeman who was brought in? He with you?"

Peter nodded. "Detective Ardley is a friend."

"Well, he has a concussion, and the X-rays showed a hairline fracture of the skull. He took a hard hit. He'll be under observation for bleeding in the brain, but so far things look good."

"Thank you."

The doctor nodded and left.

"Eugene was right," Eleanor said.

Peter looked at her. "What do you mean?"

"I didn't tell you, but the during session I had with Betty on the Ouija board, I asked Eugene if you would protect me. He said no. And I asked him where help would come from, and he said the heavens. Warren's bag from the balcony was close enough."

Peter shook his head. *Incredible*. "Eugene does it again."

Benny stood. "Well, I think it's time we go home."

"Yes," Jessie said. She turned to the others. "Betty and I came in the van."

They all stood and turned toward the exit as Detective Fred Simmons came through the double doors leading to the interior of the hospital. Walking toward them, he motioned with his hand to get their attention. "Sorry, folks. I just came from reporting to Detective Ardley, and he asked me to bring you people up to date. Frank or André, whatever you want to call him, has told us where your friend Grace is. I've got a car going there to get her."

Everyone smiled and nodded with relief.

"And, Miss Carter"—he took his notebook from his pocket and flipped through the pages—"André said—and I wrote this down because I thought you should hear it—that he wished he had had friends like you have."

Peter put his arm around Eleanor and smiled at her.

"Well, that's it," Fred Simmons said, closing the notebook and returning it to his pocket. "You all have a pleasant evening." He turned and left.

Peter looked at Eleanor. "As Benny said, it's time to go home."

They were all gathered by the swimming pool two days later. Their chairs faced the sliding glass doors leading into the building. Henny Youngman stood before the sliding doors as if the area were a stage. Eleanor still had the bandage on her head. Peter, Charlie, and Walter wore very dark sunglasses; their eyes were still sensitive to the sunlight, and they looked like the Three Blind Mice. Alice, who had been released with Ardley the day before, had her leg in a cast and bandages on various parts of her body and her arms. Ardley was there with his head bandaged; Grace had a patch of bandage on her forehead—André had hit her during the kidnapping; and

Benny, sitting by Caroline, had his hand bandaged. Betty and Henri were also in the audience. Peter had made pina coladas for the gang.

Ardley was sitting next to Peter and Eleanor, with Benny and Caroline on his other side. He was feeling better after having slept well for two days. He was still having trouble getting to sleep, but once he did, he slept well. Since he had no pressing schedule, he slept afternoons, mornings, whenever he finally fell asleep. Amanda told him that his insomnia almost got him killed, and she didn't want to visit his dead body next time. So, reluctantly, he consented to return to the hospital for a series of tests to find out what was causing his insomnia. He was still afraid to find out what the problem was, but couldn't see how he could go on trying to ignore what was happening to his health and his life. It was time to find some answers, no matter how bad they were.

"I appreciate the invitation to this event, but I must admit I accepted with some reluctance." They looked at Ardley. "Ever since you got into town, Peter, I've been a very busy man." He pointed to the bandage on his head. "The world has become a little weird."

Benny chuckled. "You want to see weird, maybe the Mad Joker will come by and show you weird."

Henri, from behind them, said, "It is very strange, this place."

"I came," Ardley was saying to Peter, "because I was hoping I could persuade you, and possibly your friend Benny here, to settle in some other part of the country."

Peter smiled, exchanging glances with Benny and Eleanor. "I'm sorry, but . . ."

"Before you make a decision in haste," Ardley interrupted, "I have arranged to take up a collection in the Police Department to pay your fare anywhere you want to go."

Benny laughed louder. "With enemies like this, who

needs friends?'' Then Benny looked at Ardley. "What's going to happen to Audrey Knitter?''

Ardley shrugged. "André confessed to killing Harry Benson. And the District Attorney is not thrilled with trying Mrs. Knitter for his attempted murder. Looks like they may drop the charges. Depends on how smooth her attorney is. And, from what I've seen, he looks sleazy enough to pull it off. He's already contesting her confession that she tried to poison Harry Benson.''

Peter leaned over. "Why did André kill Harry Benson?'' He held Eleanor's hand and gave it a reassuring squeeze.

"He said he figured any resident he murdered at the party would have an emotional impact on Eleanor. He was trying to drive her friends away, so she could suffer the isolation he felt when his friends deserted him. He wandered the party, looking for a likely victim. Harry Benson, drugged to unconsciousness, came up at the top of the list. But André's bad luck was holding up, and he killed the only person at the party nobody knew.'' Ardley took a sip of his pina colada. "So, when that didn't work, he attempted to kill Alice by running her down with a car. Alice was tougher than he thought. But he was persistent in trying to drive a wedge between Eleanor and her friends. He wanted to force her to leave Coral Sands with everyone hating her. He tried the fire, but again no luck. He was furious when Eleanor's friends stood by her, and were willing to get hurt protecting her. Then he got desperate, and kidnapped Grace. End of story.''

Ardley looked around. "Where is Ms. Cummings?''

Peter smiled. "She refused to have anything to do with this event. She was afraid that if something went wrong and she was a part of it, she could lose her job.'' He pointed to Grace standing off to the side, holding a video camera. "However, Grace is videotaping it all in case it's successful.''

Eleanor turned to Peter. "The water in the pool is

such a deep blue today. I've never seen it quite that blue.'' But everything seemed more vivid now that peace had been restored to her life.

''Well, they drained it all to remove the insecticide, and Jessie had water trucks in here yesterday afternoon refilling it. The color probably has to do with the chemicals they added.'' It was a thrill to be there with her. Just holding her hand was pure joy.

''I'm looking around at all the wounded,'' Henny Youngman was saying. ''And it brought to mind that I always captivated audiences in hospitals. Of course, they couldn't get up and walk out.

''I know you're all anxious to see Warren do his fantastic stunt. I just wanted to remind everyone that Warren spent many years doing stunts in the movies.''

''Years ago I was in the movies,'' Sailor Hat said to Gray Hair. They were sitting near the front of the crowd, facing Henny Youngman.

Gray Hair said, ''Yeah. In the balcony, groping some girl.''

''No. I mean on the screen. In a motion picture.''

''Oh, yeah. I didn't recognize you unwrapped. You were the Mummy, right?''

''They were making a film and looking in the crowd for some extras. I volunteered, and they accepted me. Got paid for it, too.''

''So what did you play?''

''A dead man.''

''Figures.''

''There was this entertainer,'' Henny Youngman was saying, ''who was down on his luck. His agent had told him the only way he could get him a job was if he came up with a great act. One day he goes to his agent. 'I got an idea for a spectacular act. I'm on stage, tied in a chair, and there's a box of dynamite under the chair. The fuse is lit, and I struggle to free myself before it explodes. I'm still in the chair when the dynamite goes off in a great roar and cloud of smoke.' 'That's a great act!' his agent tells him. 'I can get you a booking anywhere.' 'There's only one problem,' the entertainer says. 'I only do it once.' "

"Now, I would like to introduce a similar act. Ladies and gentlemen, Warren Styck!" Henny applauded, and the crowd joined in. He stepped to the side, the applause stopped, and all eyes looked up at the third floor balcony.

For a few moments there was nothing but silence. Then they heard a growing cry—"YAAAAAAAH!"— and suddenly Warren in his wheelchair shot out onto the balcony, heading straight at the railing. The chair stopped short of the railing, as if it hit a solid wall, and Warren was lifted from the chair, his body flying toward the balcony. He quickly extended his arms and grabbed the railing. The muscles in his arms tightened like steel, and using the strength of his arms, he threw himself into the air. His body did a slow somersault until he was coming down head first, his limp legs almost lying against his chest. He grabbed his legs to hold them there, as he had done in the dive into the firemen's net. Everyone watched, their hearts in their throats, hoping he would clear the concrete deck and land in the pool. From where the audience was, there was no way to tell if he was going to make it. Then, as if in slow motion, Warren's body continued to turn until he was coming down on his back, and he hit the water, sending a loud splash in the air and cries of relief through the crowd. The applause was instantaneous and, coupled with the relief everyone felt, was exhilarating.

Warren sank deep into the water, then released his legs and expertly swam to the surface. When his head popped out of the water, his face, his neck, and his hair were bright blue.

"What the . . . !" Ardley said.

At first everyone was startled, then they all broke out in a great roar of laughter.

Benny, struggling to speak through his laughing, leaned over to Ardley. "The Mad Joker strikes again!"

< A FELICITY GROVE MYSTERY > **THE**

DEAD PAST

Tom Piccirilli

Welcome to Felicity Grove...

This upstate New York village is as small as it is peaceful. But some-
how Jonathan Kendrick's eccentric grandma, Anna, always manages
to find trouble. Crime, scandal, you name it...this wheelchair-bound
senior citizen is involved. So when the phone rings at 4 A.M. in
Jonathan's New York City apartment, he knows to expect some kind
of dilemma. But Anna's outdone herself this time. She's stumbled
across a dead body...in her trash can.

BERKLEY
PRIME
CRIME

☐ 0-425-16696-1/$5.99

PENGUIN PUTNAM INC.
Online

Your Internet gateway to a virtual environment with
hundreds of entertaining and enlightening books from
Penguin Putnam Inc.

*While you're there, get the latest buzz on
the best authors and books around—*

Tom Clancy, Patricia Cornwell, W.E.B. Griffin,
Nora Roberts, William Gibson, Robin Cook,
Brian Jacques, Catherine Coulter, Stephen King,
Jacquelyn Mitchard, and many more!

Penguin Putnam Online is located at
http://www.penguinputnam.com

PENGUIN PUTNAM NEWS

Every month you'll get an inside look at our upcoming
books and new features on our site. This is an ongoing
effort to provide you with the most up-to-date
information about our books and authors.

Subscribe to Penguin Putnam News at
http://www.penguinputnam.com/ClubPPI